CW01095466

The Trumpets of Death

A story of betrayals

Stephen J Ball

True reconciliation does not consist in merely forgetting the past

Nelson Mandela

**Previously in the
Staverley series:**

The Death of an External Examiner (2020)

**Death in the Ivory Tower
(2021)**

Craterellus cornucopioides, trompeta dels morts (Catalan) or **trumpet of the dead**, is an edible mushroom. It is also known as the **black chanterelle, trombetta dei morti** (Italian).

Bolet en forma d'embut, de carn molt prima, no se'n diferència el peu del barret, de color cendrós gairebé negre, està format per plecs i no presenta làmines. Carn molt minsa, elàstica i de color gris. Olor afruitada.

Prologue

The village, or what was left of it, was ominously quiet, apart from the regular zing and thud of a sniper's bullets. The sniper was hidden somewhere on the hillside to the east of the village and was taking pot shots at anything that moved. What had been the day before a tight-knit, thriving rural community was now a smoking ruin. Hardly a single building remained intact and the muddy main street was littered with the bodies of dead villagers, killed as they attempted to flee. Immediately in front of the wall behind which the four militiamen were crouching, an older man and young girl, both shot to death, lay in the open, face up, still holding hands. Beside them lay a *horse with its belly gaping open, its guts spilling out*. The Nationalist soldiers had shown no mercy to the civilians, those not killed had been taken – who knows where and to what fate. There had not been time to run away. In the small main square the body of a man mutilated and burned, hanging from a plane tree, swung gently in the breeze. *His eyes were bulging, his swollen tongue sticking out of his mouth*. Hundreds of years of family histories, of struggles, joy, friendship, conflicts and love had been obliterated in a single morning. Political beliefs and allegiances had rendered these people less than human in the eyes of Franco's troops and therefore expendable.

The company of militia, forty men, had arrived too late to intervene but they knew in any case that they were outgunned by the regular troops with their light cannon and modern rifles and machine guns. They probably could have done little to save the village. The sniper, having no visible targets, now seemed to be losing interest and his shots were becoming less frequent. The four men in their blue coveralls and black berets nodded to one another and moved quickly across the street to a new place of cover in the doorway of a shattered and burned out bar. They were all careful to avoid stepping on the bodies of the old man and girl. None of the four had any military training to speak of, they were volunteers, as were the rest of the company, and their weapons were antiquated and unreliable. But they had learned on the job and developed a rapport and mutual trust which made them an effective unit in combat situations. That meant that their Sargent, a bellicose but basically sensible German, often chose them for the more dangerous tasks, like now, reconnoitring the village. That they had all survived this long on the front was remarkable, but something they avoided talking about, to do so was considered back luck. Inside the bar were more bodies, several of these lay face down in a line across the floor, shot in the back of the head – executed. Flies buzzed around their wounds. In the early days they all found such sights difficult to cope with, now they were inured to even the most awful of atrocities. That was also difficult to cope with. They knew they had been changed by their experiences – hardened and made cynical. They had come to know something of the darkness and evil that inhabited the souls of some men, and feared they might become like those men or were already. That was another thing they did not talk about. They each struggled in their own way to retain some compassion and humanity. Their friendship had become an important part of that struggle. It was something tangible to cling to. It was something clean. *Sudden movement inside the bar caused a rush of alarm,* as one they ducked their heads and raised their rifles, *but it was only a canary in a cage, fluttering about, bumping into the wire sides* – the sole survivor.

The four moved on to check the other buildings around the square but it was quickly clear that there was no one left to save and no one to fight. The sniper had moved on. The silence was oppressive. The rest of the company moved forward and the remainder of the day was devoted to digging graves and recording the names of the dead and to sleeping. The company had been on the move for over forty hours. Heavy artillery fire could be heard in the distance as some kind of skirmish was played out or some other defenceless village was attacked and flattened. The front was still fluid and unpredictable and the Nationalists and the Militias were raiding and probing, seeking for some kind of advantage but avoiding major engagements. No advantage was evident.

While most of the militia slept, wherever they could find shelter and keep warm, those on sentry duty collected potatoes and other vegetables from the nearby fields. The villagers would not need them now and provisions were running very low. When he woke the company cook, a tall *bearded Irishman with a huge automatic pistol strapped to his belt,* set up a cauldron someone had found in one of the village houses and began to prepare a stew. While they waited, their stomachs empty and their tin pannikins at the ready, some of the men tried to wash, others picked at their clothes, searching for the lice that inhabited their trousers and caused incessant itching, and a few tried on the boots that had been taken from the dead villagers. Boots were highly prized. Those initially handed out to the men with their uniforms were of poor quality and quickly fell apart. They were badly made civilian boots. The villagers' boots that fitted no one were loaded onto the company mule along with other useful items scavenged from remains of the massacre. *Everything was running short – clothes, tobacco, soap, candles, matches, olive oil* and most worryingly, ammunition. The uncooked potatoes would be swapped later at the commissary for some coffee – if there was any to be had and if the company were able to re-join their column. There were many mangels and sugar beets in the fields but they were too heavy to carry. Many of the men did find space in their rucksacks for a corncob or two. There would be no proper harvest this year.

The company's orders had been for reconnaissance and to engage and disrupt the enemy whenever possible. They were to use their own initiative, remain undetected if possible and report back what they saw. It was assumed that this was part of a more general plan and preparation for a battle but in real terms the purpose was unclear, there seemed to be nothing of strategic military value on this side of Huesca. That was already known. Neither the militias, of which there were many, mostly anarchists and unionists of various hues and types, nor the Nationalists, mostly regulars, seemed to have any understanding of what was going on beyond the immediate area around Huesca and whether their side was winning or losing and whether their actions were contributing in any way to either outcome. Hatred and viciousness had long since replaced planning and coordination as the basis for orders and become ends in themselves.

Fed and rested the company formed up to leave at dusk, it was cold but safer to move at night. They set off toward the east where the Sargent hoped they would find the main column digging in. The four comrades whispered to one another in an eccentric mix of English and Catalan as they marched, or lumbered more like. The name of the village was already beginning to fade from their memories.

Chapter 1

As the plane banked steeply over the Mediterranean in preparation for landing, Staverley caught his first sight of Barcelona. He tried to pick out some of the sights and buildings he had read about – La Sagrada Familia, Las Ramblas, and the statue of Columbus - but could not. He was just able to make out the orderly grid of streets and rectangular blocks of shops and houses that were the *Eixample*, the modern extension to the medieval city, built in the late nineteenth century. Some of the most famous of the buildings of the Catalan architect Antoni Gaudi were there. They were on Staverley's list of places to visit during his stay in Catalunya.

Staverley had intended to practise some Spanish grammar and do a few of the translation exercises in his beginner's book of Spanish during the flight but he had been too often distracted by the changing landscape below, and especially the Pyrenees, to make much progress. The Spanish lessons he had attended back in England were already fading into a blur of obscure grammatical rules and difficult pronunciation and he feared that he would be struggling for some time to understand and make himself understood. The whole project for the visit, about which he was so enthusiastic when still in England, now seemed very foolhardy. Staverley was a lecturer in Sociology at the University of Watermouth. His specialism was tourism. This was his sabbatical leave, and the plan was to research the impact of the recent tourist boom in Spain on the social, economic and cultural life of the Costa Brava. He would be spending nearly six months living in Catalunya, interviewing people involved in and affected by the expansion of the infrastructure of tourism and by the tourists themselves. He had done similar work in England focusing on the impact of modern mass tourism on traditional seaside towns. The sabbatical and the time away from the university was also an attempt to distance himself from events, unrelated to his work, in which he had become embroiled over the past two years: primarily, his involvement, once removed, with three murders. In the previous three months he had had to give evidence at an inquest and a trial, the first concerning the death of a student, the second related to threats made to him by violent criminals. All of that had taken its toll on his senses of security and morality and his self-understanding. He found that he needed to re-think himself, the person he was, or thought he was - which was both difficult and very uncomfortable and the task had made him rather depressed. Everyone he had talked to, his mother, his friends, colleagues and Monica - his lover and the woman he loved - thought that getting away would be a good idea.

Staverley had tried very hard not to show how much he was affected by the violence and intrigue and pain he had been confronted with, and he was able to convince most people with his brave face. However, his participation in the murder investigations, both at the behest of the police and on his own account, had left him with an accumulation of guilt, regret, doubt, confusion and uncertainty. He felt guilty about things he knew and had not told the police. He had regrets about decisions he had made and the consequences of those for people's lives. He had doubts about whether what he thought were the right things to do at the time were right after all. Altogether, he was confused about his willingness to get involved in those things in the first place. Why had he not stopped, not said no, and not left things to those responsible? Why did he *feel* responsible? But most of all, perhaps, he was uncertain whether the damage he had done to his sense of self was actually repairable. His values, or what he had thought were his values, had been displaced, and no longer fitted his actions. He could no longer find himself in the place he expected to be. He had become unmoored. The sabbatical was in part meant to fix all of that. He would be somewhere he would not have to do so much thinking about himself and just be, and sleep better. Perhaps it was all just a matter of being in the wrong place at the wrong time, and being too eager to find the truth. Sometimes the truth is better left to its own devices.

The fasten seatbelt sign came on and the landing was announced. Staverley re-fitted his seat belt and collected up his book and papers. The landing was smooth and there was a ripple of applause among the passengers as the plane slowed to taxi. As soon as the plane came to a stop on the tarmac Staverley could feel the heat from outside and he realised he had dressed wrongly - too many clothes and too heavy. This was not weather for denim. He prepared himself to sweat. The passengers were transferred to a bus for the short drive to the terminal and then they shuffled and jostled straight into passport control. Spain had not yet joined the European Union but the increasing flow of tourists had encouraged the authorities to make sure entry to the country was as straightforward as possible. As Staverley edged forward in the queue he looked at the posters and pictures on the walls, celebrating the wonders of the Costa Brava and its beaches. This was the new Spain, the democratic Spain, Europe's playground. That got him thinking about the other reason he was now here. Well, not a reason, perhaps, rather a task: a task with a long history, that he had known nothing about until just three months ago.

*

The visit to his Mother had been overdue. He had only seen her once since Christmas but they had talked on the phone each Sunday as usual. And she was very good at never making him feel like a bad son - which sometimes made him feel like a very bad son. But growing up as an only child to a single mother meant that they found it easy to talk, about both the trivial and the serious. She was very proud of what he had achieved, he knew that. He had been looking forward to telling her about his plans to travel to Spain for his sabbatical but also worried about what she would think about him being away for such a long time. When he explained what he was intending to do she had gone very quiet and he had feared the worst.

"Are you worried about me being gone for all that time?"

His mother stared at him oddly and he had difficulty reading her expression. She said nothing. She was almost never without something to say.

"What is it Mum? Tell me".

She retrieved a handkerchief from the sleeve of her cardigan. It was something he had seen her do many thousands of times and it made him smile. She brushed her nose with the handkerchief and tucked it back in place. She gathered herself and put her hand on the dining table. He reached across and put his hand on top of hers. It was soft and warm. He liked touching her.

"Mum?"

"It's just so strange," she said, "I have been waiting for this moment for so long. I had even rehearsed what I have to say, but now it's difficult to begin."

She fell silent again and retrieved the handkerchief from her sleeve again.

"Now you've got me really worried. What is this? What is it you have to say to me? I really don't understand."

His mother smiled then, as only mothers can, making him feel six years old.

"Don't worry, you don't have to worry. This isn't about me, there's nothing wrong. It's about your father and it's about a twist of fate. I suppose you could call it that. But he told me that this would happen. I don't know how but he knew. I didn't quite believe it."

Staverley barely remembered his father, who had died when he was three years old from wounds sustained in the Second World War. He had been a virtual invalid and spent most of his time, as far as Staverley remembered, in bed. Staverley would be sent to sit by his bedside at some point every day, and his father would talk to him fitfully - about what, Staverley had little recollection. But as he grew older he had begun to ask his mother questions about his father's life and his injuries but she had been very skilled at avoiding having to answer directly. Staverley had learned little beyond the basics – where he had been born, some details of his immediate family, that he had been in the RAF as a radio operator. He remained an enigma. His mother had been willing to talk about how much she had loved him and about how they had met and married and about her sadness that his life had been cut short by the effects of war, but she had always remained vague on details. Staverley had thought that the memories must be too painful for her, and he had come to accept that he should not push her to rehearse that pain. But he had always wanted to know more and have a better sense of what kind of man his father had been. He had learned a few more bits and pieces from his aunts and uncles, but his father remained as a kind of blur. There were even very few photographs of him but the few Staverley had seen showed a vital, vigorous young man with a ready smile.

"The thing is that you are going to Spain, to Catalunya, and you're going to try to learn Spanish you said. Well your father could have helped with that."

Staverley had no idea what she was talking about.

"Your father spoke some Spanish and some Catalan, not very refined but enough to make himself understood and get by, enough to order a good meal he used to say. You see he fought in the Spanish civil war. He was a volunteer, in what was called the International Brigades."

Staverley was stunned, but stunned was an understatement, he was well beyond stunned, he was astounded, shocked, flabbergasted: he found himself stuck in a cliché of reeling thoughts and stuttering speechlessness.

"Why did you never tell me?" Was the best he could manage, but it was a pertinent question.

"He made me promise that I wouldn't, or at least not until the right time he said, and he told me that I would know when the right time was. Until now I've had no idea what he meant by that, but this is it, this is the right time, it's obvious. I shouldn't have worried so much. I should have just trusted him."

She was smiling again now and remembering. She glanced at the wedding photo that sat on the mantelpiece. The one set in snow, they had married on Christmas day.

"All right, why did he not want you to tell me until the right time? It's not a little thing to not know that your father fought in a war in another country. And now I am wondering on which side he fought, and why?"

His mother gripped his hand and looked at him as though he was very silly.

"The Republic, of course, he fought for the Republic, against Franco. That's a very unnecessary question. He was fighting Fascism and for justice. He was fighting for us, for the people back in England as well as those in Spain. He was doing what most governments would not do. He couldn't stand by and allow evil to have its day. That's what he said. But he didn't want you to know because he didn't want to burden you with his politics and the decisions that his politics had led to. Your father was more than anything a man of politics. Politics defined his life and defined him as a man, but they also brought him, brought both of us, great sorrow and not a little suffering. And he came to think of that sorrow and suffering as something that you should not inherit. He wanted you to be your own person, to find your own way. Maybe that sounds a little strange to you, but in those years before he died, when he was so ill, he had a lot of time to think about how he'd spent his life. He didn't have regrets as such, but he carried with him a great sense of dissatisfaction and failure. Not just because the Republic was defeated and all that followed, but about things that had happened to him personally, things that made him doubt the possibility that relations between people could ever be honest and true. When he went to Spain he was clear about where he stood and what he believed in, when he came back he was full of doubts."

Staverley had never heard his mother talk in quite this way before. She had always been interested in politics. When she was younger she had been an active member of her union, USDAW, the bakers and shoemakers union she used to call it, but this was more forthright and immediate than her passionate dislike and disapproval of Margaret Thatcher and her cohorts.

"Perhaps I would be a disappointment to him," Staverley said. "My political commitments, such as they are, might seem pretty trivial to someone who risked his life to fight Fascism in another country."

"Don't think that. You fight where you stand, he used to say, and you do what you can do best, as long as you do something. It was different then in the 1930s, when we met. The lines of right and wrong, friend and enemy, were much clearer than now. Don't get me wrong, there was debate and argument, lots of it, but it had a point of concentration, or rather two - Capitalism and Fascism. It was very clear what it was we were up against. And I think I began to fall in love with your father as soon as I heard him speak about those things and the need for political struggle. I liked to listen to him talk about what a better world would look like. He had a way with words that you have certainly inherited. He could make people dream, he could spin a web of words that captured hearts and souls. They certainly did mine. He talked about what he had read and what had inspired him, and people responded. He was always being told that he should stand for the council or for parliament, or work for the union, but that was not what he wanted. He believed that politics was something beyond speeches and books, that it was about how we treat one another, how we value one another. That it should be about bringing out the best in people, showing them how good they might be. It's about social relations not institutions, he would say, about freedom and tolerance, about being different and being comfortable with difference. He read everything he could but he didn't just spout what he read. He was a thinker your father. Our first flat in Deptford was furnished with his books. We couldn't afford much in the way of proper furniture but we could always afford books. I was forever dusting them and rebuilding the piles that had collapsed. I worked in a laundry then, first in the washroom and then upfront in the shop. He moved from job to job, but he had done his apprenticeship as a plasterer and there was always plenty of work for someone with his skills."

Staverley had never heard these things. His father was becoming a little clearer but more of a puzzle.

"So how did it come about that he went to Spain?"

"It became a preoccupation for him. It was for almost everybody on the left. He came to see that arguments and exhortations and taking collections and expressing solidarity were not enough. He became frustrated with all the talk. And if anything the Conservative government in Britain at the time was sympathetic to the Nationalists. They were worried about the spread of communism, and Stanley Baldwin and the French prime minister, I can't remember his name, campaigned for non-intervention. Even the Labour Party supported them, at least initially. And they got their way. But the Germans and Italians were sending planes and supplies and arms while the rest of the world just stood aside and watched. They did nothing while Franco and the fascists did their worst. Anyway, your father knew several people in the Independent Labour Party, not the Labour Party, they were different then, and they gave him an introduction to Mannie Shinwell, and Reggie Reynolds I think. They were MPs. And the ILP were forming a contingent to go to Spain as part of the International Brigades and fight alongside POUM, they were anarchists and unionists, opposed to Stalin as much as Franco, and they had a big following, especially in Catalunya, where you are going. There were many late nights then, long and difficult conversations, before he decided that he actually would go. It wasn't just his decision, it was ours, he was very clear about that. We even talked about me going with him. I thought I could have been a nurse's aide or a fighter. You know the first British volunteer killed in the fighting was a woman, Felicia Browne. She was involved in trying to blow up a train. People forget that, or men do. It wasn't just a men's war. Women participated in all sorts of ways. But I had been unwell, from working in the laundry, the chemicals, and we had no idea what was possible and what hardships might be involved. So we decided that I could join him later when I was better. He went with the ILP contingent, with George Orwell part of the way. They travelled to Paris and then on a train to Perpignan and from there in a truck to Barcelona. I didn't hear from him for two months after that. But neither your father nor Orwell really understood at the beginning that the communists hated POUM as much as they did the Nationalists and that the Spanish government in Madrid was deeply suspicious of the Catalan anarchists. I was able to visit him once, in Barcelona, I went with Eileen, Orwell's wife. That was in the spring of 37. And then I lost track of him again, for a long time."

Staverley knew vaguely about some of this from a contemporary history course he had done as an undergraduate and he had read *Homage to Catalonia* and a lot of Orwell's fiction. But the idea that his father was part of the struggle against Franco and against Stalin and had known Orwell was difficult to grasp. It all seemed unreal. And he was still finding it difficult to accept that his father had not wanted him to know about his life and about who he was and what he had done. His mother had explained his father's wishes, but to keep back so much and to deprive him of a proper sense of who his father was seemed almost cruel. He would never say that to his mother, of course. She had done so much for him, and given up so much. Her life with a sick husband and a young child, and then as a single mother, had been hard. The long hours she worked as a shop assistant and floor manager had affected her health, though Staverley had never had any sense of being disadvantaged or constrained by his upbringing. His mother and her sisters, especially Aunt Alice, had made sure of that. But he did want to know more, and understand better his father and what he had experienced, and he realised that his time in Catalunya might be an opportunity for that. His mother now suddenly looked rather tired and he thought perhaps he had asked enough and heard enough, at least for now. But she was not finished.

"I can't tell you much more about your father's time in Spain. He didn't tell me everything, but another time I can explain to you about my visit to Barcelona. After he returned to England he didn't want to talk about what had happened. He sometimes had nightmares and in some ways the effects on him were emotional as much as physical. He was wounded but he had been treated well, although he never fully recovered. He couldn't go back to his plastering work. I think, though, it was what he had seen and perhaps also what he had done and what had been done to him that stayed with him most. Too much evil, he would say, too many deaths. Wait for me a minute."

His mother stood slowly, he could tell that her knee was bothering her. She went over to the chest of drawers where she kept her papers and documents and unlocked a drawer at the bottom and pulled it out with some difficulty. She retrieved a pile of documents and photographs and shuffled through them until she found a small envelope. She returned to the table and sat down again. Staverley sipped his tea but it had gone cold. His mother slid the envelope across the table toward him.

"This is for you. Your father asked me to give it to you."
"At the right time," Staverley said.
His mother smiled again.

"That's right, dear."

The envelope was old and the corners were frayed. The paper was cheap and discoloured with age. As he opened it, it tore at little. He tried to be careful. There was one sheet of paper inside, folded in quarters. On the paper was written just one short sentence, in ink that now looked green, and below that a list of what appeared to be names. The sentence was not in English, or in any language Staverley recognised. It said, "Vam ser traïts."

"What does it mean?" he asked.

"I don't know. I've never opened the envelope, and your father never said what was in it, just that you should have it..."

"At the right time."
"That's right."
He looked at the list. There were three names.

Jaume Subirachs i Muntaner
Jordi Batlló-Sabé
Joan Canoes-Mas

*

The envelope his mother had given him was in the briefcase he now carried into the baggage claim area of the airport. He thought further about what the words and names meant as he waited while the baggage conveyer went around and around, so far with no suitcases to be seen. A colleague in the languages department at Watermouth had translated the words for him They were Catalan:"We were betrayed" they said. He had talked to his mother afterwards about what they might mean, but she had no clear idea. He had also done some library research on POUM and the ILP and re-read *Homage to Catalonia*. From that, the most obvious interpretation of his father's words was a reference to the betrayal of the POUM fighters by the Republican government and the battle for the Barcelona Telephone Exchange in May 1937 - the May Days, as they were called - and the subsequent suppression of the anarchist movement and the murder and torture of its leaders by the Russian controlled secret police. All of that he had read was part of the Madrid government's assertion of control over Barcelona and the elimination of all Trotskyist influences by the COMINTERN controlled Communist Party of Spain. It was well documented in the various histories of the civil war. So why would Staverley's father write what he had, for his son to read, and how was the betrayal related to the three names? He was sure there was something more to it than a political statement. His task, the task he had given himself, was to find out. But he needed his luggage first.

A bulging, battered blue suitcase held together by a leather strap finally emerged from the end of the conveyer and began to trundle around in front of the waiting passengers. Staverley shook himself from his reverie, wondering why it was that some people insisted on crowding forward toward the belt making it difficult for others to see what was coming rather than waiting until their own bags were in sight. The oddness of human crowd behaviour never ceased to bemuse him. He assumed that some of these people were the tourists whose impact he had come to research. He could certainly hear a mix of English accents as well as several other languages. As the crowd began to thin, he caught sight of his canvas holdall making its way slowly toward where he stood.

Bag in hand Staverley made his way unaccosted through customs control and the automatic doors to the arrivals hall. He was confronted by a seething mass of faces. Some were obvious family, eager to catch sight of their loved ones. Others were holiday representatives holding signs with the name of their company on the look out for their customers. Most of the company names seemed to be in English and to include the word sun. Staverley put down his bag and briefcase looked more systematically at the crowd, he was looking for Margarida, and hoping that she was looking for him. He assumed he would not be that easy to spot among the throng of tourists. He was of average height and build, he always bought clothes medium size and they always fitted. He was ordinary looking, he thought, with nondescript brown hair and no distinguishing marks or features. The sort of person you do not notice. Margarida – and he kept reminding himself that her name was spelled with a d rather than a t, the Catalan way – was the student of a friend of Lionel, his Head of Department at Watermouth. When Staverley had explained his sabbatical plans to Lionel he had been surprised by an offer of help in arranging local contacts. Lionel was not the most sociable of colleagues and he and Staverley had an odd history, which they both worked hard to ignore. They had shared personal revelations, which were now studiously never referred to. One of the things Staverley had discovered as part of those revelations was that Lionel was an ardent fan of jazz, and had an enormous collection of jazz records and regularly attended clubs and concerts to hear his favourite artists. Evidently a network of other academics across Europe shared this passion and met regularly at jazz festivals and concerts. One member of this fraternity of adherents was Professor Vincente Montoliu, a cultural historian working at the Autonomous University of Barcelona. At Lionel's behest Professor Montoliu had very kindly found a place for Staverley to stay during his visit, and had agreed to introduce him to some useful local contacts. He had even offered to take him to hear some Catalan jazz. With even more kindness Professor Montoliu had organised for one of his PhD students, that was Margarida, to meet Staverley at the airport and take him to where he would be staying.

As Staverley waited and surveyed the waiting crowd from one end to the other for the fourth time he caught the eye of a very tall young woman with very long dark wavy hair. She smiled and waved. If this were not Margarida then they would share a moment of embarrassment and both look elsewhere. Staverley picked up his luggage and walked confidently toward her, returning her smile.

"Yo soy Staverley," he said. This was his first attempt at speaking Spanish to a Spaniard.

"I thought you were," she replied in English with what sounded like a slight American accent, "you look English but you're obviously not a tourist. They don't carry briefcases."

So he had stood out from the crowd. Well observed, he thought. Staverley did not know whether to be relieved or disappointed by Margarida's fluency in English. But on the whole perhaps it would make things easier, at least to start with.

"Thank you for coming to meet me. You are very kind."

"It's not a problem. Shall we go? It's this way."

Margarida turned away and Staverley followed her. Her car was close by in a car park directly across the road from the terminal entrance. Even so, by the time they were trying to fit Staverley's suitcase in the rear seats his head was covered in sweat, with more running down his spine.. He had had his hair cut short for the journey, shorter than it had been for many years, but it did not help, he was very hot and very uncomfortable. And with the shorter style it was evident that his hair was thinning., a nasty shock. He was only just 30.

The car was tiny, a Seat 600 of a certain age. It seemed ill-suited to someone of Margarida's height, but she curled herself elegantly behind the wheel while Staverley, much less elegantly, tried to climb into the passenger seat.

"It's a small car," Margarida said, "but you get used to it. It's a family heirloom, handed down."

Once they were underway, with the side window fully open, Staverley began to cool down a little. They were driving north, toward Barcelona.

"Your English is much better than my Spanish," he said, as an opening ploy for conversation and with the hope that they would continue in English.

"Thank you. I kind of grew up hearing a lot of English. My family moved around a lot and English was often the easiest way to communicate wherever we happened to be. And last year I had a travel grant from the university to spend a year in the US. I was based in Baltimore but travelled around as well. And it's good to keep it up, so don't feel bad. In some ways my English is probably better than my Spanish. My mother tongue is Catalan."

"Right, so maybe I have been doing entirely the wrong thing in trying to learn Spanish - Castilian, that is. Maybe that will make my research even more difficult."

Margarida turned toward him with a wry smile.

"Well, yes, perhaps. You will soon come to understand that here language and politics are one and the same thing. Franco did his best to prohibit and suppress Catalan. Education, the media, administration, everything was in Castilian while he was in power. You couldn't even put Catalan on tombstones. You will see that many street names and public signage is still in Castilian, or in both languages. But Catalan is reasserting itself, as the Catalan people begin to reassert themselves. In Barcelona Castilian is still pretty much dominant at least in public spaces but that's also changing. And where we're going now, Catalan was always spoken at home and in daily life, that was true even in Franco's time, but it's now the language of public life as well."

"So basically I am in trouble and will have to start again from scratch." Staverley said this with a huge sigh, Margarida offering another wry smile in response.

"Yes and no. It's complicated. As a foreigner, or more accurately a non-Spanish foreigner, you will probably be indulged and people will speak to you in Castilian quite happily. If you were Spanish, people might be more reluctant. I have a few friends who refuse to speak Castilian. But because of Franco's policies everyone, except very old people, were educated at school in Castilian - if you can call it education! I didn't go to school here a lot. As I said, my family moved around, but when I was here my mother used to remind me as I set off in the mornings. 'Remember, no Catalan!' she would say. If the teacher heard you speaking Catalan then, you were punished. It was like leading a double life:one that was natural and real but secret, and the other that was unreal but dangerous. It meant pretending to be someone else when you were in public. Like speaking lines in a play, and hating it, resenting it."

Staverley winced as she said this. He remembered reading that in the 19th century similar things had happened in Wales to Welsh speaking children. Children who lapsed into Welsh had been made to wear the "Welsh Not" around their necks.

"I'm sure you will find a way to make things work," Margarida said, "and to be honest Catalan is not an easy language to learn. The virtue of Spanish is that it's pretty logical and is pronounced as it's written, give or take some exceptions. Catalan is not. It has its origins in Vulgar Latin and was widespread around the Mediterranean between the 11th and 15th centuries.There are even some villages in Sardinia where they still speak it. But from then on it was suppressed in various ways. And that inhibited the development of the language even now there are rules of grammar that are in dispute."

Staverley's second thoughts about this trip and his research were now becoming third thoughts. Maybe he could just take a holiday here and then go home and spend his sabbatical in his flat writing a book about the growth of the charter holiday industry, in English. He tried to put those doubts aside.

"As I said, this is really kind of you, and Professor Montoliu of course. But I am still not clear about where you're taking me and where I'm going to be staying."

Margarida laughed.

"He didn't explain? Actually I can believe that. He's a lovely man, and a great supervisor for my PhD but sometimes he does come very close to the stereotype of the absent-minded professor. He was supposed to pass on a whole list of details to you. I even wrote them down for him. But never mind. Okay then, we are going to a very small town about an hour and a half north of Barcelona. It's called Sant Pere de Palautordera, or just Palau among the locals. It's inland, about half an hour or so from the coast, and from some of the new developments that I think you're interested in. It's very quiet, very Catalan, but it's very nice. My family come from there. It's on the edge of a group of mountains called the Montseny, spelled with a 'y' that you don't pronounce. The Montseny is a significant place in this part of Catalunya. There's lots of folklore stuff and myths, pixies and wild boars and mushrooms and legends. Anyway you can ask the locals about that, there are lots of stories. So you are staying in Palau, in my grandmother's house."

All of this was news to Staverley. It was both reassuring and a little daunting. The last thing he had heard from Professor Montoliu was that he would sort something out and not to worry. But now Staverley *was* worried. He had certainly not anticipated having to cope with living with a Catalan grandmother and whatever that might entail.

"And your grandmother is all right with this? It seems like a huge imposition."

Perhaps Margarida's grandmother ran a lodging house, Staverley thought.

Yet another wry smile.
"My grandmother is dead. She died about a year ago."
"Oh dear, I'm sorry. My condolences."
"Thank you. I adored my grandmother, and she lived to a good age. She was a real character. But her house has been empty since she died, and the family are not sure what they want to do with it. It's very small, very traditional. We've cleaned it out and done a bit of decorating, although *iaia,* grandma, kept the house immaculate. So you will be our tenant. You'll be on your own. We're charging you rent. If that's okay?"

"Absolutely, no problem. I even have a small grant from my university for living expenses, I was expecting to pay."

"Good, although in fact it won't be much, especially given the exchange rate between the pound and the peseta. And Senyora Budó, who's a neighbour and was my *iaia's* best friend, is happy to do some bits of cleaning and washing for you. You will have to pay her too. She might also do some cooking. She's a very good cook."

After the initial surprise of all of these arrangements, Staverley thought he quite liked being organised and looked after, and the idea of a little house of his own was actually very appealing.

"In fact, that sounds great. But I don't know how I'm going to make this up to you. You've gone to so much trouble for me. You still are."

Margarida tapped him lightly on the arm.

"It's a Catalan thing. Nothing is too much for a visitor. And obligation is also a big thing. So Professor Montoliu is a friend of your Head of Department, I think. And Professor Montoliu was very much involved in getting me my travel scholarship to the US. There is a whole string of obligations. So if I can do something in return. Things go around that way, and now you have obligations, d'you see? "

Staverley thought he did see, but there was something else bothering him in all of this.

"You mentioned Senyora Budó and cooking," he tried to copy Margarida's Catalan pronunciation,, "there's one thing that I didn't mention to Professor Montoliu. You see I'm vegetarian".

This time there was no wry smile but instead full-out loud laughter that continued for some time. It was a while before Margarida calmed down enough to speak.

"Now that, in Catalunya, could be a real problem. I don't think we even have a word in Catalan for a vegetarian. We are big on our meat. That's especially true in the Montseny. In fact, there's a Catalan divide. On the coast it's fish, and in the country it's meat. I don't know how we're going to explain that to Senyora Budó."

Margarida laughed again. But Staverley looked glum. It was his turn to smile wryly.

"I have spent the last three months preparing for this trip, and now it seems I'm not prepared at all."

"So why Catalunya? Why decide to spend your sabbatical here?"

"Well, there was initially a very simple answer to that. It's for research. I have a period of study leave and I want to pursue my research here, looking at tourism. Spain's economic miracle. But now I have another reason for being here. It's to do with my father and my family history. He fought in the Civil War, and I want to find out more about what happened to him. He died when I was very young."

Staverley could see Margarida tense when he mentioned the Civil War. Her hands tightened on the steering wheel and her smile faded. He could see in her face the formulation of a question, obviously an important question.

"So … On which side did your father fight?" she asked this and glanced at him.

"He fought for the Republic. He was attached to POUM, the anarchists, like George Orwell. He was wounded."

Staverley watched Margarida relax again, as she glanced sideways at him, her smile returning and then fading again.

"That's so interesting. My Phd is related to the Civil War. I'm looking at the poetry and literature produced during or about the war. So I should know more than I do about the different participants and the international volunteers. But you will find there is a general reluctance to revisit the darker side of what went on in the war. People don't talk about it. And you see, we have, -what is it in English? –the official 'Pact of Forgetting'. The idea is that we pretend that there was no repression or murder or torture back then and that it has no relevance now and just get on with being democratic and modern. No victors or vanquished anymore they say, national reconciliation, looking forward and not back. No one gets blamed. Which means that a lot of things stay the same, a lot of people stay the same. People get to keep their jobs and get new ones; people who worked for Franco. So history doesn't exist for us, all is forgiven and forgotten. All the brutality is skated over, bodies remain buried, who knows where, literally. So we ignore our pain and ignore the dead and all those who are missing and are probably dead. And yes the Republic committed atrocities too and those need to be acknowledged, but we don't talk about a rebellion and foreign intervention and thirty-six years of Fascism and all that went with it, all the crimes and the suffering and humiliation. It's not healthy."

Margarida was quiet for a moment, and chewed her bottom lip hard.

"Sorry, I'm letting off steam, I have a problem with all of the silence and pretending. I think spending time outside the country has maybe given me a bit of distance, and from there the Pact seems like a very stupid and dangerous idea. My father does, too, and is working against it. I'll tell you about him perhaps another time. Sorry for the rant."

"Don't be," Staverley said, "I need to know these things, especially if I am going to get anywhere with finding out about my father's experiences. And from what you are saying that's just got a whole lot harder."

"Don't give up too soon. There are people who might help, and there is political opposition to the Pact. But look, we are coming into Sant Pere. That's the church ahead. The town is a small place, about a thousand people, but it has all the basics - bars, shops and all that, and nothing is very far from anywhere else which makes things easy. Everything is clustered around the two main streets, the old one and the new one. The old one's too narrow for cars. *Iaia's* house is up here, on the left. This is the new *carrer principal*, it goes up to the Montseny."

They stopped outside a row of three small houses, all similar but all different. They all had front double doors set in small masonry arches. The doors were wooden, studded with iron. There were three windows, one down and two up, the lower window guarded by ancient iron bars. In every case pots of red geraniums sat on the wide sills behind the bars. Each of the houses was painted a different hue of ochre. They were obviously quite old but looked very solid. Spanish versions of the two-up, two-downs that Staverley had grown up in. Margarida fished around in her large straw bag and came up with a huge iron key. She eased out of the car while Staverley struggled to extricate himself and his luggage.

Inside, the house was cool and dark and rather spartan. Staverley immediately liked the smell of it, the smell of old wood and old stone. It smelled like a happy house – a place where good lives had been lived by good people. The bottom floor consisted of a single space, which served as kitchen and sitting room. Margarida showed him around and then led him up the open stone staircase. On the upper floor was one bedroom and bathroom. It was spotlessly clean and the bed was made. It was covered in a embroidered bedspread. There seemed to be everything that he would need.

"This is going to be good," he said to Margarida.

"I'm pleased. *Iaia* would be happy to know it's being put to use. She lived in this house for nearly fifty years, and brought up three children here. It shouldn't be left empty."

Downstairs again, Margarida began opening cupboards and the small refrigerator.

"Ah ha! Senyora Budó has been busy! You have coffee, bread, cheese, tomatoes, milk, eggs, onions and potatoes. And a fuet. You won't need that."

She brandished a large sausage in his direction, and then put it in her bag.

"And we have lunch, a tortilla." She put a plate on the table, on which was a formidable omelette about an inch thick, made with onions and potatoes, more like a cake than what usually passed as an omelette in England.

"Spain's culinary gift to the world," Margarida said. "Let's eat. I'm hungry."

She laid the table and produced a bottle of red wine from one of the cupboards. She carefully studied the label.

"Emporda, good - that's the nearest wine growing area, just north of Girona. Not classic wines, but usually very reliable. Let's try it."

Lunch was delicious. Staverley really enjoyed the tortilla, and Margarida explained how it was made. She said she would write instructions for him.

"Most important of all is patience. You can't rush a tortilla."

They ate almost all of it with the chunky bread and drank a glass of the wine, which was robust and unsophisticated but more than drinkable. Margarida then suggested that she take him on a quick tour of the town. They would have a coffee in *La Granja*, and then find Senyora Budó. Over coffee, which Staverley enjoyed -he was very particular about his coffee - Margarida asked more about his father, and he tried to explain how he came to be in Spain as a volunteer fighter. As she had said in the car, she knew little of POUM or the involvement of foreign volunteers, but said she would ask Professor Montoliu and her father and some other people she thought might be able to help with information. She did know from her research that several well-known poets from other countries had fought for the Republic, like Stephen Spender, Octavio Paz, John Cordford and Pablo Neruda. Staverley's debt of gratitude was piling up significantly, but he wanted to ask one more thing.

"Can I show you something my father left for me?"
"Of course."
"It's this." He had his father's note with him, and handed it to her.
She read it very carefully.
"What does it mean?" she asked.

"That's what I want to find out."

"And who are these three people?"

"I want to find that out too. But I don't really know
where to begin."

Margarida read the note and the names again.

"Well, one thing for sure is that they're all Catalans, with names like
that. Those are Catalan fore names and family names. There are lots of
people who would share the family names, in different combinations.
Unlike you Brits we take both our parents' names. But the only one I
recognise, and it doesn't mean it's the same person, is Jaume Subirachs
i Muntaner. There's a well-known, local ERC politician of that name.
And he would certainly be the right age to have fought in the Civil
War."

"ERC?" Staverley asked.

"Sorry, that's the *Esquerra Republicana de Catalunya*. I think it was
founded in the 1930s and, as the name says, it's Catalan, it's left, and
it's republican. They were the majority party in the Catalan
government in the years before the War and were involved in the
proclamation of a Catalan republic in 1931, although that only lasted
four days. Later, of course, the party was declared illegal by Franco but
it continued to exist in exile. They're rather overshadowed now by
Convergencia. That's Pujol's party – Jordi Pujol. Anyway, the ERC are
down to just four or five seats in the Catalan parliament, and I don't
think they have any representatives at all now in the *Cortes* in Madrid.
I should know more, especially as I voted for them in the last elections.
But it's history again and the forgetting."

Staverley had read up on the Catalan government and its President
Jordi Pujol and his party *Convergencia i Unio*. They were an alliance of
moderate but conservative Catalan nationalists with the Union which
is Catholic. Pujol had founded the party and was the dominant figure in
Catalan politics. He was briefly imprisoned by Franco in the 1960s, but
had also served in the provisional Catalan government in the 1970s.
He seemed to offer an odd mix of Catalan intransigence and
conservative pragmatism.

Margarida looked at her watch.

"Listen, I'm sorry, I need to get back to Barcelona. That's where I'm living at the moment. I'll find out more for you if I can. I'll make a note of the names, and I'll try to find out more about Subirachs. You've got me intrigued now."

She got a notebook from her bag and wrote down the three names.

"Let's talk to Senyora Budó, and then I must go. Will you be okay on your own? I'll be back tomorrow, mid-morning, and we'll go on a tour of the area and over to the coast, if that's okay with you?"

"That would be really great. Thank you again, Margarida."

As promised, Margarida introduced Staverley to Senyora Budo before she left: she was a small woman, of at least seventy. She looked severe at first sight, seeming to regard Staverley with some suspicion. But when Margarida explained his dietary disability she laughed as much as Margarida had, and gripped his arm tightly with both hands.

"*No hay problema*," she said several times and she was still chuckling to herself and shaking her head when Margarida rushed away. Left to their own devices with no translator, and relying on Staverley's basic Castilian, they established that if he wanted her to make him lunch or dinner or breakfast he would come to her house, two houses along from *iaia's*, and if she was not there he would leave a large smooth stone on her doorstep, which she gave to him to keep. She would also change the linen and do washing for him once a week and clean the house twice a week. They agreed a payment for all of this, which seemed to him to be very modest. She seemed very happy with the arrangement, and Staverley certainly was. A lot had happened since his plane had landed and he was very tired.

Chapter 2

The bed was comfortable, although it creaked loudly sometimes when he turned over, and Staverley slept well - which had not always been the case in recent months. The night had been quiet, and the house had a peaceful, calming solidity about it.. He made himself a fried egg and toast for breakfast and pottered around the kitchen checking out the crockery and utensils. Most had obviously belonged to Margarida's grandmother. They were of a certain age but entirely serviceable, although the actual purpose of two of the older utensils completely eluded him. He would ask. Before Margarida arrived, he decided on a further exploration of Sant Pere, and perhaps some shopping.

Sant Pere was a little too small to be called a town and maybe just a little too big to be called a village. As Margarida had said, it had all the necessities to manage daily life. He braved the small supermarket and came away with some jars of delicious looking beans of different shapes and sizes and various vegetables that looked freshly picked. The vegetables all looked bigger than in England. He also found a small shop in the old main street that sold wine from the barrel and he bought a litre of Priorat for 70 pesetas, including a glass bottle for re-fills, and some olives. He chatted with the shop owner, David, in an imprecise but functional mix of English and Castilian. David had learned his English from wine trade magazines and the backs of bottles. He knew a lot about wines and explained the Priorat grapes and growing conditions in great detail.

Just as Staverley got back to the house Margarida was arriving. She seemed impressed with his purchases and he left them in the house before they set off on their tour.

"I thought," Margarida explained, "that we would go to the coast first. I think that's where your research will happen, yes? And Professor Montoliu has given me the list of contacts he promised you."

"That's great, but I want to get an initial sense of what's going on for myself before I speak to anyone. I've read about the scale of investments and development but it's different when you actually see it."

Margarida turned the car around and they headed southeast away from the Montseny toward another mountain.

"We need to cross Mont Negre, the Black Mountain, in order to get to the coast. It's a tortuous route, I warn you. The road is difficult, lots of bends and slow going."

She was right, the little car chugged slowly through the wooded countryside, the road getting steeper all the time. They passed through one small town that looked about the same size as Sant Pere and from then on the bends started and seemed to go on and on and up and up. Then suddenly they were at the top and the sea was below them. They could see for miles. The sea was a classic blue, like in a children's painting. They drove downhill alongside a wide dry river bed, past a large rambling ceramics factory and through fields full of fruit trees and vegetables into the main street of a busy fishing port.

"Arenys de Mar," Margarida announced. "Not much tourism here, it's a working port and commercial centre for this part of the coast."

Once at sea level Margarida turned north on the coast road, which ran between the railway line and the mountain. As soon as they left Arenys and began to drive through the small resort towns, Staverley could see the cranes at work and the glut of new buildings, sitting between and alongside ordinary houses and shops, looming over them.

"The developers buy up what land and buildings they can. Some people are happy to sell and move to the city, some are not and it's said that pressure is brought to bear. When the developers have enough land they build. And the whole point is that."

Margarida gestured toward the sea and the broad, smooth, clean sandy beach on the other side of the railway. It was dotted with parasols and towels and bodies broiling in the full sun. As they continued on the small coast road there was a succession of such beaches, large and small, separated off from one another by rocky headlands. Some were well populated with sun-bathers and swimmers and others, less accessible, were virtually deserted. After about half an hour fields and wetlands gradually replaced the mountains and cliffs and they passed a series of new, purpose built resorts with large hotels, pools, restaurants and bars. These were busy with tourists and the beaches were packed. Sun oil encountered olive oil in a heady clash of cultures.

"This used to be agricultural land or open coast line with lagoons and reed beds, and it's here where there are the big developments that are most controversial," Margarida explained. "Shall we stop somewhere and look around?"

They parked close to the beach in a resort called Santa Susannah and found a bar near the beach with parasols under which they could hide from the sun. The temperature was rising fast and they both needed something cool to drink, Margarida also ordered pastries.

"An *almuerzo*," she said.
"In England we would call it elevenses."
Staverley had begun a list of questions in his head as they drove. The list was long.

"Would you mind if I made some notes?"

"Not at all, in fact while you do that I'll make a phone call." She went to the bar while Staverley retrieved his notebook and began to scribble down ideas.

By the time Margarida returned Staverley had filled several pages of his notebook. As with his previous research done in England the reality of seeing things first hand, in context, was very different from reading about them in the abstract. Investment, planning and building was changing the physical and natural environment and people's lives, although the material, economic and cultural impacts of development on the scale he had seen were obviously generating new jobs and local business opportunities – like the bar in which they sat. The drinks and pastries arrived and Staverley turned his attention to the clientele of the bar. The raw and pink skin of some of the people returning from the beach was painful to see. They were not used to this kind of sun and seem to ignore sensible ways of protecting themselves. He wondered what the waiters thought about all of that burnt flesh.

When making his notes Staverley realised that he was confronted by a very practical problem if his research were to progress.

"Margarida, you have been so kind and given me so much of your time already but I'm wondering how I'm going to get from place to place once I'm on my own. Are there buses or taxis I can use to get from Sant Pere and move up and down the coast?"

"There are but not from Sant Pere itself. Well there is a taxi, Josep-Maria is the driver, and you could get him to take you to Arenys and then catch the train or a bus from there. The train goes north up the coast toward Girona or south to Barcelona. But that would be tortuous and time-consuming. I assumed you would want to be more flexible, so I had an idea, I'll show you when we get back. Are you ready?"

They retraced their route along the coast to Arenys and then back over Mont Negre. Again the Seat struggled up and around the sharp bends and once or twice coughed ominously on the steepest sections. Margarida murmured words of encouragement on the steepest sections but she had no doubts about the reliability of her tiny car. Once back in Sant Pere, she pulled off the main street and turned sharply through the double doors of a large workshop, inside which several cars were being worked on. They got out and a large man in blue overalls, with an even larger moustache, emerged from under the bonnet of one of the cars. He made an attempt to clean his hands on an oily rag and leant forward to kiss Margarida, taking care not to touch her. They exchanged greetings in Catalan, and Staverley could tell that he was being explained. Margarida gestured and Staverley and the man shook hands.

"Bon Dia Senyor," the man said. He had a broad, pudgy face behind his enormous moustache, and his smile was warm and genuine. Staverley responded in his newly acquired, and as yet only Catalan.

"Bon Dia."

"This is Salvador," Margarida explained. Salvador smiled again, attempted another cleaning of his hands, and then turned and disappeared into the dark shadows at the rear of the workshop. There was a clatter of movement before he returned wheeling a tiny, green moped. He parked it and gestured toward it with another burst of Catalan.

"This," said Margarida, "is you transport. It's a ciclomotor. It's only 50ccs so you need no license. Salvador has checked and repaired it. He says it's done hundreds of kilometres and it's good for hundreds more. We have agreed a special price and it's yours to take away. If you want it."

Staverley was astonished. His first thought was the strangeness of the whole idea. His second was whether he would be able to manage the machine. But it was nothing more than an overgrown bicycle with a tiny engine behind the seat. It was a great idea and a perfect solution.

"Perfecto," he said to Salvador, who looked very pleased and gave the diminutive machine a wipe with his rag.

Salvador showed him how to start the engine and how the gears worked and then he and Margarida watched with amusement as Staverley set off on a test run. After a few wobbles and some struggles with the unfamiliar gears he was off. He tried some turns and stops and starts. The moped was light and easy to manoeuvre and everything seemed in perfect working order. He was enjoying himself. He had briefly wanted a motorbike when he was a teenager but his mother would have none of it. As he turned again and re-entered the workshop he thought of how much had happened in the short time since his arrival and how kind and helpful everyone had been. He doubted whether the same degree of kindness and help would be forthcoming in England for visitors like him. It would depend on the circumstances, he thought. After paying Salvador and as a small recompense, he persuaded Margarida to let him buy her lunch.

Staverley wheeled the ciclo, and Margarida led him to a restaurant in the old main street. The entrance was very small and easy to miss. Inside, it was nearly full and they were lucky to find a table. The menu consisted of three courses with two choices for each. Water, bread and wine were included in the set price, which would hardly buy a sandwich in Watermouth. Margarida engaged in some detailed negotiations with the waiter and when he laughed Staverley realised that the topic was his dietary peculiarities again. The bread came in a basket, the water and wine in carafes. His first course was spinach cooked with garlic, pine nuts and sultanas. His second was a huge pile of potatoes and green beans. Margarida explained that these should be mashed together with a fork into a kind of puree, and olive oil and salt and vinegar added to taste. Staverley set about the task. In the meantime she ate a salad and then attacked a meat stew, which she explained was wild boar, which were common in the Montseny and were hunted by the locals. The bread was fresh and chewy. The wine was rich and fruity. They finished with what Margarida described as the classic desert of Catalunya – *crema catalana*, which she also explained had been stolen by the French and turned into crème brulee – gastronomic booty from the peninsular wars. Coffee followed, very small, very dark, and very rich. Staverley was full. The meal had been both wholesome and delicious. He thought that perhaps being vegetarian would not be as difficult as he had first imagined. The small sum he handed over to the waiter seemed far too little compensation for everything Margarida had done for him. But there was more to come.

"Well, I talked to Professor Montoliu, and to my father, and he talked to some of his friends and you have an invitation. The politician we talked about, Jaume Subirachs i Muntaner, is speaking at a meeting tomorrow evening in Sant Celoni. That's only fifteen minutes from here on your ciclo. It's a meeting organised by the ERC to discuss local issues. The ERC are trying to re-build their grassroots support by highlighting the failure of Pujol's government to deal with the things that most affect people's daily lives. But Pujol is very popular around here with his version of Catalan Nationalism, at least for the moment. Most people like him and trust him. But he's very conservative and he's very close to Madrid and he's pro-business and does little for the small farmers. And he's also struggling with questions around the activities of his father's bank, the *Banca Catalana*. You might be interested in that. They have invested heavily with the developers."

Staverley was making notes again.

"Anyway, if you want you can go to the meeting and perhaps speak to Jaume Subirachs i Muntaner in person. It'll all be in Catalan of course, but there might be someone who can help you with the language. I can't be there, I'm sorry. My father says that Subirachs was in exile during Franco's time so who knows maybe he speaks some French or

English. He may be the person on your list or may not. It's worth asking."

"Please Margarida, don't be sorry. You've helped me more than I ever expected. Really." Dealing with kindness was sometimes difficult, and Staverley was struggling to properly express how grateful he was. Margarida wrote down the time and the address of the meeting, and drew a basic map showing how to get there.

"I also asked Professor Montoliu and my father about the other two names. They don't recognise them but they are going to ask around. I also asked Senyora Budó and Salvador. They know everyone in Sant Pere and most people in the Montseny, so if either of the other two is local they will find them for sure. Senyora Budó already has one idea she says. But realistically they could come from anywhere in Catalunya, and of course, as you must have thought. And the chances are they are no longer alive."

Staverely *had* thought about that. Indeed, he assumed that it was very likely, for all sorts of reasons; but having one possibility to follow up so soon after arriving was encouraging.

"What does your father do, Margarida?"

"He does all sorts of things. He's a kind of journalist, a broadcaster for TVE, he writes books, both fiction and non-fiction, he sits on some committees and is a trustee for a Fundación. What he does depends on the day. Sometimes he is one thing, sometimes another. I lose track, but I admire him a lot. The best way to describe him is that he's an intellectual, I suppose. He thinks and writes and speaks, and sometimes people don't like what he thinks and writes and says. He earns his living from words and ideas. I think he's extraordinary, but I would wouldn't I?" She laughed and looked embarrassed.

"I'd like to meet him sometime," Staverley said.

Margarida offered one of her trademark wry smiles.

"That can probably be arranged. He was certainly interested in your list and your father. He knows a lot about the civil war: too much, I think sometimes. He's a staunch opponent of the forgetting. Now, again I must rush. I need to get back to the University for a seminar. One of my friends is giving a paper, and she's very nervous about it."

Back in the house Staverley tried to put his notes from the day into some kind of order and to make a list of things to do, research tasks. But the combination of the lunch, the heat and two glasses of wine soon led him to succumb to that great Spanish institution the siesta.

The following day was again hot. Staverley woke early, made himself some breakfast – another fried egg – and then went for a walk before it got too hot. He explored more of Sant Pere, but there was not a lot to it. From each corner he turned he could see the Montseny looming. The mountains looked both daunting and intriguing, and he was tempted to collect his ciclo and take a closer look, but thought perhaps he should wait until he knew more about the local geography and where would be a good place to head for. When he got back to the house Senyora Budó was cleaning up the kitchen. She seemed excited to see him and an awkward but lighthearted conversation ensued. With her Staverley felt relaxed about his linguistic deficiencies. It was evident that Senyora Budó was not entirely comfortable in Castilian, and Staverley's Catalan vocabulary had now expanded to a grand total of six words, so there was a lot of gesturing and pointing, some mime and a lot of laughter and confusion while one or the other searched for the right word. But eventually Staverley thought he understood what Senyora Budó wanted to tell him and she seemed satisfied that he had grasped what she was saying. In the process Staverley acquired two more Catalan words – *muntanya*, which was fairly easy, and *cabrero* which - he grasped eventually, with the appropriate mime -meant a goatherder. Getting this had involved goat and sheep noises, ushering movements and what looked like milking. They had both enjoyed themselves. He could hear Senyora Budó's chuckles as she finished her cleaning. What she was telling him, he thought, was that Joan Canoes-Mas, or someone of that name, was a goatherder in the Montseny. She might also have been explaining that this Joan Canoes-Mas made and sold goat's cheese and there was something else about him that Staverley could not get the hang of. He pondered for a while what to do with this new information and then remembered that David's *bodega*, another new word, sold what looked like goat's cheese. He set off to find out.

The bodega was empty and pleasantly cool, and David was happy to chat, if that was the right word. This time the mix of Staverley's textbook Castilian and David's wine label English quickly established that the goat's cheese David sold was indeed produced and made by a man called Joan Canoes-Mas, that he lived with his goats in the high Montseny, and that he was a kind of recluse, which was the other thing that Senyora Budó was trying to communicate he now realised. Beyond those basics the conversation got stuck again, and Staverley had forgotten to bring his English-Spanish dictionary. He dutifully bought a piece of the cheese, called *Garrotxa*, David explained, and a bottle of wine to go with it and thanked David heartily for his help.

Back in the house Staverley could not resist trying the cheese. It was strong, firm and piquant, just like proper goat's cheese should be. It was quite unlike and far better than any Staverley had had in his sandwiches in Watermouth. That meant lunch was sorted.

Staverley decided to set out for the meeting in Sant Celoni early. Partly to make sure he could find the place and partly to give him some time to see a little of the town. Sant Celoni was bigger than Sant Pere, and quite ugly. It was a commercial and industrial centre and had obviously been marred and marked by messy modernisation in the 1960s and '70s. Old and new were jammed together, and some of the new was already looking distinctly the worse for wear. Concrete and stone did not sit happily together, a shame he thought. It was just possible to discern the structure of the old town with its tiny streets with rows of weathered stone houses, but in this instance progress was unforgiving and unsentimental. The church in the main square, with a flamboyant baroque edifice, seemed entirely out of place.

Staverley consulted Margarida's map and made his way from the centre to the north side of the town. He was looking for the *Rectoria*, which he assumed was a Rectory. So it was: a converted chapel, now a cultural centre, that stood at the side of a stretch of parkland, next to a school. There was a group of ten or fifteen people, men and women, standing outside the building, smoking and chatting. He parked the ciclo and stood on the edge of the group, trying not to look too out of place. The people all seemed to know one another. One of the men nodded to him.

"Bona Tarda," he responded – good evening. He had asked Senyora Budó about that – good afternoon. A few more people arrived, some going straight into the building, so Staverley followed. There was a small hall, which had obviously been the knave of the chapel. It was laid out with seats facing a table at which two men and a woman sat shuffling papers and talking. One of the men was older, seventy something perhaps, which might mean he was Subirachs. He was short and a little rotund but looked energetic and fit. His skin was very wrinkled and looked like crepe paper, but he had an impressive crop of well-groomed white hair and matching beard, and he wore a pair of rimless spectacles lifted back onto the top of his head. An enormous number of Catalan men wore beards, Staverley had noticed. Subirachs was wearing smart corduroy trousers and matching jacket and a red shirt. He also had a red handkerchief carefully arranged in the top pocket of his jacket, something Staverley had not seen for a long time. He wondered if the red was meant to be a visual reminder of the man's politics.

The hall was well filled now, with around twenty-five people. The younger man at the table called the meeting to order and spoke briefly. Then, as far as Staverley could make out, he introduced Subirachs. He was the older man. Staverley understood virtually nothing beyond that point. Subirachs spoke for around twenty minutes. It was clear that he was very comfortable and experienced at public speaking. He had an engaging manner and spoke in staccato sentences punctuated by hand gestures to reinforce what he was saying. Several times he pointed at the audience in a way that seemed almost accusatory. The reaction to the speech as a whole and to the pointing was mixed. Some people nodded enthusiastically and muttered noises of agreement. Others shook their heads and muttered noises of disagreement. When Subirachs finished speaking about half the audience clapped and shouted, the other half remained obstinately and disapprovingly silent with crossed arms. Subirachs sat down and the woman at the table asked for questions and responses, that much was self-evident. There were few questions as such, but a lot of responses, and again, despite the language, Staverley could easily tell which of these were supportive of the speaker and which were not. At one point two of the audience members, a young man in workman's overalls and a middle-aged woman, broke into an argument between themselves, which appeared to degenerate into an exchange of insults and finger-pointing before they were rebuked and quietened by the young woman at the table. Subirachs remained impassive during all of this and seemed to enjoy the spectacle. He was given the last word by the chair. This time he sounded more conciliatory, and addressed himself directly to some of the speakers in the audience who had seemed to be critical, although their facial expressions did not suggest that they were any more convinced than before. After two hours of non-stop talk the meeting was closed. Most of the audience left quickly but three people approached the table to speak to Subirachs and an elderly woman remained seated, she was staring fixedly at Subirachs.

Staverley waited his turn and practised a couple of Castilian phrases in his head. But they turned out to be unnecessary, as both Subirachs and the woman organiser spoke good English. Staverley was relieved.

"I was hoping you might find some time to meet with me," he said. "my father was a volunteer fighter during the civil war and I think you might have known him. I'm trying to find out a little more about his time here. He died when I was very young."

Subirachs was clearly surprised by the request, but recovered himself quickly.

"That is possible. I fought alongside several comrades from other countries in the war. His name?"

"Jack, Jack Staverley."

Subirachs searched his memory for a moment and then his face lit up with recognition.

"Jack, of course, Jack. How could I forget him? So you are his son. Welcome."

He held out his hand to shake and pumped Staverley's arm vigorously.

"Of course we can talk. Indeed I will be here at the *Rectoria* again tomorrow. We could meet then, perhaps for coffee. Yes?"

"Yes, that would be wonderful. What time shall I come?"

"Let's say eleven." He glanced at the young woman and she nodded,."Eleven then."

"I shall be here, and thank you." Staverley turned to go and almost knocked over the elderly woman, who was standing behind him now supporting herself with a cane. She was still staring intently at Subirachs and then very slowly lifted a gnarled finger and pointed at him. The finger trembled. She seemed upset and angry, perhaps she had been offended by the speech. Subirachs seemed unphased and smiled. He spoke to the old woman gently in Catalan, and again glanced to the young woman, she moved around the table and took the older woman by the arm and began to walk her to the door. The woman was not physically able to resist but looked back over her shoulder at Subirachs.

Staverley shared the embarrassment of the moment, although he had no idea what had just happened.

Across the street from the Rectoria was a small bar with tables on the pavement. He decided to treat himself to a drink before returning to Sant Pere, a brandy perhaps, a Fundador. He had seen the name on several advertising hoardings. There were some members of the audience also drinking and the debate, whatever it was, continued. There were loud voices and a great deal of shaking of heads and blowing out of cheeks. As everywhere politics provoked a great deal of hot air and frustration. He enjoyed watching the interaction but wished he understood what it was that was causing such consternation and quarrelling. The only things he could make out with any certainty were 'Pujol', who he knew about, and 'Banca Catalana', which was already on his list of things to find out more about. The Fundador was smooth and rich. Nice.

The next morning, having left the stone on Senyora Budó's doorstep, he was brought breakfast.

"Pa amb tomaquet," she explained, "i truita a la francesa."

This was thick slices of very crusty bread spread with garlic, olive oil and salt and rubbed with a juicy tomato, with a French omelette. He liked it - a lot.

Chapter 3

As Staverley made his way back to the *Rectoria* the following day, on his ciclo, he kept thinking about the old woman from the night before and her finger pointing. He did not really know what it was that intrigued him about the encounter, especially as Subirachs had not seemed in the least put out. He did not think that he was bold enough to ask directly what had happened and who the woman was. Subirachs was waiting at the entrance when he arrived, talking with the younger woman from the night before. He introduced her.

"This is Nuria, she is my assistant, and also more importantly my daughter."

They shook hands and exchanged polite greetings. Her English was even better than her father's but her accent was very different. She was about Staverley's age. She was polite but eager to go.

"If you will excuse me, I will leave you to talk, I have work to do."

Subirachs took Staverley by the arm and they crossed the road to the bar where he had had his brandy the night before. They sat outside at a table under a parasol. After a quick consultation Subirachs ordered a *cortado* for each of them and two small pastries. The *cortado* turned out to be a small coffee with a good splash of foamy hot milk. The pastries were miniature croissants.

"I have been thinking about your father," Subirachs said. "It is so many years since we fought together. I have wondered often what had become of him. After the suppression of POUM by the Republic and the merging of the militias into the People's Army there was much confusion and we lost contact. I know he needed treatment for his wound and I assumed that after that he had returned to England. But perhaps after the war I should have made more effort to find out what had happened to him. I am sorry for that. But it was a time of much upheaval and unpleasantness. It was often difficult to understand what was happening."

"Please no, I understand a little of how difficult things were both during the war and afterwards for those who had fought for the

Republic. My father was treated for his wound but he stayed on in Catalunya for some time after that before returning to England. I don't know why he stayed or what he was doing, I don't think he returned to his unit. My mother said he was reluctant to go into detail about what happened. I had hoped you would be able to tell me something."

Subirachs looked pained and shook his head slowly.

"Unfortunately not. As I say, we lost contact, as I did with other comrades from POUM. Those who survived the fighting with the government troops and avoided arrest by the secret police mostly joined the regular Republican forces. I certainly did so. After my time in POUM I was initially assigned as a motorcycle messenger and was lucky to survive that, as most messengers were picked off by Nationalist snipers or ambushed. I had some near misses. After Ebro in '38 the Republican army was broken and the air force such as it was, was all but gone. The Republican generals, urged on by the Russians, constantly launched attacks when they should have been defending what they had. There were huge losses on both sides but Franco had the upper hand by then and the manpower and the weapons, supplied by the Germans an Italians of course, and the Nationalists pressed on into Catalunya. Ebro probably just delayed what was inevitable. I was re-assigned again near the end to the border with France and when Girona fell in February '39 I abandoned my post and slipped across the border. I'm not proud of that but like many others I was tired of war and afraid of the consequences of Franco's victory for myself and my family. Many relatives suffered as well as those who had actually fought. Thousands were being executed and imprisoned, and the reprisals went on for a long time. So it seemed sensible to disappear. The French were not welcoming, to say the least, but nearly half a million refugees crossed the border and the camps the French set up were over-crowded. Food was short, there was a lack of organisation, and dysentery and other illnesses were rampant. It was a really cold winter that year. People died of exposure. The French government did not want the refugees to stay and many were repatriated against their wishes, some were even handed over later to the Germans. Others, a few, were able to move on to places like Mexico or Chile. Again, I was lucky. One of the French border guards I had got to know while I was on duty provided me with some travel documents and I was able to make my way to Perpignan and then to Le Havre and a ship, then for a while I lived in the Dominican Republic, but eventually I was able to return and settled in Paris. I found work there through some political contacts and did not return to Spain until the 1960s. I met my wife in Paris and my daughter was born there. What of your father, after the war?"

Staverley was trying to take in what Subirachs had said, and grasp the extent to which the country had torn itself apart during the war. From his reading he knew that the Republican/Nationalist divide had cut through families, communities and friendships. But also that there were many divisions and conflicts on the Republican side, Communists, Anarchists and Socialists fought among themselves and murders and assasinations were commonplace, especially just before and in the first year of the war. He also had some sense of the brutality of Franco's reprisals and the ways in which supporters of the Republic had been hunted down or ostracised after the war had ended.

"My father joined the Royal Air Force in early 1940 and trained as a radio operator. From what my mother told me he was very skilled and he moved on from direct involvement in bombing missions to become a trainer, and worked with the Americans after they joined the war. But in late 1944 he was seriously injured when a training flight he was on crash-landed. He was invalided out of the forces and never really recovered his health. He died when I was three years old. And it was only recently that I knew any of this about him being a volunteer in the civil war here. He was adamant that my mother should tell me only when the time was right. And the right time was just three months ago."

Subirachs stroked his beard and squeezed his chin between his fingers. He seemed uncertain of what to say, or whether to say anything.

"That does not surprise me young man. Many of my comrades even now want to say nothing about the war here and their part in it. I rarely speak about my experiences and then only with people with whom I shared those experiences. In war we see despicable things, and to be honest we, some of us, do despicable things. I saw too much death, too much viciousness and suffering. You read about heroism and bravery and self-sacrifice, but for the most part war is both mundane and unrelenting evil. And it's not just evil in terms of what we do to others; it's evil in terms of what it does to us. It was years before my nightmares faded, and even now they sometimes recur. There were things done that were just inhuman. Sometimes when I walk the streets I see the faces of fallen comrades among passers by, the faces of the dead, and I remember when and how they fell, and I cry – not for them, but for myself, for in surviving I must live with everything I saw and everything I did. We went to war as idealists, as defenders of freedom, but we had no idea of the reality of war. Especially at the beginning I saw brave men throw down their weapons and run, and I had that same urge myself. It was only because I was among friends that I did not succumb. But I was not brave, I was foolish and naïve. When we had returned to Spain and she was old enough to understand what had happened here, my daughter began to ask me questions about the war and my part in it. But I was never able to answer her questions properly. I did not want her to know what I had witnessed and what the war had made me into. I am sorry to say I became angry with her and she stopped asking. Perhaps your father was the same and did not want you to think of him as a man of violence, as someone who could kill his fellow men and do other things much worse than killing. And if you think you want to know more about what he did here you should ask yourself why, and what may come with that knowing. Sometimes not knowing is a blessing."

It was Staverley's turn to pause for thought. Despite his mother's explanation of his father's wish that he not be told about Spain, he had not really thought through what knowing might mean and what he might learn about his father. He was curious and wanted to understand his father better and wanted him to be someone he could admire. But that was not necessarily what knowing would deliver. Perhaps he should reconsider his need to know and accept that his attempts to find out more might end badly. But over and against that there was the message and the names. His father had wanted him to have them for a reason.

"I understand what you are saying, Senyor Subirachs, about the dangers and sensitivities involved in asking questions. And I will think carefully about what I want to know and why, and therefore what it is

I ask. But for now can I show you something that you might help me with?"

Subirachs nodded reluctantly. "If you must," he said. He seemed disappointed not to have put Staverley off from further questioning.

"My father left me this." Staverley removed the note his father had left for him from his notebook, unfolded it and laid it on the table for Subirachs to see. The old man took his spectacles from his jacket pocket and put them on. He read the words and the names and his eyebrows raised. He tapped the paper several times with his finger.

"What does this mean?" he said.

"I was hoping you would be able to tell me. Do you recognise the other names?"

"Of course. That is me of course, and the others, I know them both, they were with you father and I in POUM. We fought together; we were part of the same unit and we became inseparable – Jordi, Joan, Jack and Jaume, the four Js. What is it the Americans say? We watched each other's backs, we depended on one another, trusted one another, and when we were not fighting we talked, we talked all the time, and in that way Jack taught us some English and we taught him some Catalan. We shared a great deal, good and bad."

Staverley asked what is was they had talked about. Subirachs was still reluctant, but he did reply.

"Our talks were mostly about before the war and especially the things that we missed from that time or things we would do after the war. We learned a lot about one another in that way and about the men we used to be and hoped to be again. To pass the time and entertain one another we would construct elaborate fantasies about what we would do if the war ended the next day and we could return to our previous lives. Joan's always began with bread, bread and cheese. The bread we were given at the front was often days old and poorly made. It was stale and hard to chew. Joan would talk about the *panaderia* near his house in Barcelona and the smell of newly baked bread and how he would go every morning to buy fresh bread for breakfast for his family. And the bread always led on to the cheese, and especially the goat's cheeses that his grandfather made. He loved to describe their different smells and textures and consistencies. By the time he had finished we all had the taste of those cheeses in our mouths and for a few minutes we could remember what it was like to eat well and feel replete. And then Jaume would start. He loved wine and he loved to dance, to waltz of all things. Before the war after work he would go to cafés and dance and drink. He was very skilled and a much sought-after partner, or so he told us. And he could recite all of the wine growing regions of Catalunya and compare their qualities. If Joan could make us feel full, then Jaume could make us feel giddy and drunk. Your father's fantasies were different and focused on soap and hot water. He told us that in London he had once been to a Turkish bath and had spent hours there enjoying the heat and steam and had, for the only time in his life, a massage. He intended to go back and to sweat the stink and dirt of the trenches from his pores. I remember that your father found that the hardest thing, being dirty all the time. He hated the thought that he would smell bad, but I think we all did, we just didn't know it. He was constantly cleaning his nails with his bayonet and searching the seams of his uniform for fleas, But worst of all was the lice. The lice were resilient and the fleas were as hungry as we were."

"And you, Senyor. What was your fantasy? What did you talk about?"

"Ah, my preoccupations were very frivolous. I hated the uniform, blue boiler suits, the coveralls, we all wore, they were a mark of POUM and what it stood for. I knew its importance and significance but the sameness and drabness depressed me, everyone wearing the same ill fitting, poorly made boiler suits - and they were itchy and hot in the daytime and cold at night. I had always dressed well before the war and hoped to do so again after our victory. I would describe for the others my visit to the tailor, and the fitting and the exact style and fabric I would choose for my jacket and trousers, and shoes and shirt and tie to match. It made me feel like an individual again. At the same time I remember that at the outbreak of the war, in Barcelona, men in suits, wearing ties, were regarded with great suspicion, as possible Falangists or fifth columnists. It became dangerous to dress that way or to shave even. It seems ridiculous now but then what you wore could get you killed. But our fantasies were a kind of escape from out of that, for a short time we were able to indulge ourselves and divert the others from the tedium and the dangers and the frustrations of being on the frontline. I don't think any of us expected to survive the war. It is a miracle that we all did. The militias like POUM were full of foolhardy men, and women, and full of ridiculous bravado. Many of your countrymen, and foreigners who fought with us, mostly good men, were killed or maimed seriously wounded. I remember one young man who had cycled all the way across France to join us. He was killed on his very first day by a stray shell. There was so much tragedy and stupidity that sometimes it was difficult to remember that what we were doing was worthwhile, or so we believed. Now with hindsight it seems less clearcut.

In late '36 and early '37, before the suppression of POUM, we were at the front in Aragon. We were poorly armed, I remember they gave us Mausers from the nineteenth century, rifles that had not been fired in decades. Many were unusable but that was all we had. And they often jammed and the ammunition sometimes didn't fit. At the beginning some comrades had only pitchforks or sythes, it was insane, they were slaughtered. Even when more guns started to arrive from Russia they were old and primitive compared with what the Nationalists had. But for a long time there was little fighting where we were, just exchanges of insults. We shouted at the Nationalists and they shouted back at us. We insulted their mothers and they insulted ours. It sounds strange now but we were bored a lot of the time: it got so we wanted something to happen. We sat in our trenches, we dug, or some of us dug. Some of our more outrageous comrades thought digging trenches was cowardly. We slept and we tried to keep clean and find enough to eat, and we constantly scavenged for firewood and candles – the nights were very cold and very dark. There was little to read apart from the party newspapers like *La Batalla*. But I was lucky. I was made *cabo*, corporal I think you would say, and I was elected by our company to the representational council. Each militia operated as a political organisation in its own right and POUM was big on democratic processes. Even our orders were sometimes subject to debate. Some of the officers were reluctant to issue direct orders at all and there were certainly no salutes. But being a representative meant I was able to go back to Barcelona on occasion for meetings at POUM headquarters. That's where I learned my public speaking, I suppose. Eventually we were moved to the siege of Huesca, which was under Nationalist control, and we fought alongside the Durrati Column on one side, also anarchists, and a PSCU unit on the other, communists. 'Tomorrow we'll have coffee in Huesca', we were told when we arrived, but we didn't. It was a stalemate but the fighting was constant, us attacking them, them attacking us, often for no clear purpose. Our unit was given the task of ambushing the Nationalist patrols, which gave us the opportunity to take their weapons. We got very good at that, scrambling around as quietly as we could among the shrubs and the tinkling limestone rocks. But that was when your father was wounded. He was shot in the hand. It didn't seem serious at first but then the wound turned septic and he was sent to a field hospital and later back to Barcelona. Joan went with him. He had some stomach problem, and could no longer fight, and that's when we lost touch. By then Barcelona was in chaos, the militias were fighting in the streets with the government assault troops and the Russians had already rounded up the POUM leaders. Jordi and I stayed together for a while but when the POUM militia was broken up we were assigned to different units. I never again had friends and comrades like them. We had a bond, and it was something special. It was political, yes, we saw things the same way; but it was deeper than that. I can't describe it."

As he spoke Subirachs seemed to visibly age, the memories he normally kept buried and avoided now sapped his vitality and etched themselves on his face. He now looked all of his seventy years. Staverley experienced a wave of guilt for having made him talk about his friends.

"I should not have asked. I am sorry. Perhaps you are right that these things should be left unsaid. I will not bother you further. I should go and leave you to your work."

Subirachs straightened his back and drained the last of his *cortado*.

"It would be very contradictory to say that I miss the comradeship, the sense of purpose, the clarity about the rightness of what we were doing but there is some truth to that. The memories are not all bad ones, so don't apologise. Why not speak to the others? They might be more or less willing than I to share what they know. They may have different memories and other stories to tell about your father. It's up to them."

"Sorry, I don't understand,.What do you mean - the others?"

Subirachs' expression softened. As before, he was wearing a handkerchief in his jacket pocket, a green one this time, that looked like silk, and he used it to dab the small drops of sweat that had formed on his forehead.

"Ah yes. I did not finish my autobiography. When Franco died and we began the so-called transition to democracy I found again first Joan and then Jordi. They might tell you their own stories. Both survived the war and its aftermath, but very differently. Jordi, like me, escaped to exile and he lived in Germany for many years. He is now a wealthy man and seeking to become wealthier by very kindly building hotels and resorts on our much-abused coast." Juame said this with pointed sarcasm.

"Joan did not prosper in the same way. He went into hiding. He was one of *los topos*, you know, the moles, like Quero and de Vega. Have you heard of them? Anyway, he spent over three decades waiting for the knock on the door by Franco's police, until the amnesty in '69. That experience of isolation and solitude gave him the taste for a different sort of life and he lives alone now in the Montseny. He's a goat herder. We have met, the three of us, a few times. But it's more an obligation than something we enjoy, I think. There is a lot of silence. In many ways we do not know what to say to one another. Regret haunts us, as so many others, and our differences now are greater than the things that held us together then. If you want to talk to them, Jordi is easy to find. He has offices in Barcelona and is often on the coast supervising the despoiling of its beauty. His company is building in Lloret del Mar at the moment, I think. I'll get Nuria to give you his phone number. Joan will not be so easy. He certainly has no telephone and he spends most of his time walking the mountain with his herd. He rarely comes down. Ask in Sant Pere. Perhaps someone can give you directions." Subirachs consulted his watch. "Now I do have to go, I have yet another meeting, my life sometimes seems to consist entirely of meetings. We had an interesting conversation, I think."

Staverley paid and shook hands with Subirachs, who seemed quite emotional now, which increased Staverley's feelings of guilt further. Subirachs held onto his hand long beyond the normal.

"Listen, next week our local ERC branch is meeting for a meal. It's something we do every year around this time, to enjoy mushrooms together. It's a social event. Why don't you come?"

"Actually, that would be great. I haven't told you about my main reason for being here in Catalunya. I am doing research on the growth of tourism and I am very interested in the effects of the major developments, like those your friend Jordi is involved in. The chance to meet with people who might talk to me about what is happening on the coast would be so helpful."

Subirachs chuckled. "And talk they will, my young friend. Be prepared for some fiery opinions. Nuria will get in touch with the details."

"But how will she do that?"

Subirachs chuckled again. "Don't worry she will find you. You are living in a very small world now, Senyor Staverley, very small."

Staverley was pleased that he was leaving Subirachs in a lighter mood, and even more pleased with the invitation. It was just what he needed to move on with his research work. That, and a possible contact with Jordi Batlló-Sabé, was a really good start.

Back in Sant Pere Staverley went straight to the bodega and asked David for help in finding Joan Canoes-Mas. It was obvious that, over and above the problems of language, explaining how to find Joan would not be easy, and David resorted to drawing a rough map, which he re-started several times before producing something that Staverley thought he could understand and follow. David made it sound as though it would be a major expedition, and was insistent that Staverley prepare himself carefully and take food and drink if he were to venture into the mountains alone and also to wait a couple of days until the hot weather had abated. Staverley was disappointed. He had hoped to set off the next day, but he was beginning to realise that the Montseny were serious mountains. The tallest, *Turó de l'Home*, the Tower of Man, was higher than anything in the British Isles. He hoped he would not have to climb that in search of Joan.

The other thing he wanted to do was to write to Monica. She was a research chemist, working at the University of Cambridge, a junior member of a team developing a new kind of long-life battery for electronic equipment. She and Staverley were able to get together only intermittently, but he was really missing her now. They had talked about her coming to visit him but that would probably not happen for a while. The letter was a long one; he had a lot to tell. Another goat's cheese sandwich kept him fortified. Once finished, the next challenge, he realised, was to find a post office. But that would have to wait. It was now after 2.00pm and everything, except the bars and restaurants, would be closed until 5.00pm. He surmised that the nearest post office was probably in Sant Celoni. Which turned out to be the case.

For the next few days Staverley explored the coast and tried to estimate the scale of the building currently underway and make a record of the on-going work. He also returned to Santa Susannah and wandered in and out of the bars and hotels that stretched out along the beach behind the railway line. The feel of things here was totally different from Sant Pere. The lingua franca was Castilian rather than Catalan, leavened with English, French and German. The bars tended to specialise in one nationality or the other with food and drink on offer to match. The absence of Catalan, he discovered, was partly due to the backgrounds of many of the hospitality workers. The waiters and barmen and hotel workers were usually not Catalan, many came from Andalusia or other parts of southern Spain. It also became apparent that there were tensions between the Catalan locals and the immigrants - as the Catalans called them. Each dealt with the others through the medium of derogatory stereotypes. The Catalans saw the southerners as lazy and untrustworthy; the immigrants regarded their hosts as cold, calculating and arrogant. He gathered most of this from conversations with the one or two waiters who had picked up some English through their work, and receptionists in the hotels who were employed in part for their language skills. His willingness to listen to disgruntlements elicited some lengthy accounts of the travails involved in moving from home to what was regarded as a foreign land. There was also plenty of eye rolling and finger waving when he asked about the tourists. Further stereotypes were recounted, but with a degree of indulgent humour. The Germans were pushy and promiscuous, the French were haughty and mean with money, the British got sunburned and drunk. Staverley also explored parts of Santa Susannah away from the beach, the old town, or what remained of it. It was interesting but not exactly picturesque, a dusty collection of narrow streets clustered around another improbably large church. The town seemed to be still mainly oriented to serving the needs of the agricultural hinterland but some of the small shops stocked items that might attract tourists, and the bars and restaurants that lined the tiny main square were clearly making an attempt to offer local colour to tourists in search of something more authentic than the dull international cuisine that was served up by the beachfront hotels. He had lunch in a couple of these and ate well and very cheaply, although on each occasion he had to negotiate the disbelief that his vegetarian diet provoked. He was developing a small vocabulary to manage this, but at the same time was aware that he was now beginning to talk using a confusing mish-mash of Catalan and Castilian words and already forgetting which was which. *Bon dia* and *sius plau* now came more naturally to him than *buenos dias* and *por favour*. But Catalunya was complicated and unlike Castilian was not pronounced as written.

Staverley's first notebook was full, and he bought another at the *librería* in Sant Pere. That was a good sign, lots of notes, lots of ideas, and lots of questions. That was, for him, how research worked, a process of immersion, of attending to the mundane, of listening to stories and hearing emotions, seeing and experiencing and sharing, set against a material world of structural problems and economic opportunities and constraints. His work as a sociologist, as he saw it, was to relate personal problems to public issues.

On Friday morning he ate breakfast in *La Granja*. He tried a sweet pastry, an *enseimada*, a speciality of Mallorca, but was slightly disappointed. His preferred taste was savoury, and the coffee did not quite live up to the standard he had become accustomed to either. Even so, sitting on the roadside in the sun, watching the people of Sant Pere go about their business was engrossing. He was particularly fascinated by the old men whose breakfasting on bocadillos and a brandies. When he returned to the house there was a note sitting on the doorstep, his first post. The note was from Subirachs' daughter

Nuria. It contained Jordi Batlló-Sabé's address and telephone number, and the details for the ERC dinner the following week. He had no idea how it had arrived.

Chapter 4

Jack was waking up and he was happy. He was happy for two reasons. One was that he was clean; for the first time in months he was not ashamed of how he looked and how he smelled. The other was the residual effects of whatever medication he had been given the day before when he arrived at the hospital. He suspected a strong opiate of some kind. Whatever it was it had dulled the pain in his hand and reduced the swelling and inflammation. The doctor in the field hospital had muttered darkly about the possibility of an amputation but hopefully that was less likely now he was in a proper hospital. He tried to open his eyes but the light was too bright. He covered his eyes with his good hand and tried again, peeking between the fingers. He was in a long, narrow and cavernous ward, which was lined with beds - perhaps fifty or sixty - every one occupied. The light came from a series of skylights set into the high ceiling. There were several nurses bustling about or tending to patients and one of them noticed that he had awoken.

"*Cómo te sientes*?" she asked in rather stilted Castilian. Jack guessed she was not Spanish herself, nor Catalan. He tried some English.

"I'm feeling a lot better, and a lot cleaner, thank you."

That made her laugh, and she switched into English.

"You're welcome. You had quite a fever. The infection was well advanced; one more day and I don't think we could have saved the hand. As it is it looks like you get to keep it, but the doctor will take a look this afternoon."

Jack guessed from her accent that the nurse was American. She had short blonde hair and a button nose and freckles, all of which made her look totally out of place. She also looked very, very tired, probably close to total exhaustion, but her manner was confident and reassuring. Jack felt his bad hand was in good hands.

"American?" he asked.
"Sure am, a mid-westerner, born and bred. Detroit. D'ya know it?"

"Not really."

"It's a car town, slap in the middle of the US."

"And how did you end up here?" Jack asked.

"Now that is a long story."

"I'm not going anywhere"

"But, I am, I've work to do. The short version is I'm with the Abraham Lincoln Brigade. I joined the AMB, that's the American Medical Bureau, back in Detroit. I was organising events and collecting money for the fight against fascism. Most of the organisers now are women. But I thought I could do more by being here rather than there. I'd started at nursing school and it seemed the right thing to do. So here I am. To begin with I was driving an ambulance down south but the damned Nationalists blew it up and there was no replacement, so I was assigned to a field hospital with Salaria Kea, and then ended up here."

"Salaria Kea?"

Jack was a little embarrassed by how little he knew about other parts of the International Brigades.

"I thought everyone knew about Salaria. She's amazing. She's a negro lady, from Georgia I think, and she's married to an Irish guy. She organises and runs field hospitals for the Republic. She got captured by the Nats but escaped. My pa heard her speak back in the States and he doesn't impress easily but he was mightily taken with her."

The nurse seemed a bit frustrated with his lack of knowledge.

"My Pa brought us up, my brothers and sisters and me, to see direct action and political struggle as a natural part of a proper life. It's all for dignity and freedom he would say. So you now know my life history, but I must get on before I get into trouble with Sister. She's great but she's a stickler."

The nurse turned to go.

"Wait, wait, you haven't told me your name."

"It's Haywood, Helen Haywood. That's Nurse Haywood to you." She wagged a finger in his direction and hurried away. Jack had heard many stories like Helen's during his time in Catalunya, told by people from all parts of the world. Stories which all ended with a decision to travel to Spain and confront Fascism directly, in person, and to fight against the threat of Hitler and Mussolini and Franco. He had even spent one rather drunken evening in Barcelona hearing this from Winston Churchill's nephew. He found the stories humbling and they gave him a sense of hope in the face of carnage and stupidity. Jack began to drift into sleep again but as he did he was still reflecting on the incredible variety of people he had met in Spain, both the locals and others, who were united in their commitment to democracy. That seemed like a third reason to be happy. He slept with a smile on his face.

When he woke again he was hungry. He opened his eyes to find another nurse changing the dressing on his hand. She was very tall and her very black hair was pulled back in a tight bun. She had a stern face with elegant, sharply defined jawbones and nose. The sternness might just be her work face Jack thought; at home she would probably be beautiful. She said something in Catalan, which he did not understand, and then she tried Castilian, which he did not understand, and then French, which he did not understand. He tried to explain himself.

"*Ho sento, no ho entenc,*" he said, a Catalan phrase he had probably used more than any other, usually wrongly: I don't understand.

The nurse seemed to appreciate his effort.
"Ah! Vostè és, American?"
"English".
"Ah! My English is small - no, little, yes?"
"My Catalan is also little, very little, I'm sorry."
This nurse wore a more ornate uniform than Nurse Haywood, with a rather fussy cap. He presumed she was the Sister Nurse Haywood had mentioned, and that turned out to be the case. While she took his temperature and replaced the dressings on his hand, exchanging bits and pieces of her little and delightfully flawed English with his even littler and more flawed Catalan, he got her to tell him her name – Mercè Fàbregas. As they chatted, her stern look loosened somewhat. He discovered that she was a native of Barcelona and had moved from a civilian hospital where she worked normally to take charge of two wards in the military hospital soon after the outbreak of the civil war. He also gathered that her father had some role in the Catalan government. He asked her what the political situation was like in

Barcelona. At the front the news was always old and often wrong, he explained.

"It is now a most difficult time. There is shooting, killing. We are killing each other. The troops of the Republic and the assault guards attack the Catalan militias, they fight back. Dangerous I think is the right word, yes?"

Jack nodded. It was very much the right word.

"I worry much about my father. Now you are done. The hand begins to heal. You rest and I have duties."

And she was gone. His questions had seemed to disturb her air of stern efficiency. Her answers had given him considerable pause for thought. What should he do when released? Would he be fit to return to the front? Would the militia and his unit still exist? Was he in danger?

By the following morning, Jack felt refreshed and much stronger. It was several months since he had slept so long and so peacefully. Nurse Haywood brought him some breakfast and gave him permission for a short walk. She looked even more exhausted than the previous day and he assumed that the nurses did not get to sleep much. She was too busy with other patients to stay and talk. Jack walked the length of his ward and into the next and he was horrified to see the number of men with missing limbs or serious head wounds. He recognised, despite the dangers of his infection, how lucky he was by comparison. He stopped a couple of times to exchange greetings and to hold water glasses for those who could not manage for themselves. The eyes of some of the men he helped were empty and sunken and they seemed to be detached from their immediate surroundings. Some were clearly reliving the horrors that had brought them to the hospital. Jack thought they were probably struggling to come to grips with their injuries and to think about what the future might hold for them, or not to think about it. These were wounds inflicted by countrymen one upon the other, and if the Nationalists were to defeat the Republic the future for these defenders of the democratic government might be even grimmer than it looked now. That raised again the question of Jack's own future.

While walking, Jack was also on the look-out for Joan. He should be here somewhere; they had been admitted together. And there at last he was, in a dark corner of the third ward that Jack had explored. He looked a lot better than when they had parted two days before. He had been diagnosed with a kidney stone and told that he might need an operation but he was not a high priority for treatment, which he understood entirely. He had been given some medication that might move or dissolve the stone. He was to be discharged that day. He was very agitated and more than ready to leave. He waved Jack close and whispered to him.

"Last night," he explained, "two of the wounded were taken. The nurses could not stop them."

"Sorry, Joan, what do you mean. Taken? Taken by who?"

"Look, Negrín has become Prime Minister in Madrid, right, and he wants to impose law and order throughout the Republic and unify the army, and he's allowing the communists to take over in Catalunya. They will surely make POUM illegal and the NKVD will purge us. Purge, yes, is that the word? I've heard they're sending six thousand civil guards from Valencia. We are no longer safe. We are not safe here."

Jack was more than a little aware from his own experience in England of the tensions on the political left between those affiliated to Stalin and Comintern, and those sympathetic to Trotsky, as POUM was. In Spain tensions was the wrong word, a massive understatement. The Russians wanted to exterminate anyone they considered deviationists, and POUM with its anarchist leanings and links to Trotksy was certainly viewed as one such organisation. The Russian NKVD even believed that Trotsky would come to Spain in person. The NKVD was the People's Commissariat for Internal Affairs, but their name did not delimit their activities to within the Soviet Union. NKVD agents together with the Communist Party of Spain were a major and growing influence within the Spanish republican government and had even accused POUM of having contacts with Franco's Falange party in their newsheets and the posters that were appearing in the city. Jack, like many others, could not come to terms with the idiocy of all of this. Rather than focusing all of its efforts and attention on the Nationalists the government were using resources and energy to undermine and attack the leadership of the Catalan militias that were fighting on the frontline. The dead and wounded were being called cowards and spies in the communist newspapers. They were accused of deliberately interfering with the war effort. It was like having to fight Hitler, Franco and Stalin all at the same time. But he had also become aware that what was happening in Barcelona now was also the playing out of an older form of politics that centred on Catalunya's wish to be an independent country, as they had been in the past, and Madrid's resistance to that. For the first time in the last few days Jack had begun to wonder whether he had done the right thing in coming to Spain and to think that he was somehow intervening in an historic process that was not his business and that he would never properly understand. Joan pulled him closer and whispered again in his ear.

"Jack, you come with me. It's not safe for you here, come with me now. I have friends. They will help us."

"I don't know Joan, I don't know what to do. Let me think. I should contact my ILP people perhaps. When is your discharge?"

"I think at 2.00pm."

"I'll decide before then and come back, wait for me."

Jack shuffled back to his own ward and was surprised to see Sister Fàbregas waiting by his bed.

"Where you go Senyor Jack? Come back to bed now."

Jack slipped back into bed and Sister Fàbregas leaned close to him as she made a show of tucking his sheets back into place.

"Listen, some people ask about you. I think you need to go soon. Under the mattress I leave address where you are safe, also clothes and shoes are under the bed."

With that she turned away and began to attend to another patient in the bed opposite. Jack was rattled and took a few moments to recover his composure. Joan had obviously been right. It was not safe in the hospital. He slipped his hand beneath the mattress and recovered a sheet of paper. He then felt beneath the bed and found a pile of clothes and a pair of old espadrilles. He collected his papers and passport and money from the small cupboard by the bed and carried these and the clothes to the latrines in the corridor, trying to seem casual and unhurried. The clothes were those of a workman, clean but well worn. The trousers were too big and too long and he made adjustments the best he could. He folded the hospital nightshirt and left it on the side of one of the sinks. Now he began to think of the best way to leave the building without drawing attention to himself and what to do about Joan. He edged along the corridor trying hard to be inconspicuous and looked into Joan's ward. The bed Joan had occupied was now stripped and empty. It was possible that he had been discharged early, but why had he not come to see Jack before he left? Jack considered trying to ask what had happened but that would only serve to draw attention to himself. At the nurses' desk a very tall man wearing a black suit was looking through a set of papers - he might be a doctor or he might not. Jack decided to leave immediately. No one paid much attention as he made his way to the main entrance of the hospital. Wearing the clothes he had been given he looked more like a labourer than a soldier and his bandaged hand could just as well be the result of a work injury as a battle wound. Outside, the street was unusually quiet. There were very few civilians but several small groups of men in Republican uniforms. Jack did not know who they were or what they were doing. He noticed that the Catalan flags and anarchist flags, which had been everywhere around the city until recently, had been replaced by those of the Republic. There was an atmosphere of anticipation. It seemed as if the city was holding its breath, waiting for something to happen – something bad. He turned into the first side street and then again into a narrow alleyway. He had only spent a short time in Barcelona before joining his unit and later just a few days on leave, and had only the very vaguest sense of its geography. He certainly had no idea where to find the address that Sister Mercè had given to him – 36 Carrer de Roger de Flor. He knew the city was laid out between the sea to the east and mountains to the west. The oldest part, the Barrio Gótico, was immediately adjacent to the sea, and the nineteenth century modern *Eixample* was neatly laid out between that and the mountains, with the *Plaça Catalunya* between. The wide streets and octagonal blocks of buildings in the *Eixample* - the expansion, it meant - had been carefully designed for better ventilation and better transport than the narrow dark passages of the Barrio Gótico allowed for. He somehow could not imagine Mercè living or having friends in the old part of the city, so turned west, but kept to the small side streets wherever he could. Twice he picked his way over piles of sandbags that had previously served as militia barricades but were now abandoned. He thought he could see trails of blood on the pavement, and there were some black and red neck scarves in the gutter. The majority of shops were closed. Once or twice he hid in doorways as military trucks passed by. After about fifteen minutes walking he thought he could hear machinegun fire in the distance and turned again in the opposite direction. He was already tiring and his hand was aching. On the next corner, down a short flight of steps, there was a *Tabac* that seemed open. He hesitated for a moment but then decided he must ask for directions. Behind the counter was an elderly man with rheumy eyes who smelled distinctly of cheap alcohol. That seemed like a good thing in the circumstances. Jack mustered his best Catalan and showed the man the piece of paper with the address. The man took it from him and held it close to a small lamp behind the counter but still seemed to find it difficult to focus. After several attempts the man turned away and huskily called out a name that sounded like Alphons. A small sickly looking boy appeared from the back room and the man gave him the paper. The boy read it and whispered something to the man. This was all taking time and Jack was becoming increasingly nervous. He was trying hard not to reach across the counter and snatch the piece of paper back from him and run. After further whispers and several bouts of pointing the old man spoke to Jack. After asking him to repeat twice, Jack thought he understood that the address was about ten minutes away and that he should cross the junction and turn right. As he thanked the man and turned to go the boy ducked under the counter and took him by the hand. The hand was cold and very fragile but the boy's grip was confident. He led Jack up the steps and across the street. They took a right turn and after a further few yards the boy stopped. He let go of Jack's hand and held on to his arm instead. With his other hand he pointed along the street and then raised four fingers. Jack understood at once, and began to search in his pocket for some coins, which he gave to the boy. The boy looked at the coins carefully in his palm, picked up three of the four and returned them. "*Gràcies senyor*," he said.

Jack began to walk again. When he turned to look back, the boy was still standing where they had parted, he raised his hand and waved, and Jack waved back.

The fourth turning was indeed the street he was looking for, but as he approached the corner he could see a group of Republic soldiers setting up a roadblock using wooden barriers topped with barbed wire. He retreated and edged as far as he could into the nearest shop doorway, hoping he had not been seen. But the soldiers were having problems manoeuvring the barriers into place and paid no attention to the one or two passers-by, some of whom were carrying white handkerchiefs. Jack's heart was pounding and his hand was throbbing. This was worse than being at the front. Here he did not know what was happening and what the danger was, or indeed if he was in danger at all. He looked again at the soldiers and beyond them to the house of which he had the address. The house was very unusual in design; he had never seen anything quite like it. It looked like something made up by a child from a toy box of bits and pieces. The front included some brightly coloured tiles, stone pillars around the windows that might have come from a church, an enclosed wooden terrace at the top, and a set of small balconies with ornate ironwork. Jack did not understand it, which was for him a strange response to a house. He did not pay much attention to the buildings in London. He could recognise the landmarks and had enjoyed visiting the Tower of London with his mother when he was a child but this was different. This was a building that made you think, a disconcerting house. The distraction of the house calmed him a little and he looked more carefully at the soldiers and the rest of the street. The barriers were still not properly in place and he thought it was probably safe to pass until they were. But as he leaned forward on the opposite corner from where he stood he saw another man, also standing in a doorway. He wore a long raincoat, tightly belted at the waist and was holding a dark hat in one hand; he was smoking a cheroot of some kind. As Jack watched him he realised that the man was watching the house - and he did not look like an admirer of unusual architecture.

Chapter 5

Staverley had established a workspace for himself in the bedroom so that he could sit and look out of the window while he worked. The occasional change of focal length was good for the soul and the eyes. In the small outhouse at the rear, he had found a pair of trestles and an old door which, when dusted and washed, made a serviceable desk. In the *llibirería*, which was a few doors down the street, he had bought a set of files and a block of notepaper and was beginning to transfer his rough notes, putting them into analytical categories as he did so. The categories were crossed-referenced to types of respondents. He had made a modest start but he was pleased with his progress.

The trip into the Montseny was still on hold, awaiting a change in the weather, which Senyora Budó assured him would come soon. He had made a couple of trips to the *Granja* to use their telephone and now had an appointment to meet with Jordi Batlló-Sabé on the coast in Lloret de Mar. The idea of trying to speak in Castilian on the telephone was daunting and he had made some notes to help him but Batlló-Sabé's secretary had switched into English as soon as he began to struggle. Virtually everyone's language skills seemed better than his. Not for the first time he reflected on the reluctance of the English to learn other languages and the inadequacies of language teaching at his Grammar school. He had planned to spend an hour a day working on the exercises in his Castilian textbook but some days that did not happen. Nor was the vocabulary in the exercises very relevant to his research needs.

He was to meet Batlló-Sabé in the lobby of the Hotel La Palmera. The hotel, new and still pristine, was built in a V-shape with a large pool area between the two wings. It was constructed in concrete and painted an eye-watering white. It had seven floors and each room on the inner side of the wings had a small balcony overlooking the pool and out to sea. Presumably there were cheaper rooms at the back with views of the countryside and the service entrance. It was perhaps a little up-market compared with other hotels he had seen and visited in the resort. The reception and the lobby were glass-fronted and dotted with mini-palms and olive trees in terracotta pots. Staverley found a vacant spot next to one of the olive trees and sat to wait, he was as was his custom a little early. He recognised Batlló-Sabé at the same moment Batlló-Sabé recognised him. Both stood out, neither being dressed as a tourist. Batlló-Sabé was wearing a freshly ironed, white, short-sleeved shirt and faun coloured summer trousers, both looking expensive. He appeared younger and fitter than Staverley had expected: slim and upright, his sparse grey hair neatly barbered but left long and swept back in leonine style. This was a man who clearly took care of himself and who was careful with self presentation. He had a strikingly large hooked nose, which in comparison made his eyes seem small. His complexion was reddish, and his facial skin smooth.

"Senyor Staverley, I presume. *Encantado*. Shall we take a drink?"

Batlló-Sabé had obviously been briefed on the limitations of Staverley's Castilian.

"Shall we speak in English or would you prefer to speak in Castilian?"

The precision of Batlló-Sabé's English suggested expensive lessons and lots of practice.

"I should say let's try Castilian but if you don't mind I think I can ask my questions more effectively in English."

"As you wish." Batlló-Sabé ushered him toward the bar and they found a table overlooking the pool area. When the waiter came, Batlló-Sabé ordered a vermouth, *un vermut*, and Staverley followed suit. *Vermut*, Staverley had learned, was a local speciality and most bars served their own brand. It came with slices of lemon and lots of ice. They both sipped appreciatively and then Batlló-Sabé was quickly down to business.

"I understand from my secretary that you used the name of my friend Jaume."

"I did, yes. He suggested I might do that. I met with him a few days ago and asked about you. He thought you would be willing to talk to me."

"And what did you ask about me, and about what will we talk Senyor Staverley?"

"Two things I hope, different things. One is your business here."
Staverley gestured to their surroundings. "I am a sociologist and I'm
researching tourism in Catalunya. The other is my father. I wanted to
ask you about my father."

Batlló-Sabé looked perplexed.
"I am sorry, your father?"
"Jack Staverley, your colleague in POUM during the civil
war."
Staverley thought Batlló-Sabé may have paled slightly. He certainly sat
back in his chair and scrutinised Staverley more carefully than before.
He rubbed the side of his nose with one finger and then leaned
forward again. He delicately sipped his vermouth.

"I apologise for my hesitation. I am unused to speaking about the war.
It is a topic that is generally avoided. Most people prefer not to talk
about it. Sometimes, if you will excuse my crudity, there are situations,
when men of my age are gathered, in which the war lurks in a room
like a fart, but nobody acknowledges the smell. We all know it is there
but nothing is said. But of your father I am happy to speak. He was a
good man, a good friend, and a good soldier. We were not together for
long he and I and the others, I presume you also know of Joan also, but
we became close, like brothers. War can do that. It can forge strong
relationships. – shared danger and fear draw people together. Now I
look at you more carefully you resemble your father somewhat, your
eyes and hair especially. Is he alive and well?"

"I am afraid not. He was badly injured in the European war and died
when I was very young. I barely got to know him. Which is the reason
for my questions and my interest in his time in Catalunya."

"I am very sorry to hear that. My belated condolences to you and your
mother, I remember her. We met once when she came to Barcelona to
join your father."

"Thank you, I will tell her that. She will be pleased that you remember
her. Senyor Subirachs explained to me something of your time
together at the front, the four of you, and my father's wound, and the
attacks on POUM, and the dark days in the city, and how you lost
touch. But I wondered if you knew anything of what happened to my

father after he was sent to the hospital in Barcelona. Did you have contact with him again? But please, I have realised though from my conversation with Senyor Subirachs that such questions might be painful and unwelcome. You must tell me if you would rather not rehearse the memories."

Batlló-Sabé sat back again and rubbed his nose again.

"I appreciate your concern, and there are memories that I would prefer to keep to myself and not revisit. But I would be pleased to tell you what I know of your father. I still have a great affection for him. He was an interesting man, and a kind one, although very intense. He took his politics very seriously and we had many long debates and arguments. Let me see."

Batlló-Sabé paused to gather his thoughts, he sipped again his vermut and replaced the glass gently on the table.

"After our unit was disbanded - or militarised, as they called it - it was a chaotic time and a dangerous time for those of us identified as syndicalists and anarchists. Jaume and I were together for a short while after your father and Joan were sent to the hospital unsure of what would happen to us. We did then return to Barcelona for a few days before our reallocation to the regular Republican army, but we were assigned to different regiments. I was sent to join a battalion of engineers. In the time I had before that I tried to trace your father. I asked at the hospital and one of the nurses remembered him, but he had disappeared she said. He had left suddenly without a proper discharge and she was worried that he may have been snatched by the Republican police. You probably know that by that time the anarchists and the communists were in open conflict, there were tit-for-tat killings, and exchanges of rifle fire in the streets were common. The battle for the telephone exchange became well known from the writing of your author Orwell, who was there at the time. The exchange was controlled by workers from the CNT union. Each of the cities services were held and run by a different union or party, and the Madrid government wanted to remove them and assert their control of the city. After those days in April and May we were all afraid, and no one wanted to speak about POUM and the militias. The atmosphere in the city changed and some terrible things were done. I was certainly fearful. None of us knew if our name was on a list somewhere. To be on a list was a very bad thing. I also spoke about your father to a man called... what was his name? He was a political representative from London who had links with POUM. It was, yes, I remember, it was John McNair. Do I pronounce that correctly?"

"You do, quite correctly." Staverley found himself mimicking the precision of Batlló-Sabé's speech and told himself to stop.

"This McNair had also tried to obtain news of your father but had also failed. He was worried that your father had become involved in some way in the street fighting and had been killed, or perhaps that he had been taken against his will from the hospital. He promised to let me know if he heard anything more, but we both knew that that would be impossible. The order of things was changing. I think he also left Barcelona at that point to evade the communists. I visited one or two places where POUM militiamen would spend time when on leave in Barcelona. The Hotel Falcon was used by many of the foreign volunteers but was almost closed when I got there and even the party contacts I had were unwilling to talk with me. Everyone was suspicious. There were informers everywhere. It was difficult to know who was a friend and who might be a communist spy. The POUM offices were ransacked and empty by that time. With regret I had to join my new battalion as ordered. I heard no more of your father. I could do no more. I am sorry."

Staverley could see that Batlló-Sabé was embarrassed and wanted to reassure him. He shrugged his shoulders and avoided Staverley's eye.

"I think you did more than could be expected in the circumstances Senyor Batlló-Sabé and put yourself at risk. I have begun to understand, as you said, how chaotic and dangerous things were in Barcelona at that time. And my father did eventually make his way safely back to England. I was just hoping to know more of what occurred in the missing time after he left the hospital and how he managed to escape."

Batlló-Sabé shrugged again. He did that a lot.

"May I ask about you and what happened after you joined the engineers?"

"Of course. I spent the rest of the war doing many strange things, both constructing things and blowing things up. But I learned much, many skills, and in some ways what I learned then has led me to this, to here, and my business. At the end of the war I was rounded up with thousands of other Republican troops, and I spent a year in Mallorca, again building, roads this time, in a work camp. We engineers were useful to Franco and fared better than many others who suffered badly at the hands of the Nationalists. After the first year I was allowed a short release from the camp to visit my mother in Tarragona,who was unwell, and I was able to find a place on a foreign ship, as I think you say a 'stowaway' - is that right?"

Staverley nodded.

"I was very frightened when the ship moved on first of all to Barcelona and then Naples but after that it docked in Greece, Piraeus, where I disembarked. By then I had been discovered, but the Captain and crew were sympathetic to my plight and allowed me to work my passage. After some time in Greece I was able to obtain papers and I spent the next years moving around the Mediterranean, and always it seemed the war was right behind me. Every time I settled in one place the Germans or Italians or the British would arrive with their ships and planes and tanks. This time I was building things and they were blowing them up. At the end of the war I was in Palestine, again building, and again there was fighting, first between the British and the Jews and then the Jews and the Arabs, but I stayed this time and founded a company of my own and after the fighting stopped and with the many people arriving as refugees from Europe there was a great demand for new houses and factories and roads. I prospered there and in the mid-1950s, through contacts I had made, I expanded my business to Germany. Again there was much demand, much rebuilding to be done, and again I prospered. You could say that I benefitted from war, or its aftermath. And now I am back in my own country and again I am building, but as you know, this time it is hotels, like this one." He gestured toward the surroundings with his right arm.

"So this hotel and others were built, or are being built, by your company?"

"Not exactly. The investment involved here is large, too much for my business to carry alone. I coordinate a group of investors - some companies, some individuals, and some German and Spanish banks. My role is one of liaison between the money and the work, so to say. I ensure that funds are available for costs, and that the funds are spent properly and building is completed on time and as contracted. We have now completed eleven hotels big and small, including this resort, and there are several other projects, work is underway on a further five hotels at various locations."

"And is the work always completed properly and on time?"

"In most cases yes. At the moment we do have a problem with one project, but I think you will understand if I do not go into details about that. Let's say it is a local problem where the funds and the work to be done do not quite come together as they should."

"Of course, I understand that these are complicated matters. But one last thing, if I may, is there any documentation that I might see about the investment group and its projects?"

Batlló-Sabé thought for a moment and there was more nose rubbing.

"There is a prospectus that you could have I think, nothing more than has been reported in the financial press. It lists our investors and our plans and projects, dates and timetables and such, and gives some general sense of the sums of money involved. It also explains the benefits of our developments for the local communities. I will speak to my secretary and perhaps you could telephone her in a few days. Would that be acceptable?"

"I would be grateful. And thank you for being generous with your time today."
"Not at all, I am pleased to have met the son of my friend Jack."
"Perhaps if I had further questions...?"
"Of course, I am often on the coast."
They both stood and shook hands warmly. After Batlló-Sabé had left Staverley sat for a few minutes to make notes. He was beginning to get a sense of the situation in which his father had found himself in those turbulent times in Barcelona but still had learned nothing of the time

between his leaving the hospital and returning to England. Staverley estimated that there were five or six weeks unaccounted for. His father may simply have been in hiding, or travelling. He knew now that the movement of volunteers across France, either way, had become difficult as the international non-intervention agreement was implemented. Perhaps the gap would remain a mystery or perhaps now that he had traced the names on the list his mother would be willing to say more about his father's experiences in Catalunya and his return to London. Batlló-Sabé's account of his business activities had been useful but very general. Staverley had a lot more specific questions he wanted to ask but knew from experience that it was not always a good idea to rush things and push people too hard. He would try to speak with Batlló-Sabé again.

When it came, the promised change in the weather was dramatic. On Friday morning the skies clouded over and by midday the clouds were black and ominous. The wind got stronger and then came the lightning and the thunder and then the rain. The downpour was biblical. Within a few minutes the gutters in the road outside the house were full, the drains were flooded and pools and puddles of water were forming everywhere. The old house took all of this in its stride. The thunder could not shake its elderly stones and the tiled roof remained stubbornly watertight. Some water did creep under the wooden front doors, which had shrunk away from the floor over the years, but no damage was done. After three hours during which the thunder and rain stopped and then returned several times the sky began to lighten and by five o'clock the sun was back and was beginning to dry the roads, and the temperature had dropped a little. Staverley ventured out to see what effect the storm had had on the town. Other people were reappearing and normal life was quickly resumed, and apart from a few puddles there was little to see. The storm had come and gone. He sat outside *El Mos*, a bar in the small main square of the town, and had a beer. As he watched the comings and goings, people exchanging greetings, the shops re-opening, children playing. As he sat, he realised that his mind was calm, he was undistracted by dark thoughts, indeed he was content and happy. That was all very welcome. It felt good. The events of the previous two years seemed at last to be fading from his conscience and the dull but persistent sense of guilt he had been carrying was abating. His body felt more at ease, his muscles less tense. Coming here had been the right thing, and learning more about his father was also a source of positivity, if also somewhat frustrating. It connected him with a sense of personal history, and filled in what had been a blank space in his awareness of who and what he was. It was also beginning to break down the insularity of his Englishness, fastening him to a broader and richer identity as a European, as someone who shared in a collective memory of political conflict and struggle that cut across national borders. And - if he was honest - not having to deal with the micro-politics and bureaucracy and petty rivalries of university life was also a great relief.

The next day was sunny again but the dry heat had been replaced by a softer warmth and the rain had cleared away the accumulation of dust that had covered the town and the countryside. Everything looked fresher, brighter and sharper. It was time to tackle the Montseny, he thought. Senyora Budó prepared some *bocadillos* and fruit – wonderful peaches and nectarines – and two bottles of water filled from the spring that provided a source of mineral water that was bottled and sold in the area. She also lent him an old canvas knapsack. He filled up the small tank of his ciclo at Salvador's workshop and set off. Between the town and the mountain the terrain was flat and the fields were intensively cultivated and filled with row after row of plump vegetables and canes heavy with green beans. The generally held low opinion of vegetables as a food source seemed to Staverley to make little sense given this abundance, but as he was discovering from Senyora Budó's cooking and his meals at the local bars and restaurants there was actually a wide variety of delicious vegetable dishes that were staples of Catalan cuisine. Most of these were simple and relied on the taste of the vegetables themselves, which were harvested within walking distance of the town, and interesting combinations of flavours. They were also a quotidian history of Catalunya on a plate, with influences and ingredients traceable to the Moors and, before them, the Romans. The latest addition to his list of favourites was boiled potatoes served with *alioli* – a garlicky mayonnaise.

After about three kilometres the road -there was only one road through the Montseny - began to twist and turn and steepen dramatically. The twists and turns then became sharp hairpin bends. On these bends the road crossed narrow deep ravines – he now knew to call them *barrancos* - over small stone bridges. The ciclo was beginning to struggle but kept going, if very slowly at times. After twenty minutes of steady climbing Staverley stopped for some water and to allow the ciclo engine to cool, and he was able to look back toward Sant Pere which was now far below. The view was impressive and the grandeur and uniqueness of the Monsteny was apparent. The mountain range was designated as a UNESCO biosphere reserve, with protected status. The individual, over-lapping mountains of differing heights were all densely forested, although every few kilometres there were small pastures that had been created around farmhouses, some of which seemed impossibly high up to be habitable. He could only imagine that making a living from the land in such a setting was very hard. The highest peaks rose above the tree line, the trees replaced by a mix of rough grass and a variety of heathers and gorses.

Staverley consulted David's map and tried to orient himself before continuing. As he was putting the knapsack on his back a farm lorry careered by and an arm waved from the cab. It was only the third vehicle he had seen. He estimated that he was perhaps another ten minutes from the turn-off to Joan Canoes-Mas' house. David had tried to describe it. It was just beyond a ravine, he had said, which had a longer bridge than most of the others, between some tall pines on the right. It was a rocky track that was signed with a wooden board nailed to a post. At the slow speed that ciclo was capable of Staverley had no problem spotting the post, even though the board had fallen off. He turned onto the track, which was lined with lavender and rosemary bushes and clumps of thyme, but realised very quickly that the ruts and fractured sandstone rocks were beyond the capability of the ciclo, which was beginning to shake and rattle alarmingly. He dismounted, stood the ciclo behind a large boulder at the side of the track, and set off on foot. Even on foot it was not easy going and gradually got steeper and more uneven, leaving him sweating and panting. He had neither mountain legs nor mountain lungs. His urban, flatland muscles were unprepared and found wanting. He finished off one of the bottles of water but made himself wait for another stop before starting the second. After half an hour of solid climbing his legs were aching from

the exertion and his feet and ankles were getting sore from walking on
the fissured rocky surface. He needed proper boots. He decided to stop
for sustenance and sat in the shade of an alzina – a tree he had looked
it up that was a type of oak, a holm oak, that grew everywhere in the
Montseny. He ate a *bocadillo*. As he chewed the crusty bread, which
came fresh from the *panaderia* in the town that morning, he thought
he could hear something in the distance an unfamiliar sound like bells,
a faint disjointed melody of tinkling and banging. He climbed up the
side of the track to find a vantage point from which to look around,
and above him. Just beyond the treeline, about half a kilometre away,
was a herd of goats. He could also just make out a solitary figure
carrying a long stick walking slowly behind the herd. He finished the
sandwich, re-packed the knapsack and stumbled on. The sound of the
bells got louder, a pleasing cacophony. As he turned a bend in the track
he could see the herd more clearly. It was actually a mix of goats and
sheep. The goats were mostly brown, but there were a few white ones,
and a couple that were a mix of grey and white and had shaggy coats.
Most had small horns, presumably does, but some, presumably bucks,
had impressively long broad horns that you would not want to be on
the wrong end of. The does had full udders. The herd was nibbling its
way across the mountainside. Their lungs and legs had no problems
with the terrain. When he was close enough Staverley stopped and
shouted a loud "Bon Dia." The man, who was carrying a long thumb
stick, stopped and considered the interloper for a long time before
responding. He raised his stick, which Staverley took to be a welcome.
He approached while the man waited, assuming this must be Joan
Canoes-Mas. The goat herder was slight and wiry and wore a heavy
beard that was entirely grey; his hair was long and made into a short
ponytail at the back, held in place with string. He wore patched work
trousers, a collarless shirt and an ancient waistcoat. A small cotton bag
was attached to the waist of his trousers. Staverley did not get too
close too quickly. He had no idea of the etiquette in such a situation.
The man's eyes remained fixed on him as he approached, they were a
startling light blue and stood out from behind his beard and his sun
reddened skin like gem stones. Staverley took a deep breath and tried
to speak the phrases he had been practising.

"Mi nombre es Staverley. Creo que conosistes ma padre, Jack Staverley." – My name is Staverley. I think you knew my father, Jack Staverley.

Staverley waited; there was a long silence. The man moved his stick and rested both palms on the grip.

"*Mi nombre es Joan Canoes-Mas. Te paraces un poco a tu padre.*" – My name is Joan Canoes-Mas. You look at little like your father."

Staverley was relieved.

"*Lo siento, perro mi Castellano es muy, muy, pobre.*" – I am sorry, but my Castilian is very, very poor."

The old man's eyes sparkled and he may have smiled, it was difficult to tell beneath the beard.

"Then let's speak in English," he said.

This was not what Staverley had expected, although Subirachs had said that his father had taught the Js some English in exchange for Catalan lessons from them. Perhaps his assumptions about Joan the goat herder were misplaced. Joan looked around; the herd had wandered off some distance but seemed to know where they were going.

"It's hot and we have been out long enough today. Let's go back to the house," Joan said. Then he turned to follow the herd and Staverley followed him. Joan was much more agile and moved much more easily across the sheets of rock than did Staverley. They walked for about twenty minutes, by which time Staverley's legs were burning with pain. In a slight dip in the mountainside, partially shaded by bushes and shrubs, was a solid-looking stone house, and next to it a stone-walled enclosure into which the herd filed of their own accord. When the last was in, Joan pushed closed a rough wooden gate and propped a stone against it to keep it shut.

"Come," he said. He laid his stick against the wall of the house and pushed hard against the heavy wooden door which had been weathered by sun and wind to the colour of pewter. The door was held together with iron rivets and moved slowly with a very loud creak. Inside, the house was cool and dark.

"I think you need some milk, sit," Joan said. He moved off into the far corner of the dark room, and Staverley gratefully sat on a wooden bench. Joan returned with a red ceramic mug filled with pungent-smelling goat's milk. It was cool and tasted wonderful. Staverley drank most of it immediately in a series of long swallows.

"Food and drink in one," Joan said.

With his thirst quenched and his legs resting and his eyes adjusting to the dim light Staverley looked around the room with growing astonishment. The ground floor of the house was entirely open. In the left corner a wooden staircase led to a galleried second floor, where he presumed Joan slept. The entire right and back walls were lined from top to bottom with bookcases, every shelf of which was filled with books. There were hundreds of them, perhaps thousands. He pointed to the shelves.

"May I?"

Joan nodded. Staverley got to his feet with some difficulty, his legs were already beginning to stiffen. He crossed the room and looked at the titles on some of the shelves. The books were in various languages, mainly Castilian, French and English, but also some Catalan and a few German and one or two in other languages that Staverley did not immediately recognise. There was fiction, many classics that Staverley knew well, but also philosophy, politics, some science, a smattering of poetry, and books on art and music and a lot on myths and mysticism. He turned around.

Joan was sitting in a roughly made wooden armchair lined with cushions, sipping from a cup. Staverley smiled.

"You read."
Joan's eyes sparkled again.
"I read."

Staverley explained that he had written one book. It was a study of tourism, a case study of one seaside resort in southern England. It was drawn from his PhD. Joan asked several questions about the book and about Staverley and that enabled him to explain his presence in Catalunya and his meetings with Subirachs and Batlló-Sabé, and

David's help, which had led him to Joan. He also explained his curiosity about his father's experiences in the civil war and some of the things he had learned thus far.

"I was hoping you might be able to tell me more," he said.

There was another of the long silences before Joan spoke again.

"This house belonged to my grandfather. He also was a herder and also made goat's cheese. He taught my father how to make the cheese and tend the goats, and how to live on the mountain and to use all that it can offer. My father would have passed all that to me. I would have learned from him as he worked. But that did not happen. Instead the war came and I learned to fight and to kill. I learned that men could be evil and do evil things. Although some of the men I met in the fighting, men like your father, were good-hearted and righteous, and I valued that, but the war robbed me of my heritage, of my family. My father was killed in 1938 and my mother died soon after, of both sorrow and starvation. And because of all that I became disconnected from my identity and from the land, the mountains. I did not become the person I should have been. I did not live my life as it was meant to be lived. So I can understand that you want to know more about your father's life and how it might relate to your own and how you might have been different. What can I tell you?"

Staverley was both moved and saddened by what Joan had said, but also encouraged by his openness.

"Jordi, your friend, told me of his efforts to find you and my father after your time in the hospital in Barcelona. Can you tell me what happened there and whether you saw my father at the hospital and again after that?"

Again there was a silence, Joan stood up, and from a cupboard brought a chunk of hard cheese, presumably goat, from his own goats, and a jar of pate. He cut two generous slices of the cheese and poured two very small glasses of dark liquor. He handed Staverley a piece of cheese and a glass.

"Ratafia," he explained, "made from walnuts, collected from the mountain. And the pate is made from the mushrooms I collect while walking with the herd." He sat back in his armchair, took a bite of the cheese and a sip of the ratafia and began.

"I was due to be discharged that day. In the late morning a man arrived, with two government soldiers, assault guards. He was tall and officious and spoke roughly to the nurses, and he carried a list. He consulted his list, looked at the patient records and pointed to three men in my ward. I was one of them. He ordered us to dress but one of the men was too ill to get out of bed and the soldiers were reluctant to drag him. A nurse arrived, the Sister I think, and she harangued the man and protested his actions. They shouted and he accused her of obstructing the business of the Republic. When he spoke it was clear that he was not Spanish, probably Russian I thought, which turned out to be the case. The shouting attracted other nurses and a doctor and more patients and the man backed down but threatened repercussions. The other militiaman who could walk and I were made to dress and then led away and put into the back of an army truck. There were four other men already there and it was quickly evident that we were all militia of one sort or another. The two government civil guards sat with us and gesticulated angrily with their weapons when we talked together in Catalan, which they did not understand. But they were also clearly uncomfortable about their task. One of them offered us cigarettes. When the truck stopped at a police checkpoint in the centre of the city I looked the one who had offered cigarettes directly in the eye and he looked away. I jumped down from the truck and walked away. The truck moved on. I was expecting someone to shout that I was escaping, even that someone would open fire, but when I had looked the soldier in the eye I knew at once he did not have the stomach to shoot an unarmed man in the back, and when he looked away I knew that I would probably be safe.

I had some friends in the city, and some cousins. My cousins were not at home and my friends were unable to help me but they did give me an address, somewhere I could go, a bookshop."

Chapter 6

Jack did not believe that the man's presence in the doorway was a coincidence. Nor did it look as if he was waiting for someone. His attention was too fixed, too professional. Should he approach the house anyway? Jack was unsure, but he was very tired and needed to rest. He wondered how long the man had been standing there. He noticed after a while that the man had begun shuffling a little from foot to foot - a full bladder perhaps? Despite his own need for the toilet Jack decided to wait him out. Another five minutes passed, then ten. It may have been Jack's imagination, but the man seemed to be shuffling more urgently. At last, he threw down the cheroot he was smoking and left his post. He walked quickly away and turned down a side alley. As soon as he was out of sight Jack also walked quickly from the shelter of his doorway. The soldiers had finished positioning the barricade but were now taking a cigarette break. Jack tried to be casual and purposeful at the same time and nodded confidently to the sergeant as he passed by. The sergeant nodded in response, glanced at his bandaged hand, and returned to the banter he was sharing with his detail. Jack approached number 36 and used the large brass knocker in the shape of a lion's claw. He looked nervously back to the corner but the watcher had still not returned. Perhaps he had other needs? After a second knock the door was opened by a middle-aged woman. She was wearing a colourful apron over a plain black dress - a housekeeper perhaps?

"Sister Fàbregas, Mercè, sent me," he said in his best Catalan. The woman's expression changed as he spoke and she peered over his shoulder into the street before ushering him inside. She then looked out to the street again before closing the door behind him.

There ensued a series of confusions as Jack's limited Catalan vocabulary failed him entirely. After several attempts at explaining himself he handed over the note he had been given with the address. Perhaps the woman recognised the handwriting. Her demeanour certainly changed. She explained, as far as Jack could understand, that Mercè was not at home, that her own name was Montse, and asked did he want something to eat? His Catalan did extend to giving his name and saying that he was very hungry and that he needed to use the toilet. When he returned from the bathroom Montse settled him in a large dining room and very quickly produced a large bowl of stew, some bread and water and a bottle of wine. The dining-room was like the exterior of the house - an extraordinary mix of styles and materials. He ate the stew as slowly as he could, which was not very slowly at all. He mopped the bowl with the bread. Montse watched him eat and when he had finished she took the bowl and returned with a pastry filled with a soft custard, which he also ate as slowly as he could, which was also not very slowly at all. Suddenly the food and wine hit him hard, and with some desperation he explained to Montse that he needed to rest. She led him up two flights of ornate, wooden, curved stairs to a small bedroom.

When he awoke he was disoriented. It took him a while to reassemble his day and make sense of where he was and why. He sat up slowly and began to think about what would happen next. What should he do? Where should he go? How much danger was he really in? On a wooden blanket box at the end of the bed there was a change of clothes: underclothes, trousers, shirt, jacket, shoes and socks - a distinct step up from what he had been wearing. He gathered them up and went in search of a bathroom, which was next door. He washed himself thoroughly, appreciating once again the feeling of being clean, it was still a novelty. Then he dressed, the new clothes fitted a little better than the ones he had been given at the hospital. As he descended the stairs he began to recognise the incredible care and attention that had gone into the design and making of every detail of the interior of the house – the door handles, light fittings, windows, bannisters. Each had a unique form, and many were patterned or shaped as leaves or flowers - such odd and eclectic beauty.

He could hear voices on the ground floor and followed the sounds to the rear of the house. Montse and Mercè were in the kitchen. Mercè was seated at the kitchen table picking at a plate of cold meats. She smiled when he entered and signalled for him to sit with her. Her severe professional face had been left elsewhere but she looked tired and worried.

"You found us," she said.

Jack explained how he had found the house and tried to convey a sense of how grateful he was. He could not find the right words in any language. He also told her about the watcher and he could see her worry intensify.

"It is my father I think that he watches for."
"But you said he was in the government?"
"That is right. But now the question is which government. My father belongs to the ERC, which is part of the *Front d'Esquerres*, the Popular Front you would say, and that is a majority in the government of Catalunya – the *Generalitat*. This includes the trades unions and the anarchists - and the Republic does not want them. Catalunya has already declared itself a federal republic once in 1931 and in parts of Catalunya now the workers and trade unions control the economy. The Republic does not want this and the middle classes do not want this. There are many fears and compromises and pressures, and now the Russians they are everywhere. Their influence in the Republic grows. The independent police patrols have been replaced and there are thousands of civil guards in the city, like those across the street. It is impossible anymore to know who to trust, who is a friend, who is the enemy. My father is working to keep things together but with tensions between the socialists and anarchists and trade unions, and now communists, it is very difficult for him. He is very exposed."

"And the man outside?" Jack asked.

"Who knows? The secret police, perhaps, or a Russian even?"

The atmosphere was grim and they were all quiet. Montse spoke first and offered Jack something more to eat. He was hungry again and readily accepted.

Mercè changed the dressing on Staverley's hand and suggested he rest again. Her father had still not returned and he could see her worry escalating by the minute. She had tried to telephone but there was no connection to the parliament, a bad sign. He thought she would not be sleeping well that night and with the demands and long hours of her work of the hospital that would only add to her exhaustion. But Jack still had sleep to catch up on himself, and he was surprised how easily he fell asleep and how restful the sleep was. The months on the front and never quite being properly asleep and usually feeling very cold had left its mark, in more ways than one. At least his hand was throbbing a little less.

It was light when he awoke, and he allowed himself time to savour the clean sheets and being in a room alone - more of those small things he had missed. He washed again, shaved and dressed, and made his way downstairs. He found Mercè and Montse together again in the kitchen. He had still not quite grasped Montse's position in the house and the relationship between the two. They certainly did not behave toward one another as mistress and servant or as sisters – cousins perhaps? Montse prepared an omelette for him while he sipped something that was a vague approximation to coffee. The city was running short of basic foodstuffs. While he ate, Mercè explained something of the house to him. It was a *modernista* house she said, designed by a Catalan architect called Puig i Cadafalch. She went on to say that the *modernista* movement had developed as a reaction to industrialisation and set its ubiquitous organic motifs and themes and colours against the hard machine edges and greyness of the factory. When he had finished eating his omelette she gave him a tour of the house.

They were on the first floor when the knocking on the door began. The insistent bangs did not sound friendly. Montse appeared from the kitchen and opened the door tentatively.As soon as she did so, it was pushed open from the outside and she was knocked to the ground. Two assault guards with rifles entered, followed by the man that Jack recognised as the watcher from the previous day. A fourth man, very tall, two metres at least, entered next, and a fifth stood in the entrance without coming in. He was formally dressed, with a large grey hat pulled down so that his face was in shadow. The tall man was clearly in charge. He pointed to the staircase, and the assault guards ran up toward Jack and Mercè. Jack thought about trying to escape but the tour of the house had not suggested any means of exit from the upper floors. One of the guards grabbed Mercè by the arm and pushed her roughly down the stairs; she almost fell but maintained her balance by holding on to the bannister. The other guard took Jack by the arm and walked him down the stairs more slowly. The watcher checked Jack for weapons and then gestured with his head to the guard.

"Take him."

Mercè shouted in Catalan, "No, no, you can't."

The tall man raised his arm with amazing speed and caught Mercè by the neck. He pushed her backward against the wall and squeezed hard, so that she began to choke.

Jack shouted this time in English: "Stop! Stop that! I'll come!" He freed himself and both guards raised their rifles toward him. The tall man said nothing but continued to squeeze. Mercè was struggling as hard as she could, hitting his face, but was unable to break from the man's grip. He smiled and squeezed harder. Jack continued to shout. Someone pushed past the fifth man at the door. It was a man in his sixties, with silver hair. He wore a tailored blue suit and was carrying a black cane. For a moment everything stopped, the guards raised their rifles, the silver-haired man pulled at the handle of his cane and drew a short sword from the base. With this he slashed at the arm of the tall man, who released his grip on Mercè and tried to stem the flow of blood from the cut with his other hand. Mercè collapsed to the floor. The watcher pulled a gun from the pocket of his raincoat and shot the sliver-haired man in the head. He fell heavily to the floor, blood beginning to pour from his wound. Jack knew that he was dead. Mercè leapt up, screamed and pushed past the tall man, she fell on her knees and lifted the dead man's head with her two hands.

"*Pare, pare, pare,*" she said. It was her father.

The tall man had recovered himself and he signalled to the guards to take Jack. Jack jostled against them and then pulled away. One of the guards hit him on the side of the head with the butt of his rifle. He fell to his knees and with the guards holding his arms he was dragged toward the door, his feet scraping across the tiles. He looked back from the door and watched in horror as the tall man picked up the swordstick from the floor and plunged it hard and deep into Mercè's back. She emitted a horrible groan and collapsed across her father's body, her blood mixing with his. The tall man left the weapon embedded in Mercè's body and followed the guards out the door. The watcher was the last to leave. He moved Montse's body out of the way with his foot and closed the door gently behind himself. The fifth man was already hurrying away down the street.

Jack tried to struggle again but the guards bundled him onto the floor of a waiting car and he sank into semi-consciousness, his senses dissolved. He had no idea of how long they travelled or to where. When he awoke again properly he was seated in a wooden chair. His legs were tied to the legs of the chair and his arms to its arms. His head ached and blood had run down the side of his face and into his right eye. His hand was throbbing again, and he was very thirsty. He was in a large room with a high ceiling that looked as though it had once been a workshop of some sort. The floor was covered in grease and grime, and a set of tools hung from hooks on the walls. A row of bright lights dangled from a crossbeam. The only other person in the room was the watcher. He was leaning against the frame of a doorway which led to a small office, he smoking another cheroot. When he saw that Jack was waking he turned and called over his shoulder.

"Orlov."

In a few seconds the tall man appeared. Jack experienced a surge of anger, and threw himself forward. He wanted to beat the man; he wanted to kill him. But the chair did not move; it was fixed firmly to the floor. All that happened was that he strained painfully against the ties on his arms and legs. The tall man smiled. He had, Jack could now see, a small moustache. He had changed his clothes and now wore a checked suit, dark shirt and a tie. He looked out of place in the grimy workshop. He had brought a chair with him and put it down about two metres in front of Jack and sat. Jack could see no evidence of the wound Mercè's father had inflicted with the swordstick. The man leant forward and put his elbows on his knees and his chin on his hands. He studied Jack as if he was some kind of biological specimen and then spoke for the first time. He spoke in English but with a thick accent, Russian Jack surmised. He spoke gently and calmly.

"Mr Staverley. I welcome you to my office." He gestured to the room with his right hand and Jack thought he winced a little. That pleased him.

"We are here to ask some questions. You are here to answer. Very simple, yes?"

Jack said nothing; he was finding it difficult to get past his anger and his need to kill the man.

"There are three questions."
The man leant back and began to number the questions with his fingers.
One finger. "One, we want to know, where is Orwell."
Two fingers. "Two, we want to know, where is McNair."
Three fingers. "Three we want names of others with whom you travel here.
Simple, no?"
Jack said nothing. Orlov looked disappointed.
"Perhaps not so simple. Pity."
Orlov stood and moved very slowly closer to Jack. He pulled a long bludgeon that looked like a police baton from the belt of his trousers. He leant down and whispered in Jack's ear.

"One, where is Orwell?"

Jack looked straight ahead and firmed his jaw. He said nothing. In a swift movement Orlov raised the baton and brought it down hard on Jack's bandaged hand. The pain shot through his body like an electric charge, his back arched, his head shot back and he screamed like an animal. He would never have thought himself capable of producing such a sound. He then found it difficult to draw breath, he could not fill his lungs, and his arm spasmed. Saliva and bile drooled from his mouth. He wanted to hug himself, to protect himself, to ease the pain in some way, but he could not, he remained firmly bound to the chair. Orlov leant down again.

"Two, where is McNair."

Jack was unable to speak, he was struggling to draw breath, but Orlov took no account of that. He raised the baton again and hit the hand again with all his strength. Jack strained against the ropes and urinated. His brain seemed unable to register what was happening to his body and he blacked out. It was a short-lived relief. He was awoken by cold water being poured over his head from a petrol can by the

83

watcher. In his state of heightened sensitivity Jack could smell the residue of petrol. He shook his head to clear the water from his stinging eyes and as he did so Orlov leant down again.

"Three, names?"
This time Jack did manage to speak.
"I don't know."
This did not satisfy Orlov. He raised the baton again, hit Jack's hand again, and again Jack's body convulsed. He screamed again and the scream turned into a long high-pitched groan. When the groan died away he breathed out a series of fast exhalations with his head tilted back. Orlov studied him for a moment and handed the baton to the watcher.

"I think this may be enough for a while. Mr Staverley can make a recovery and take time to think about what comes later if he does not answer my questions. I think such contemplation will be beneficial before we begin again. And I need to rest from my exertions and take a drink perhaps. Yes, I think so. But not for you Mr Staverley, no drink for you until you behave. Come."

He gestured to the watcher who picked up Orlov's chair and followed him out of the room. Jack drifted back into unconsciousness.

It was the pain that woke him. And his first thought was how long he had been unconscious and how soon Orlov would be back. His second thought was that he could not cope with more pain. His hand felt huge and distorted and blood was seeping through the bandages. If the throbbing before had been uncomfortable, it was now unbearable, each throb pulsing through his body. It felt as though his whole arm was on fire, and the fire ebbed and flowed every two or three seconds from a high intensity to a low intensity and back, on and on. More pain or less pain, both unlike anything he had ever experienced, on and on. He tried to formulate a third thought, to distract himself, but the pain would not cooperate, it wanted its due and his full and undivided attention. He tried harder. What he wanted to think was that he had no idea where Orwell was and he had no idea where McNair was. But he knew that Orlov would not believe him and that meant more pain. He did know the names of some of the ILP people he had travelled with, and fought with in some cases, but surprised himself when he realised that he would not tell Orlov what he knew. Anyway, what was the point, if he could not answer question one and question two? There was no way of stopping the pain and stopping more pain, until his body could stand it no more and gave up. He needed to think about something else, something more constructive, more distracting. But the pain was adamant, it needed to be felt, it needed to be in control. It had somehow become something in itself, an enemy inside his body that needed to be defeated. He tried to breathe more deeply and slowly and to isolate the pain, to focus on it, to combat its control of his senses. A plan of escape, that's what he needed to think about. He tried but he could think of nothing. The bindings on his legs and arms remained as tight as they had been when tied. There was an array of tools on the walls, but the chair was fixed to the floor. As his fragile creative energy waned the pain took its opportunity and overwhelmed him again. He sagged and suffered. He could sense that the good friend of pain, despair, was sneaking up on him, overwhelming him. He tried again to concentrate - ties, chair and tools, ties, chair and tools. His mind settled on an idea, perhaps not a great idea, but it was something. He began to rock back and forward in the chair as hard as he could. This created new sources of pain in his arms and legs but these were pitiful rivals to the pain in his hand. His hand wanted all of his attention, but he kept rocking. Back and forward, back and forward, back and forward, back and forward. He got into a rhythm and began to imagine that the movement was increasing just a little in length each time and that the fixings were loosening. But maybe it was not imagination. One of the back legs of the chair was beginning to creak loudly, and suddenly the chair dropped on one side. It took him a moment to realise that the cross strut between the back legs had broken. He pushed away the pain again and tried to think for a moment. He began to rock again, this time from side to side. This was more difficult, he could not shift his weight so decisively, but with the broken strut the chair was unstable and he could concentrate his effort on one side to apply more pressure. He rocked and rocked and there was a loud crack. Another side strut had given way and broken away from the left front leg. He returned to the back and forward movement. There was more play now with the broken struts and he could feel the back legs lifting slightly from the floor. He began to fling himself forward on the forward movement, ignoring the pressure this put on his arms and the insistent pain in his hand. He was in a world of movement now. That is all there was. Nothing would stop him. Backward and forward, backward and forward, and then suddenly the forward movement did not end, he crashed toward the floor and managed to turn his head at the last moment, landing on his right cheek bone, which broke he thought. Then he was unconscious again.

When he woke his first thought was the same first thought as last time. How much time had passed, and how soon would Orlov return? It was not a thought to be indulged. He tentatively moved his left leg, and while it was still tied to the leg of the chair the leg was no longer attached to the floor. He tried the right leg. The same. He tried his left arm, but that was more difficult: the arms of the chair were still attached to the backrest. The backrest was no longer attached to the seat, however, enabling some movement in his upper body. At the very least, he could wriggle – with enormous effort, and with small movements from each arm and leg in turn, he could move, slowly, across the floor, like a wounded tortoise. He began to do so, a few inches at a time. As he leant to his left, his damaged hand was pressed into the floor with his weight on it. He tried not to scream. It was not until the fifth or sixth cycle of small movements that he realised that he did not know where he was going. He needed to rest, and felt himself drifting into oblivion again, but he knew he had to stay awake and free himself before Orlov returned, as he inevitably would. He tried to turn over onto his back, but the backrest of the chair prevented him from completing the turn. He tried to raise himself onto his knees, but without his hands to help him the strength in his back was inadequate. Perhaps if he could reach the wall he could rest one end of the backrest of the chair against it and push sideways with his legs to turn himself around and flip himself over. Once over, he was sure he could stand, and if he could stand he could reach the tools or smash the remaining parts of the chair against the wall. He had made plenty of noise already, but evidently Orlov and the watcher could not hear him. He resumed his wriggling. Slowly he got closer to the wall. He was just two or three feet away when he heard noises, first wood breaking and then glass being smashed. He began to panic, but a calmer voice somewhere deep in his head said wait, why would Orlov and the watcher be breaking glass and smashing things? Even so, he tried to wriggle faster. Then there were two loud popping sounds that he recognised as gunshots. Then a shout, then two more shots, another shout, another shot and someone ran into the workshop. Face down on the floor, he could not raise his head far enough to see who it was, just a pair of muddy black boots. He had no idea what was happening or what was going to happen next.

"He's here." The voice spoke in English, American English. More people entered the workshop and someone began to very gently undo his ties. He strained his head to look up and was met with the smile and freckles of Helen Haywood.

"You are quite a mess, militiaman Staverley," she said. He tried to reply but slid into unconsciousness.

Joan finished his ratafia and wiped his mouth with a large grey white handkerchief.

"The bookshop was not hard to find. It was well-known, Sempere and Sons, in Carrer de Santa Ana. When I arrived I was surprised to find it open for business, as most of the shops in the city were still closed because of the fighting. I stood outside for a while and watched. The streets were quiet and there were few customers but I saw two enter and both left with packages under their arms. Perhaps books were not a necessity when a city is divided by political battles, or perhaps that is when they are very necessary. In part I waited because I did not know what to do and what to say. 'I am a political refugee from Stalin, please give me asylum.' That seemed stupid. I almost left. To be honest, I was embarrassed. Asking for help was difficult and a great risk, for them and for those I asked, but I had nowhere else to go. If I kept walking the streets I was sure that the assault guards would eventually pick me up. So in I went. A bell tinkled as I opened the door. As soon as I was inside I knew I had found a haven of calm and somewhere I would be safe. The books would protect me. It was like entering a different world, one where any violence would be confined to the page and sad stories had an ending. The bookshelves were enormous, higher than the tallest man could reach, and there was little space between them, you had to shuffle sideways, which made the book titles difficult to read. I got the impression that this was a bookshop for people who knew what they wanted and where to find what they wanted, not a place for idle browsers or indecisive readers. I was unsure what I was or how to behave, how to fit in. I shuffled and browsed as best I could but I was aware that a man behind the counter, who was unpacking books from a wooden box, was watching me from over his half-moon reading glasses. After more shuffling and browsing I summoned the courage to approach him. This was far more daunting than fighting at the front. I was exposed before the whole of western literature and its keeper and I feared I might not be worthy. It was not the man that bothered me, it was the books, perhaps they would judge me harshly. I remember even now what I said.

"Can you help me?"
"Of course Senyor, what is it you are looking for," the
man said.
"Help," I said, "I am looking for help."
"Ah!" he said, "help. I see. Who sent you?"
I explained who had sent me and I could see that he recognised the names of my friends. He took off his glasses ushered me around the counter and into the cluttered office behind. Beyond the office was another room, a kitchen, a warm welcoming kitchen. He made me a coffee, or something approximating to coffee.

"Si Senyor, Senyor Cervantes shall we say. It is probably best if I do not ask your other name," Senyor Sempere, said, "and that I do not ask more than you have told me already. You are welcome to stay and browse among our books, our rare books, those we keep for special customers. Let me show you."

Senyor Sempere led the way beyond the kitchen, along a corridor lined with more books, to a large storeroom, filled with boxes of books. In one corner of the storeroom he approached a rough wooden bookcase and pulled out a book from the top shelf.

"Fifth from the end," he muttered to himself.

The bookcase swung away from the wall to reveal a hidden room. It was also lined with books but was well furnished, it had a bed, some chairs and a small table, light came from a set of narrow windows set high on one wall.

"I think you can be comfortable here."

"I think I can," I said.

I ate that night with Senyor Sempere and his wife and slept well in my secret book room. While I knew it was dangerous I knew there were things I had to do the next day. The most important of which was to find your father. I discussed this with Senyor Sempere over breakfast and he agreed that it needed to be done and he insisted that if I found him I should bring him to the shop. He suggested that there were three places I might begin to look, places that might, like Sempere and Sons, take in political waifs and strays. I knew that sharing the addresses with me meant that I was trusted. I think I had been checked up on. I set off, taking care to avoid the barricades and patrols. It was as though the city was being occupied by an invading army, which in effect it was. I heard several bursts of gunfire and I changed my route each time to avoid those. I saw lorries filled with armed men, some were civil guards, others were militia. The black and red flags, which had previously hung everywhere, were less common now and some had been ripped down and trodden into the rubbish which was accumulating in the streets. The first address I had was a men's clothing shop, a rather up-market establishment from the looks of the display windows. But the shop was closed and the interior seemed to be in some disarray. I knocked several times and waited but no one answered. I thought someone across the street was beginning to pay too much attention to my efforts so I moved on. I entered a bar, one of the few still open, and left again by the back door. The next address was near the harbour, the workshop of a farrier, but I was met with suspicion and reluctance. In the circumstances I could understand people not wanting to talk with a stranger and answer questions. I could have been anyone, a spy, a provocateur, they did not know me, and I did not know them. After I had been turned away I watched the building for a while but saw nothing that was helpful. I thought then that my attempts to trace your father were probably foolish and dangerous. But I had one last address, a house in the *Eixample*. It was a long walk and I felt very exposed in the nearly deserted streets and when I arrived I found a barricade that was manned by civil guards blocking the street of the house. I was very tempted to return directly to the bookshop but I made a circuit of the block and entered the street from the other end. There was a large official looking car parked outside the house with a driver at the wheel. I hid behind some steps and watched, almost immediately two civil guards came out dragging your father between them, they bundled him into the back seat of the car. Two other men followed and got into the front. One of them was very tall, the other wore a gabardine raincoat. I only saw them for a few seconds. A fifth man wearing a hat walked away down the street as the car moved off. I don't know why but I watched the man in the hat hurry all the way to the corner and through the barricade he was not stopped by the soldiers. If it were not for the barricade I would have followed him. Instead I walked as quickly as I could back to the bookshop stopping several times to see if I was being followed. I could see no one.

I told Senyor Sempere what I had seen and he took a particular interest in the tall man. He said he would make some phone calls, if the phones were working.

"Let's see what we can see."

I had begun to realise that he was a man who knew things and knew people and could get things done. There was nothing more that I could do except wait. I was frustrated and angry with myself. I felt impotent. I had no idea where your father was being taken. Senyor Sempere sent me to rest in the room of books and I think I slept. My back was painful after all the walking. It was several hours before Senyor Sempere came.

"It was difficult," he said. "Things are falling apart, people are missing or have fled and the telephone is unreliable, but I think there is some progress. There are other lives at stake. The tall man is known. He is a Russian, from their secret police, an agent of Stalin, the NKVD *rezident* in Spain – he is Orlov, but uses other names. He is organising a secret police force for the Republic and he is tracking down the leaders of POUM. Many have already been arrested. It is being said that POUM are spies for the Nationalists, which I know to be ridiculous. I spoke to a friend, who spoke to a friend, who spoke to friend, who may know someone, who may know where Orlov can be found. But nothing is certain."

All of that was disconcerting and I feared for your father in the hands of the Russians. We had heard stories of what happened to those they took. They saw friends of Trotsky everywhere, and wanted them destroyed.

I ate again that evening with Senyor Sempere and his family. I was overwhelmed by their willingness to take risks for someone like me they had never met before. Amidst all of the distrust and fear in the city, a name or a piece of paper with the right words could ensure shelter and safety, at least for a time. As we ate Senyor Sempere told me something of the history of the bookshop, which he had inherited from his father. We all glanced repeatedly at the telephone. It finally rang as we were preparing for bed. Senyor Sempere snatched it up quickly. He said nothing but just listened. Whatever was said was brief."

"Something might be known, something might be done," he said, that was the message. All we could do was wait again. That night I slept little, and to be honest with you I wept. I wept for your father, for my country, and for my family. I had lost touch with my parents and grandfather while I was at the front and had no way of contacting them. I wanted to ask Senyor Sempere if he could find out anything of them, but I had asked enough already. I also had no idea of what I could do next, and where I should go. I wanted to fight Franco, that was why I had joined the militia, but I would not fight alongside the communists and the Russians, not after what I had seen.

The telephone rang again near dawn and Senyor Sempere came to the hidden book room in his dressing gown and he was smiling. It was the first time I had seen him smile.

"We have him, we have your friend" he said, "but he is injured, he was treated badly by Orlov and he is still in danger."

It was some time before I came to know how badly your father had been treated and perhaps it is better not to talk about that now. The important thing is that he was freed and he survived. I only saw your father one more time after that, and then only for a short time, as he was being moved out of Barcelona."

Staverley had a tear running down his face. He was deeply shocked and moved by his father's predicament, but also by the willingness of so many people like Mercè and Joan and Senyor Sempere to help him and save him. Joan's story was one that told of the worst and the best of people, it was both harrowing and uplifting. It took Staverley several minutes to gather himself again, but he was not embarrassed by his emotions. They seemed of little consequence over and against what had been told to him, what Joan and his father had experienced. He understood even better his father's reluctance to talk about his time in Catalunya.

"And this man Orlov, do you have any idea what became of him?" Staverley asked.

"I do not. There were some rumours concerning his involvement in the removal of the bullion reserves of the Republican government to Russia as payment for war materials. He was said to be responsible for the logistics of the transfer, over 500 tonnes of gold was taken. Beyond that, nothing."

Chapter 7

It was several hours, so he thought, before Jack became fully conscious again. He had drifted in and out of wakefulness several times but each time a welcoming black hole had opened up for him to fall back into. When he did come round his first thought was how much time had passed and how soon Orlov would return. Fear coursed through his body like a fever before he remembered the rescue and that he was no longer tied to the chair, waiting. Now he was lying in a narrow iron-framed bed in a small windowless room. There was no furniture, but there were several religious statues and a very large wooden cross fixed to the walls. His damaged hand had been re-bandaged, there were more and thicker bandages this time, but for the moment it was quiet, more opiates at work he suspected. His head and wrists and legs had also been cleaned and treated, and he was pleased to see that his urine-soaked clothes were nowhere to be seen. He looked beneath the thin sheet that covered him, and saw that he was wearing a long cotton nightshirt – a first for him. After about ten minutes the door opened and two people came into the room. He experienced another spurt of fear until he recognised Helen Haywood. There was a man with her, and he could see three other men gathered outside the doorway looking in. They were smiling.

"Well, Jack," Helen said, "how are you feeling? I have the strong sense we may have come along in the nick of time." She grinned at him and he felt so glad to see her freckles again,

Jack tried to answer, but for a moment the memories of what had happened over the last two days overwhelmed his ability to speak. He tried very hard not to cry.

"I ache and I hurt, but I think I might ache and hurt a lot more without something you might have given me? And if it's all right with you I will stay where I am for a little while."

The whole group smiled again. He realised they were all wearing some kind of rough and ready military dress, including Helen, but with no identifying patches or insignia.

"Look, I just don't know how to say this, I don't think there are any right words or enough words for how I feel and how I am going to be grateful to you, all of you, for the rest of my life. You saved me. You saved me from him, from Orlov. I am certain I wouldn't have survived another set of his questions, and to be honest I wouldn't have wanted to. Until I found myself in that room I had no idea of the meaning of pain or what pain could do to a person."

The other man in the room spoke for the first time, also an American.

"We were glad to do it, buddy, for a comrade. The only pity is that we missed that Ruskie bastard. We were hoping to show him some US hospitality."

The others nodded in agreement.
"But who are you people, and how did you find me?"
Helen answered.
"We're a motley crew. This is Chuck, another yank as you probably guessed, he was with the George Washington boys; by the door, that's Emiliano, he's with the Garibaldi Battalion, Italian obviously," Emiliano gave a mock salute. "Then there's Josef and Miguel from the Palafox. Josef is Polish, Miguel from Galicia." The other three raised their arms in greeting.

"And you know me."

"But why are you together, and why rescue me? And how did you find me? I don't understand."

Chuck answered this time.

"Okay, my friend, that's complicated and a long story, and you need to rest. But I'll give ya the short version. Everything's going haywire out there. It's no longer us against the Nats, it's us against each other, or rather the Ruskies and Spanish communists against everyone else. A lot of the International Brigades are being disbanded or merged and some, like POUM, your lot, are being purged. The Brigades are anti-Fascist all right, but not everyone in the Brigades is for Uncle Jo Stalin, you know that. There are a lot of other affiliations out there. And some of us are not happy standing by while good people are being murdered and tortured by the damn Russians, so we have a kind of network of volunteers who are willing to help out when necessary, and you seemed necessary, and you were spoken for. The word came and we did our best. That's probably all I should say. We try to keep things close, if you know what I mean. But we can't carry on with this much longer, the way things are going."

Jack was trying hard to listen but he knew he was slipping away again. Helen waved the others away and sat down on the side of the bed.

"Let's take a quick look at your wears and tears and let you get some more sleep. That hand of yours took a beating and most of the bones are broken. With any luck it will mend. It'll take a while, and I'm sorry to say it won't work like it used to, but we'll do our best. Okay?"

Jack heard no more.

Over the next week he began to recover his strength and was able to eat, but his hand continued to cause him a lot of pain despite the medication that Helen gave him. She explained that there was a shortage of morphine and that she did not want him to get too used to it either. She also explained that they were in a convent, the headquarters of a nursing order. She worked alongside some of the nuns in the military hospital and they were turning a blind eye to his presence as a favour to her. But he could not stay for too long. As soon as he was able to walk properly he would be moved and then got out of the country and back to England. Plans were being made, she said.

"But why take so much trouble for me. Don't get me wrong, I think going home is a very good idea right now, but I can't see that I'm much of a priority. There must be plenty of others out there needing your help."

Helen gave him a look that suggested his ordeal might have damaged his ability to think clearly.

"You saw things Jack, and you were not meant to live to tell the tale. From what we've pieced together you saw two people attacked and a senior Catalan politician killed in cold blood by a Russian agent. Orlov and his secret police buddies are gonna want you back, they're gonna want you real bad, and then they're gonna want you dead. But they can't have you. We've got you now and we're keeping you out of harm's way, okay. There might be opportunities to tell what you saw to others willing to listen to what's really going on here and that's important right now. You are a precious commodity, my English friend, even if you're a damaged one."

Put that way, getting him out of the country sounded like an extremely good idea. Another encounter with Orlov was the last thing he wanted. He was not going to argue. He did have one more question, which he had not wanted to ask but really needed to.

"You obviously know what happened when they took me. Can you tell me anything about Mercè and her father and her friend Montsé? They were kind and brave to shelter me and I think I'm at least partly responsible for her death and for her father's."

"You can't think that, Jack. All of us involved in this know the risks we are taking. We do it because we believe it needs to be done, whatever the consequences. Mercè and her father and Montsè were taken care of by another group of our friends. The father is dead, as you probably knew already, Montsè was not badly injured and is recovering, she was the one who told us about Orlov and the others and what they did. As a witness she's probably in great danger now. Mercè survived but is very seriously ill. To be honest, from what I've been told, I don't think she'll make it. Her injury is a bad one. But she's being well taken care of, I promise you. She's an important person in the world of Catalan politics, and not just because she's her father's daughter. Montsè is with her."

Helen's answer made Jack feel a little better and offered a glimmer of hope, a glimmer that he was determined to hang on to.

Early in the morning two days later Emiliano came, now in civilian dress, to help Jack leave. He had brought clothes and a few necessities in a small leather bag. Jack realised that he had nothing of his own. All of his possessions and papers had been taken or left behind in Mercè's house or had just disappeared. With Jack leaning on Emiliano's arm they slowly descended several sets of stairs and emerged through a tiny wooden door at the back of the convent. A van was waiting for them - a florist's van, so the sign of the side announced. Emiliano helped Jack into the back, shook his hand and then waved him on his way. The driver was a young woman Jack had never seen before. She did not speak. Jack was already tired from the descent. By looking through the small window in the backdoor of the van he could see that they were heading out of the city, driving west, roughly in the direction of Lleida. After about an hour the van pulled off the road and turned into a barn by a rambling farmhouse. Jack was ushered out of the van by the driver, then she drove away. He stood in the farmyard for a moment uncertain what to do. The door of the farmhouse opened and there was Joan. They moved toward one another and embraced. They held each other for a long time.

"I was beginning to think that I would never see you again my friend," Joan said.

"The same for me, Joan, the same for me. I was so worried about you when you disappeared from the hospital. When I returned your bed was empty."

"I was taken by the assault guards, but I was lucky, I escaped and I was helped. You were not so lucky I think."

They had very little time but Jack explained as best he could what had happened to him, although he found it very difficult to describe his time with Orlov and what the man had done to him. It was as though the experience was not quite real. It was real in the sense of the pain involved and the pain he still felt, but it seemed as though it had happened to someone else. Someone he used to be. The torture and the pain were inhuman, and had made him less than human he felt. It had lessened him, taken something from him, something that would never be returned. He now knew his limits, in a very visceral sense – he was limited by what his body could tolerate and by what his mind could cope with. His relationship to his body was changed. He tried to convey some of that to Joan but was not sure he was making proper sense, even to himself.

They went inside the farmhouse and there was food, very good food, and for the first time since he had been taken and despite his tiredness he had a proper appetite. The food was served by a weather-beaten, middle-aged woman wearing farm clothes, and after they had eaten she carefully checked his bandages and treated again his cuts and bruises. Her hands were rough and chaffed but her touch was gentle and delicate. She spoke a few words of sympathy in Catalan while she tended him. More kindness. He thanked her, but again his gratitude and trite words seemed totally inadequate. Then it was time to move on, and Jack said his goodbyes. He embraced Joan again and said no more: nothing more needed to be said. Jack understood now that it was Joan's persistence that had saved him. Another debt of gratitude he knew he would probably never be able to repay. Kindness and help were becoming a burden, which was not right.

This time a dilapidated farm lorry, fully loaded with huge logs was waiting. Jack sat alongside the driver, a young man who looked too young to be driving such a heavy lorry, but who handled it with ease. As they set off the young man reached across to shake Jack's hand. "Josep-Maria," he said. Jack offered his name in return but avoided another thank you. He soon fell asleep. After two hours he was dropped off by Josep-Maria outside a small town deep in the Catalan countryside. He would never know its name. There, he was picked up by Miquel-Angel, a tailor. And so it went, with several more changes of vehicle and driver, on through the night. Some talked to him, some did not. Some wanted company, others preferred silence. He asked each of the drivers if they had news of what was happening in the city, but none had anything new to tell him. Fighting continued and the militias were losing control. He also asked after Mercè, but was not sure they knew who he was talking about. Shoulders were shrugged and heads shaken. Twice more he was fed and had his wounds checked, before arriving in the early morning at a town in the Pyrenees, Camprodón the signs said. There, Javier, a lieutenant in the Republican army, dropped him off outside a shoe shop. Jack had experienced a tremor of fear when he first saw the uniform but all was well. It was too early for the shop to be open for business but as soon as Javier drove away the door of the shop opened and he was ushered inside by a young man.

Hipolit, the young man who owned and ran the shop, took him to a tiny flat above and allowed him to sleep for a while. Jack heard the bell on the shop door tinkle several times, and mid-morning Hipolit brought him a coffee and a pastry. The flat consisted of just five small rooms on two floors, and it was littered everywhere with a mix of shoe boxes and the paraphernalia for hunting and fishing. Hipolit was obviously a devotee of outdoor sports and the killing of fish and animals. Indeed, as he explained proudly over lunch, he was president of the Camprodón Society of Hunters and Fishermen. He also told Jack that as soon as it began to get dark he would be collected and taken to cross the border into France. Hipolit had a set of identity papers for Jack to carry, in the name of William Montagu, a dead volunteer. It was hoped they would not be needed, Hipolit said. The crossing would be clandestine, but they might be useful once in France. The French were unpredictable Hipolit warned, some were welcoming and helpful, others did not want Spanish refugees or other outsiders in their country. Bad things were happening in France he said.

The journey over the Pyrenees was demanding, especially in Jack's fragile state. It began by car, then in a horse-drawn cart for a few kilometres, but mostly after that it was on foot. The paths, when there were paths, were steep and rocky and several times Jack got to the point where he thought he could not go on. His two companions were patient and he always found some reserve of energy somewhere in his legs and lungs. Thinking about Orlov helped, his memories of the man and what he had done invariably producing a surge of adrenalin. At one point, unmarked and unheralded, Jack's guides announced that they had crossed into France and that they would soon be passing him on to French colleagues. The new French companions were also Catalans. They spent the day out of sight in an isolated hay barn and Jack was glad of the rest. His sleep was both deep and troubled. His body was exhausted but his mind would not rest. This was not the way he had expected to leave Spain, secretively, in the dark, in fear for his life. He had imagined, very foolishly he now knew, marching in triumph as part of a victorious Republican army, seeing Franco and his generals imprisoned, the foundations of a new socialist democracy set in place, and fascism in retreat across Europe. He remembered the many conversations he had shared with international fighters from different parts of the world who shared his hopes. They were united in the belief that fascism was an evil that had to be stopped and that it could be stopped in Spain. How wrong they were. Apart from the Russians the rest of the world was standing back and allowing the

Nationalists to do their worst. The war was far from over but already the plight of the Republic was dire.

Jack found it difficult to wake in the late afternoon. His body wanted more rest. But there was another long walk ahead. Before setting off they ate some stale bread and hard cheese, with a sip of brandy and water from a stream. The guides promised him a hot meal later. Jack had learned from the guides, Carles and yet another Jordi, that he was the latest in a series of foreign fighters that they had escorted across the border, and most of these were escaping from the Russian purge of deviationists. They seemed philosophical about this pipeline of disappointed men, and some women, with their broken hearts and dreams. Carles and Jordi shared the disappointment. They were both inheritors of a long tradition of Catalan anarchism and nationalism, both had been organisers for the CNT trade union and had been involved in setting up a large agricultural commune near Girona, which had been attacked and destroyed by Republican troops. Troops that had been pulled out of the frontline to deal with the anarchist counter-revolutionaries, as they were called by the government in Madrid. Now they were trying to contribute in a different way. Their own fate was uncertain.

The eventual destination of the long walk was the French town of Pau, where Jack was handed over to his next minders. He ate a last meal with Carles and Jordi and as they said goodbyes they wished him well and surprised and moved him by offering their thanks for his service in the fight against Fascism. Jack was relieved to find that the next leg of his journey was motorised - a 200 kilometre drive from Pau to Arcachon in a vegetable truck – but with several stops on the way to collect produce from farms. Arcachon was a bourgeois seaside resort for the wealthy of Bordeaux who had villas there, but it also had a thriving mussel-fishing harbour where Jack was given a change of clothes and loaded on to a small coastal trading vessel. The crew were friendly but left him to his own devices and they asked no questions. Again he got the sense that he was not the first escapee to travel with them. He offered to be of help but the captain took one look at his bandaged hand and refused politely. The ship pottered along the coast dropping off and picking up cargoes at small ports. He changed ships in Brest, to a coastal trawler and was delivered to Falmouth very early in the morning, before dawn. No longer being a fugitive felt strange and the peacefulness of the town was oddly disconcerting. From Falmouth he was on his own with a small amount of English money for the train fare to London provided by the trawlermen. Yet more kindness accumulated. His Spanish adventure was at an end and he had little sense of what might lie ahead. His political idealism was as badly damaged as his hand. More than anything, he wanted to see Edith again and after that determined that he would tell people what he had experienced and witnessed in Spain.

Joan asked Staverley whether he would like to spend the night, and perhaps even help with the milking of the sheep and goats. He was tempted, he had so many more questions to ask, but he was worried about what Senyora Budó would think, and might do, if he did not return. Not having a toothbrush also niggled. Despite his concerns he accepted Joan's invitation. Milking turned out to be a lot more difficult than Staverley had thought, and the goats were not particularly tolerant of an amateur, the sheep even less so. Overall his contribution to the whole exercise was pretty minimal. Joan enjoyed watching his efforts, and they laughed a lot. It was light relief after Joan's account of his experiences and those of Staverley's father. Dinner was simple but delicious, and Joan was unfazed by Staverley's vegetarianism. He produced an enormous salad with walnuts and hot mushrooms, topped off of course with cheese, a soft, fresh one this time. While they ate Joan explained the different types of cheeses he produced. After dinner, and over another glass of *ratafia,* Staverley broached the possibility of asking more questions about the war and its aftermath.

"I don't mind to talk about these things. I have had a long time to think about the war, as I can explain. I have resolved many issues for myself, with help from my reading, with help from the books. There is a lot of wisdom here," he gestured toward his collection. "I have worked on myself, you might say, my relation to myself. I won't tell you that I have eliminated all of my torments and fears but I do understand them better and can keep them in check, most of the time. And as you see there is little opportunity for conversation here. The animals have little interest in anything but eating and reproducing themselves, they do not listen to me or take me seriously. But I will admit that I do talk to them anyway and to myself sometimes – so a human listener would be welcome. Go ahead with your questions."

Staverley was impressed by Joan's calmness and equanimity, and his quiet humour.

"I could not help but be curious about what happened to you after my father left, and how you managed with your predicament of being sought by the Russians and the Republican police?"

"Of course, but you should not think that I was that important. I had been a member of the JCI, that was a socialist youth organisation, before the war, but never as part of the leadership. Nonetheless, it was evident that my name was on a list somewhere and it was sensible to not make myself obvious. My illness made me unfit for active duties and a doctor sympathetic to the situation of people like me was willing to write and sign a certificate to that effect and more importantly to make the certificate in a different name. I then took the certificate to a Republican army centre in a small town outside Barcelona. I explained that I had been recuperating from my illness but was ready to be re-assigned. It was easy to say that my identity papers were lost in the turmoil of battle. I was given a post as a supplies clerk and for most of the rest of the war I sat behind a desk trying to find and distribute food and materials to units fighting at the front. That was a frustrating task but in some ways I enjoyed the challenge. I was good at my job. But after Ebro, the battle there, everything degenerated into chaos, many thousands of soldiers surrendered or were captured. The International Brigades, or rather the survivors, returned home. Then the reprisals and killings began. The Nationalists also had lists. Maybe even the same lists. And I knew that my certificate would not be good enough to protect me for very long. So I returned to Barcelona and resumed my previous identity."

"Wasn't that even more dangerous?" Staverley asked.

"It was difficult, without proper papers I would be suspect, with my papers I was also vulnerable. And from a friend I did learn that Fanco's police had listed me, and that would mean a prison camp or worse, hundreds of thousands were executed. So I decided to hide. I became *un topo,* one of the disappeared people, do you know of this?"

"It was explained to me, yes."

"So for the next thirty years I did not exist, I rarely left my place of hiding, I waited to be discovered, or to be given up - until the kindness of the Generalissimo and his amnesty in '69, to celebrate the anniversary of his great victory." Joan gave a hollow laugh and sipped some of the *ratafia.*

"Many times I had thought of walking to the local police station and giving myself up. There were many dark periods and moments of fear and despair. But do you know what saved me and allowed me to survive as *un topo*?"

"Sheer strength of will, perhaps?" Staverley offered, somewhat lamely he recognised. But Joan waved a hand in the air behind his head.

"No, it was these, my books. Many of these books I accumulated during those thirty years. They were my friends, my companions. I read, I learned languages, I educated myself, and I tried to engage with debates in science and philosophy – and I came to understand that they were often about the same things. Books became my life and sometimes I think that that was a great privilege. Few people have the opportunity to devote themselves to a life of reading. And if you look in the books you will see that many are marked with my comments and thoughts, and objections. Those were my conversations, and all of that happened in my head. I imagined myself debating with the great writers and great minds of history. I could rarely leave my hiding places but in my imagination I travelled to ancient Greece, to renaissance Italy, to the laboratories of Cambridge and the studios of Paris. In my mind I was a free man. And that kept me sane, or I thought it did, who knows? Perhaps it was all madness after all."

"And where were you all this time?"

"At first when I returned to Barcelona I spent a few days again enjoying the care and hospitality of Senyor Sempere and his family, but it appeared that the bookshop was being watched and I had to leave. Both for my safety and for theirs. Luckily for me my cousins had returned to the city, and one of them, Pascual, was willing to take me in. He was a carpenter and in his small apartment he constructed a false wall that made a secret compartment for me. It was a very small and uncomfortable space, although I got used to it, but during the day when my cousin and his wife were at work and their son was at school the apartment was empty and I could move around - although I had to be very quiet. Unfortunately, the neighbours could not be trusted: there were rewards to be claimed for turning in those sought by the police, and life was hard for many after the war. Inevitably, some succumbed to temptation or settled old scores. I learned to exist in a world of careful silence. Sometimes in my loneliness I wondered whether perhaps I had ceased to exist. I was no longer of the social world. I became a spectre, a phantom. The estimable Senyor Sempere sent me books regularly and my collection began to build. The books restricted my space even further but I never resented that. I was happy to share. After four years living in that way my cousin's wife became pregnant again, and their first child, a lovely boy, began to talk about 'the man who lives in the wall' and we were worried that he might say such things at school or to his friends. So there were two problems and I knew I had to leave. Oddly, my next accommodation was with Oriol, the farrier I had visited when looking for your father in '37. His workshop was now a garage for car repairs. The farrier was now a skilled mechanic. Again Pascual was able to build me a space in which to hide, in the attic, under the eaves. This time I had to remain in hiding during the day but I could explore the workshop at night when it closed. Sometimes I would sit in the cars that were awaiting repair and conjure up journeys to the places I had read about, turning the steering wheel and changing the gears, like a child at play. Twice while I was there, there were searches - once *La Guardia* and once the secret police. Both times Oriol was sure that someone had informed. But I was not found. Pascual was both careful and clever and his construction stood up well even to close inspection. A very few times, at night, on the days of fiestas, when the streets were full and the police were busy with other things, I ventured out, never for long, and always with great care and well disguised. If it felt safe to do so I would take a glass of wine at a café. I would never linger and never return to the same place but the brief interaction with a waiter or the pardons and thank yous exchanged with other customers were precious to me. If they could see me and speak to me and I to them then I knew I did exist, and that I would go on existing. And the books kept coming, both from Senyor Sempere and from Oriol, who I learned had wanted to be a sculptor when he was young and had a secret passion for art. Some nights when work for the day had finished he would stay behind and we would talk about art and he would explain his ideas for sculptures constructed from iron, made in his furnace. His great disappointment in life was that he could never translate his ideas into reality. The demands of work and family life were paramount, but he enjoyed those opportunities we had to speculate about the impact his works might have made in the world of art. He wanted to shock and provoke and entertain. I spent seventeen years with Oriol, can you believe that, until he became ill. He developed lung cancer. He smoked cheap cigarettes all day while he worked on the cars, despite the constant nagging of his wife. His illness developed quickly but even so he planned very carefully for me, for my future. In all those years his family and his mechanics knew nothing of my existence. We had become great friends and his death was a great blow to me: apart from waiters I talked with no one else. I discovered beneath his grease and his brute strength, and his great knowledge of metals and engines, a man of great sensitivity, a man of imagination and creative drive, who had to make a living for his family but could never express what lay in his soul. Our conversations allowed us both a kind of freedom that was rare and brilliant. I often would think of what Marx wrote in *The German Ideology*, that in a proper communist society we might became hunters, fishermen, shepherds and critics – critics after dinner. And of course here I am, a shepherd," Joan chortled but behind his amusement there was sadness in his eyes. Staverley assumed that he was remembering his lost friend and companion. After a moment Joan rubbed his eyes with his knuckles and began again.

"For the last nine years of my voluntary incarceration I lived in a house near San Feliu de Guixols, that's on the coast. The house belonged to a Fundación and was before the war a centre for writers Sometimes during my time there it was used for events or meetings, but mostly it was empty, with just a caretaker, who also took care of me. And others, other *topos* and people seeking sanctuary from Franco would stay on occasion, but no one stayed more than a few weeks. I was the only long-term resident. For a long time I did not understand how Oriol had found the place and why the Fundación was willing to risk the repercussions of me being discovered. That became clearer much later. There was more opportunity for me to be outside while there. In the winter especially, the beaches were deserted, and I even made friends with some local fishermen. But then awkward questions were asked or remarks were made and I would retreat to my hidden space in the basement, behind the furnace, where my books kept me company. For me, compared with other *topos* I think it was easy. Some suffered badly from the deprivations and loneliness and fear. Many were informed on and were imprisoned or executed. Others took their own lives when there seemed to be no end to their confinement. But I always had my books, and good people to protect me. People who took great risks."

Joan suggested a last *ratafia* and then bed. He would be up early to walk with the herd, he explained.

"And the amnesty?" Staverley asked.

"I had expected the worst when that came, questioning by the police and a period of imprisonment perhaps, but it was very straightforward and within a few days I was re-registered as a citizen of Franco's Catholic state. I was suddenly back in the world and part of it, which was not easy to begin with. There was so much that was different, so much that I did not know. There were new fears to be confronted. The world had speeded up and become more complicated, and other things that I remembered had disappeared. It took time to adjust and to learn to engage again with people and to curb my suspicions. There were certain jobs that were forbidden to me, and I had to contact the police if I moved from my registered address. But I was able to register myself as living here. As I told you, my father had died. My grandfather also was dead by then. I never knew, of course, and I have always regretted not being able to say goodbye to either of them and let them know that I was still living. They must have assumed that I perished in the war. The house had suffered a little from neglect and the herd no longer existed but no one was interested in such a remote place and the hardness of the life here. I discovered that my grandfather had left me a little money that had been held for me by a lawyer. I spent months repairing the house. I bought furniture, Pascual's son, also a carpenter like his father, built these bookcases for me, and I began to rebuild the herd, and learn to care for them and to make the cheese. The skills of making goat's cheese were almost extinct in this region when I began. I had read about these things during my time as *un topo*, but the realities were more challenging than the words on the page. I made many mistakes but slowly I became a herder as well as a reader. I have a market for my cheese now and I have a life, one that is worth living I think. And all of those years of silence and solitariness prepared me well for the mountain. I think I am content, and every day I look at the sky and the rocks and the wildlife and I wonder at their beauty. Every day is different, and of course I still read. There is still much to read. Books from Sempere and Sons are delivered to Sant Pere regularly for me. Senyor Sempere is dead now but his son Daniel still runs the shop."

Staverley saw in Joan a remarkable and admirable man. Instead of mourning the life that had been taken from him, he had made a different life, but then eventually had returned to where he wanted to be and to who he wanted to be. Staverley fetched his father's note, which he had brought with him, from the canvass bag. He handed it to Joan.

"My father left this for me. I have now met the three men he listed, and you have each been able to tell me things I did not know, things I had no idea about. But I still do not understand the message."

Joan looked at the paper for a long time before he replied.

"I have no great revelation to offer you I am afraid. And it is possible that it refers to different things rather than one thing. What I mean is that he could be referring to politics, and the betrayal of the militias and POUM by the Republic, the suppression. Or perhaps it is philosophical and the betrayal of principles and of Revolutionary Catalunya and all the possibilities that that held for a different kind of democratic future. Or perhaps he was thinking about the hospital or the Fàbregas house and that someone had informed on him and that was the betrayal, it might have been someone he knew or someone he did not. Or it could be a reflection of his state of mind. At that time we all became wary of others, of looks and whispers, of who could not be trusted, of not saying too much, not saying the wrong thing. It brought out the worst in us all. We began to live in a world where collective paranoia became the norm – you see I also read psychology – where you would not walk to buy bread without looking over your shoulder, where every knock on the door created a tremor of fearfulness, where your neighbour might be paid by the secret police, or have fought for Franco and committed atrocities, where any official might refuse to stamp your papers or might ask you questions that you could not answer. Franco ran his country that way. He kept us all in a constant state of unease and apprehension and thus timidity."

Staverley recognised that any of those interpretations could be valid and realised that he might have to accept never knowing exactly what his father meant. They prepared for bed. Staverley was tired. Joan set up a bed for him alongside the books, a wooden-framed bed with broad leather straps that supported the mattress. It was much more comfortable than it looked. They did rise very early and after a small coffee and a piece of bread and cheese they set off with the herd. Joan said they would return to where they had met the previous day and from there Staverley could find his way back to his ciclo. Joan had given him a slab of cheese to take home and another for Senyora Budó. Before they parted Staverley had one more thing to say.

"Forgive me for so many questions, and could you forgive one more?"

Joan smiled, which Staverely took as a yes.

"I wonder if I might return before I go back to England and see you make the cheese?"

Joan seemed pleased with this and said that he would be delighted with Staverley's company and to offer a lesson in cheese making. With that he embraced Staverley tightly and then turned away to walk with the herd.

"Adieu, my friend," he said and waved his stick in the air.

Going downhill back to the road was easier on the lungs but harder on the knees, and Staverley was pleased to be back on the seat of his ciclo, which was just as he had left it behind the rock. The journey back to Sant Pere was also easier, almost entirely downhill. Staverley turned off the motor and coasted a good part of the way. He enjoyed the wonderful views and the thrill of the tight bends and also thought back to his visit with Joan and the serenity of Joan's house. He now knew a lot more about his father now, and Joan's suggestion that the meaning of his father's note referred not to a specific act of betrayal but a more general sense of a life and a way of life betrayed by the forces of evil made sense. Perhaps that was enough. As soon as he dismounted from the ciclo outside *iaia's* house Senyora Budó appeared. She was drying her hands on a kitchen towel. They began one of their complex exchanges of mime and meaningful looks, mixed with bits of Catalan and Castilian and a good deal of misunderstanding. Staverley thought he understood that Senyora Budó was only a little worried when he did not return, that she was sure he would find Senyor Canoes-Mas and he would be safe, and she had heard nothing to the contrary. So all was well and she had taken the opportunity for a good clean of the house and would he like lunch? He would. Staverley gave her the cheese and she was very pleased.

Staverley was hungry. Lunch was a potage with chickpeas, potatoes, tomatoes and peppers and a local green leaf vegetable, called *acelgas* – somewhere between spinach and winter greens. It was thick and wholesome – delicious. He ate two large bowls.

Chapter 8

The ERC dinner was going to be an opportunity to make more research contacts and hopefully for getting a better understanding of the struggles taking place at various places along the coast between developers and those who wanted to preserve the environment and the local way of life. Staverley had already travelled further north along the coast to speak to people involved in setting up the Natural Park of *Aiguamolls de L'Empordá*, now an extensive bird and animal reserve that had been opened in 1983. The establishment of the park was emblematic of the tensions between nature and tourism and its creation was the consequence of a long and hard-fought defence campaign, which had begun in 1976, to stop a project to build a residential marina for 60,000 people in the coastal lagoon system. The conservation protesters had camped on the site, and a variety of grassroots organisations had lobbied the Catalan government to legislate to create the reserve -which they did. The protected area now extended to cover a large tract of inland farmland surrounding the coastal marshes and teeming with birds. But to both the north and south of the park there was extensive new building underway. For every victory for those defending the Costa Brava, like *Aiguamolls*, there had been several defeats. The *Platja del Castell,* a beach near the town of Palamós, was becoming another major focus of dispute between the two interests. Staverley thought that might make a good case study for his research, and from his initial discussions with local campaign groups it appeared that Batlló-Sabé's company was one of several who were making plans to build on the beach and establish a major resort.

The material from Batlló-Sabé's secretary had been delivered by hand and had proved to be interesting reading, although there were no great revelations. As Batlló-Sabé had explained, the funding for the building work on the Costa Brava came from a group of investors including several German banks, like Deutsche Bank, some private equity funds and individual investors, and until recently the *Banca Catalana* had had a major involvement. Staverley had done some investigating of the bank, and waded through newspaper reports in the library in Sant Celoni, with the aid of Catalan and Castilian dictionaries and numerous visits to the library desk where there was a very helpful assistant who spoke some English. He read that the father of Jordi Pujol, the President of Catalunya, had originally established the bank in 1959. The bank had expanded at great speed in the 1960s and 1970s, taking over several smaller banks, and by 1980 had over 350 branches and offices in various Spanish cities, making it the largest financial institution in Catalunya, employing over 5000 people. But in 1982 the bank had gone into crisis and there had been a major exodus of deposits, leading to the intervention of the Bank of Spain, which discovered a significant asset imbalance and irregularities related to some of the bank's dividends and loans. Despite a large deficit the bank had continued to make sizeable dividend payments to its shareholders, pay bonuses to its directors, and make loans, including one to Pujol himself. In 1983 the bank had been taken over by a consortium of other Spanish banks, led by the *Banco de Vizcaya*. The whole affair was now subject to a criminal investigation, which included Pujol, who had been interviewed at length by prosecutors from the State Attorney General's Office. The publication of the preliminary report of the investigation was eagerly awaited, especially by Pujol's political opponents.

What Staverley found particularly interesting was that in the 1970s the bank and Pujol himself had participated in the funding of two major housing developments, both of which had subsequently failed, and the purchase of a tunnel-building company. Directors of the bank, including Pujol, had acted in various different capacities in these deals - and others - as investors, sellers and buyers, suggesting serious conflicts of interest and financial mismanagement. Within all of this activity, large amounts of money had gone astray. Staverley wondered if Batlló-Sabé would talk to him about the bank and its participation in the hotel-building programme - probably not. There was no harm in asking, but Staverley was already aware from conversations with people on the coast and in Sant Pere that there was a degree of reticence and ambivalence around the investigation into Pujol's involvement in the bank's activities. Pujol was generally held in high regard, and there was a stubborn unwillingness among many of those who had voted for him to believe that he was a deliberate participant in fraud, apparently believing that the investigation was a political ploy to undermine him.

The ERC event took place in a large and impressive *modernista* villa. The villa had been built for a wealthy Catalan industrialist, who had left it to the town of Olzinelles in his will. It was now a cultural centre. Like other *modernista* buildings the house was a deliberate mix of styles and materials, part country house, part castle – a kind of architectural joke thrown back in the face of brute industrialism. Cava was served on arrival and there was a period of general mingling. By the time Staverley got his glass there were already about forty people chatting in small groups. Staverley had a plan, and sought out Subirachs' daughter Nuria. He managed to detach her from one of the groups and asked if she would introduce him to people who might be helpful in his research. She was happy to do that. Several of these introductions came to a quick end as Staverley's Castilian or the interlocutor's English proved inadequate for anything more than convivial greetings and queries as to health and wellbeing. But fourth time lucky he was introduced to Raul, an ERC official who had relatives in London and who had spent several holidays in the city, acquiring good English in the process. They agreed that Staverley would ask his questions in Castilian, as far as he was able, and that Raul would answer in English, as far as he was able.

Staverley asked his usual questions about the difficult balance between the economics of tourism and conservation – natural and cultural - and Raul rehearsed the political line of the ERC, which had become a little less clear-cut since the party had entered in the government coalition the year before. He was a little more frank about the problems of the *Banca Catalana*, and talked about the pressures on Pujol and what they might mean in the next round of elections. He also gave Staverley the name of a journalist who could be helpful to him. As they talked, Staverley noticed new arrivals being greeted at the door. One was the elderly woman he had seen at the public meeting in Sant Celoni, the one who had been so fixated on Subirachs. She was again using her cane and had some difficulty accepting the glass of cava she was offered. Staverley asked Raul if he knew who she was.

"That is Senyora Puig. She is an elder stateswoman of the ERC, although only recently returned to Catalunya. A great lady," Raul explained.

"In what way?"

"Well it is a long story but perhaps I can tell it to you while we eat. I think it is time."

Indeed, they were being invited into the dining room. There were two long tables covered with dishes of food and several large round tables with chairs and place settings. Raul explained that the event was both a celebration of the season of mushrooms and an opportunity for social and political conviviality, and the idea was to help oneself and sample the different dishes and discuss the merits of the mushrooms with others. The variety of food was remarkable, different mushrooms featuring in an impressive range of combinations. Quite a few of the plates clearly included meat, but plenty did not. Staverley was used to uniform, white button-mushrooms, and could recognise none of the ones represented here. They varied in colour, shape and size. The colours ranged from deep black to bright yellow, the shapes from the classic stem and umbrella to those that looked like plates and ears and cups, the sizes from those with thin stems no more than an inch long and tiny heads, to enormous, thick, bells that were three or four inches across. Staverley wanted to try them all, and Raul was very pleased to offer the names and to describe the different qualities and how they were used and prepared. The different textures and tastes were extraordinary, and Staverley thought he had discovered the real vegetarian heart of Catalunya – the mushroom. A disturbingly black mushroom particularly intrigued him, with a texture like velvet and an earthy flavour not unlike meat.

"What's this one, Raul?"

"Ah! That's the famous *trompets dels morts*, um, that would be in English, something like trumpets of death. You can see why, the shape. Perfectly harmless, though, despite the name and very sought after."

"Mmm! I really like it."

After more sampling and eating, accompanied by some very robust local red wine, Raul was ready to talk about Senyora Puig. Looking across the room, Staverley noticed that Nuria was very attentive and helping the Senyora with her plate.

"Well, she's a bit of a legend, if that's the right word. Her father, Luis Fàbregas, was in the Catalan government, highly respected and very instrumental in managing the coalition of parties in '36/37, although that did not last. But he was killed. It's not clear how and what happened. There are many stories and rumours – that it was a Nationalist assassin, or political rivals, or even a revengeful husband. Given how things were then, there was no proper investigation. Whatever happened, the daughter, Senyora Puig – she married Puig later – was also seriously wounded in the attack on her father and was not expected to survive, but, as you see, she did. Again there are stories and it's difficult to know what to believe but it is said that she was smuggled out of the country by supporters of her father and ended up living in Mexico. Mexico was one of the few countries that refused to recognise Franco's government at the end of the civil war, and one of the few willing to accept refugees from the Republic. Anyway when she had recovered Senyora Puig took up her father's mantle and became very involved in the Catalan government in exile, first in 1945 and then in a more organised way in 1954. That's when the people who were part of the government in exile elected Josep Tarradellas as President of Catalunya, although he was by then living in France. After Franco's death, Tarradellas was called by Suarez to Madrid in 1977 and recognised by the new Spanish government as President. But Senyora Puig remained in Mexico until very recently, I believe, and it was there some time in the fifties that she married Puig. He's also very interesting, in a different way. He was an entrepreneur and industrialist before the Civil War, beer and biscuits I think, but a very strong supporter of the Republic and Catalan nationalism. And he experimented with worker participation in the running of his businesses. He left in '39 at the end of the war but returned soon after. I think his wealth made that possible, protected him, but Franco always regarded him with great suspicion and his business activities were much curtailed. Then in the 'fifties he set up Fundación Puig, supposedly as a charity and cultural organisation intended to encourage the appreciation of Catalan culture in Europe and Latin America, but again there are rumours that the Fundación was involved in other activities that were not well regarded by Franco's government, and Puig was questioned by the security police on a number of occasions, I believe. After '75 and now, the Fundación has a different purpose. It is building an archive of atrocities carried out during the Civil War, and campaigns for a programme to find the missing victims of the reprisals, and more generally it lobbies against the Amnesty and the Pact of Forgetting. Do you know about those?

"I do a little."

"Well, Puig and some others want to write a different version of the history of the Civil War, different from that of Franco, which was what was taught in schools and written about in newspapers. It's all very controversial. Puig himself died a couple of years ago and I think that's why the Senyora returned, to pursue his work."

"What an extraordinary story. Perhaps I could arrange to meet with the Senyora at some point? My father was here in Catalunya during the Civil War, as an international volunteer fighting with the militias, and he was also smuggled out of the country after he was wounded. I've been trying to find out more about what happened to him here."

Raul looked surprised.

"It's sometimes incredible how lives and histories become intertwined. My own relatives in London were stranded there by the Civil War. There was an uncle who worked as a newspaper correspondent, for a Republican paper. They could not return."

Staverley and Raul talked for a while about London, and made a tentative arrangement to meet the following week for a beer. The event was winding down. Some people had settled in to stay longer with bottles of spirits on their table, other more timid souls were preparing to leave. Staverley was not sure what to do. Then there were several loud exclamations. Something was happening on the other side of the room just inside the main door. A group of people quickly gathered, and two or three were kneeling on the floor where someone lay. There were calls for someone to summon an ambulance.

By the time the ambulance arrived, Staverley had learned that it was Senyora Puig, who had collapsed as she was leaving, She received some treatment where she lay and was then taken away. Those who remained were obviously shocked and upset. One woman and one man were in tears, some sat forlornly heads in hands, some others talked quietly and then left. Raul excused himself. He wanted to return home, he explained, his wife would want to know what had happened, but he volunteered to drop Staverley in Sant Pere on his way. Just before he got into Raul's car Staverley saw Batlló-Sabé, who was also leaving. He asked Raul if he could take a moment to speak with the man.

Batlló-Sabé was as surprised to see Staverley as Staverley was to see him.

"Senyor, I did not see you inside. I wanted to thank you for your time last week,"

Staverley said.

"Of course, I am pleased to be of help. You are here to pursue your research I assume?"

"I am, yes, but I was also enjoying my introduction to the wonders of the Catalan mushroom. It has been spoiled by the illness of Senyora Puig, of course."

"Indeed so, tragic, very sad, a wonderful woman." Batlló-Sabé shook his head.

A chauffeured car drew up alongside Batlló-Sabé. He shook hands with Staverley as the driver got out and opened the rear door.

"Senyor, could I possibly take a little more of your time, to follow up on some things I have come across in my research since we spoke?" Staverley asked before the door was closed. Batlló-Sabé did not look pleased.

"Phone my secretary. She will arrange something."

Staverley had taken to buying a daily paper most mornings from the *tabac* in Sant Pere. He tried the Catalan ones but could understand more of those in Castilian. He was attempting to keep up with things happening locally as well as back in the UK. He particularly enjoyed the coverage of Spanish football, which took up a lot of print space in most editions. Barcelona were the current *La Liga* champions but in the new season were trailing behind their arch rivals Real Madrid, *los merengues*: so called because they played in an all-white strip. Two mornings after the ERC event there was an item that he understood as saying that Senyora Puig had died and that a police investigation into her death had begun. He was both sad and disappointed. He would now not get the opportunity to meet with her - such a feisty and interesting-sounding woman. Later that morning as he was working at his improvised desk there was a knock at the door. Any knocking on the ancient door resounded through the house loudly enough to wake the dead and unsettle the centuries of memories that were inscribed in its walls. When Staverley opened the door he found Margarida standing outside. He was very pleased to see her. She kissed his cheek and swept into the kitchen. He was getting to like being kissed by the women he had got to know. Margarida said she needed coffee urgently and set about making some for both of them.

"So how is our researcher in residence?" she asked.

"He's well, getting settled into some good work I think. The contacts you gave me initially have set me off in all sorts of directions. I have been making progress both with the tourism work and with finding out more about my father and his time here. I have talked with all three of the men on his list. It's quite extraordinary that they are all alive and all here now in Catalunya, and all willing to speak with me. They remember my father with affection and speak well of him."

There followed a long account of Staverley's conversations with the three men. Margarida had many questions and was impressed by how much Staverley had found out.

"You know you should talk with my father about these things. I think he would be interested, and you might find him interesting too."

"I would be pleased to meet him, you make him sound like a fascinating man, which I am sure he is. Maybe I could come to Barcelona next week? You know I've not been there once since I arrived, and there are a couple of other people I was hoping to see and talk to there."

"I'll talk to him. But sorry, I am forgetting why I came." Margarida became very serious.

"You went to the ERC dinner at the weekend, yes?"

"That's right, it was a really interesting thing to do, quite a privilege for me, but it was marred by Senyora Puig being taken ill, I'm sure you know all about that. And I read this morning that she had died yesterday. That's awful."

"Exactly. Well, that's why I'm here."
Staverley was unsure what she meant by that.
"Don't look so worried," Margarida said. "The police are now investigating her death, and they are interviewing everyone who attended the event. So that includes you. You were on the guest list, obviously. The police asked Nuria, Senyor Subirachs' daughter, how they could get in contact with you, and she telephoned me, and I spoke to the police and explained about you and offered to accompany you as interpreter, if that's okay with you. We agreed a time this afternoon. We have to go to Granollers, it's about 45 minutes drive. Is that okay? I know it's all a bit sudden."

It sounded a little daunting. Staverley was very pleased to have someone to go with him if he had to deal with the police. He had become wary of dealings with the police over the previous two years, and even more wary of suspicious deaths. The arrangement was also a good example of how a small country, or a would-be country like Catalunya worked. People knew other people who could arrange things. Information and knowledge could be moved around and shared quickly. Special arrangements could be made.

"I really don't know how I am ever going to repay you for all of the things you are doing for me, Margarida. I seem to be a high maintenance visitor."

"Nonsense. And if I'm honest Senyora Puig has always been a sort of heroine of mine. My father told me all about her when I was growing up and she was the sort of strong and principled woman I wanted to be, or hope to be someday. So anything I can contribute to finding out what happened to her I am pleased to do. So if that is agreed, I want to see Senyora Budó, and I have some other errands to run in the town. Why don't I come back for you at 1.30 and we can have lunch before we go for your interview."

Over lunch Margarida grilled Staverley further about what he had been doing on the coast and the people he had met, and she offered the name of someone she knew who was involved in the defence of the Palamós beach. He countered by getting her to explain more about her PhD. They stayed with water during the meal, both wanting to be alert for the interview.

Granollers appeared at first sight to be an industrial satellite town of Barcelona, surrounded by factories, warehouses and commercial buildings, but the centre was very different, a small network of narrow cobbled streets, full of small shops. There were also several art galleries and a small theatre. The *Policia Nacional* offices were in a square on the edge of the old quarter, in what looked like the palace of someone very important but long dead. Inside, the building had been painfully modernised and institutionalised. During the drive, Margarida had tried to explain the different police – Nacional, local, municipal - and their respective responsibilities, but Staverley remained confused.

"This is the National Police right, so everything will be in Castilian?" he asked.

"Unfortunately that's true, but it's probably not a moment for engaging in the politics of language."

They checked in at the front desk and were escorted to the second floor. The name on the door to which they were led said *Inspector Jefe Rodriguez*. The Chief Inspector was sitting behind a cluttered desk but rose to shake their hands and gestured for them to sit. There were two metal chairs in front of the desk. The Chief Inspector was a youngish, fit looking man, but he seemed to be waging a losing battle against hair loss and his baldness was very obvious through the few remaining strands plastered carefully onto his scalp. He ran his hand across his head, maybe in search of the missing hairs. He was in uniform. Another man stood behind him leaning against the wall with his arms crossed, next to a set of photographs of Rodriguez at various different stages of his police career. The other man was tall but bulky and looked as though he had been stuffed hurriedly into his brown baggy suit. His face was blotched, and his eyes rather puffy, his nose was a sort of blur: the morning after the night before, perhaps. His expression combined boredom with a kind of sullen aggressiveness. He raised his chin as a minimal greeting. Rodriguez spoke very quickly, but Margarida translated with equal speed.

"We have just a few questions for you, Señor Staverley, just routine. My colleague Capitán Lopez," Rodriguez gestured behind him with his head, "is from UCO, *Unidad Central Operativa*, the *Guardia Civil*. His agency has now taken a keen interest in this case."

Rodriguez consulted the papers in front of him. Staverley got the impression that Lopez's presence was making him nervous.

"How long have you been in Spain, Señor?"
"For about six weeks."
"And your purpose here?"
Staverley explained his sabbatical and his research interests. Lopez expelled a long breath through pursed lips, which suggested he regarded Staverley's research as a waste of time.

"In relation to the unfortunate events that bring us together. Did you know Señora Puig prior to the event?"

"I did not, I saw her once before at a political meeting but we were not introduced." Staverley found himself mimicking Rodriguez' formal speech.

"Did you interact directly with Señora Puig at the event?"

"I did not. I saw her across the room but we never spoke."

"Did you witness anything untoward during the event which might contribute to our investigation?"

"I did not. I was enjoying my mushrooms and talking with an ERC official for almost all of the time."

Rodriguez consulted his papers again.
"That would be Señor Balada?"
"It would."
Rodriguez made some notes.
"And finally, are you aware of anyone who might have born ill will toward Señora Puig?"

"I am not. As I said I never met her directly and her background was explained to me at the event. I knew nothing about her until that day. I am afraid I have nothing useful to contribute."

"In that case, I think we are done here."

Rodriguez turned to look at Lopez who gave an almost imperceptible nod.

Staverley was about to stand, but then stayed put. Despite the discomfort of the interview situation he wanted to know more about Senyora Puig's death and the police investigation. Although he had never spoken with her he felt a connection to the old woman.

"Inspector, may I ask you a question?"
This seemed to fluster the Inspector.
"A question?" He glanced again over his shoulder. "Of course."
"I was told something of Senyora Puig's history at the event, as I said. Is it the assumption of the police that her death was related to that history?"

Before Rodriguez could assemble a response Lopez spoke for the first time.

"It most certainly is not, Señor. A ridiculous suggestion." He spoke in English.

Rodriguez was obviously embarrassed by the brusqueness of his intervention. Staverley got to his feet and reached across the desk to shake the Inspector's hand. As the Inspector took his hand Staverley tried one more question. He was not sure what led him to ask.

"Inspector, was the Senyora's death related in some way to the mushrooms served at the event?"

Again Rodriguez was flustered and quickly dropped Staverley's hand.

"I cannot possibly comment on an ongoing investigation." The Inspector said.

"Of course, I apologise." That seemed like an answer to Staverley.

On the way out he nodded towards Capitán Lopez but was ignored. The Capitán was studying his fingernails, looking even more bored than when they had arrived.

When they were outside the building Margarida suggested a coffee and they found a nearby bar. She smiled broadly at Staverley when they were seated.

"I think you may have disconcerted the Inspector. The *Policía Nacional* does not expect that they will be asked questions in such a situation. It was amusing. I think the presence of his colleague from the *Guardia* may also have contributed to his discomfort. It is unusual to find the *Policía* and *Guardia* working together. If that's what it is."

"So what's UCO?"

"Ah, also interesting. As far as I understand they are the Judicial Police, and they get involved when crimes are particularly complicated or politically delicate. Which would suggest that the Capitán's denial of there being a consideration of Senyora Puig's history was a lie. That is exactly why he would be there. But why did you also ask about the mushrooms?"

"I don't know really. It's something I've been thinking about since the event. Raul Balada was telling me about how important it is that if you collect mushrooms you really need to know what you're doing and can distinguish between those that are tasty and those that are dangerous. He also said that in Catalunya every year a few people are poisoned by mushrooms. That put the idea in my head I think. But that's all probably fanciful anyway. No one else was taken ill, as far as I know."

Margarida took a moment to consider what he had said.

"It does seem possible, I suppose, although, as you say, you would have expected other people to be affected, but then she was an old lady and a little frail, and the Inspector didn't say no, so perhaps you are right. I'll ask around. There are always *Policía* who are willing to leak information to the press when it's in their interests to do so, and the cooperation of the Policía and the Guardia might well generate a divergence of interests, if you see what I mean."

Staverley thought he did.

Their conversation drifted off to other subjects and Margarida asked what Staverley thought of Sant Pere and the Montseny and whether he was settling in well. Staverley found it difficult to respond to that. He was in a sense settling in. He was getting to know places and people, he could find his way around in the locality and could just about fend for himself. At the same time he knew that he was still heavily dependent on the help of people like Margarida herself and Senyora Budó and that he would never be seen as or feel of the place. He was an oddity. He did not speak the language, he asked strange questions, he made mistakes of etiquette. He was liminal. Which in fact also gave him a certain leeway when it came to behaviour, and enabled him to view things that were taken for granted by others as needing to be explained. But he did feel settled emotionally to the extent that the violence and intrigues with which he had become involved in the previous two years now seemed less distressing and disruptive. He was taking care of himself, healing and beginning to be able to find himself where he expected to be. He was grateful for that. The only thing missing was Monica..

"Hello!" said Margarida. She was waving her hand at him.

He had drifted off into a private reverie, and they both laughed.

"Sorry, your comment set my mind running, I was thinking about how much I had learned about Catalunya since I arrived, thanks to people like you, but also how much I don't know, and will never know. But everyone has been welcoming and very tolerant. It all feels good. I feel good, I like it here."

That seemed to please Margarida. On the way back to Sant Pere Staverley quizzed her on the mysteries of making an international telephone call. He had decided that he needed to convince Monica to come for a visit and he also wanted to talk to her about mushrooms. Margarida also undertook to speak to her father about meeting with Staverley the following week, and he wondered whether he could arrange to see Batlló-Sabé in his office on the same day, along with the journalist that Raul Balada had suggested he talk to. More telephone calls.

It turned out that Monica was more than willing to come for a visit. She was excited by the idea of staying with Staverley in his house and seeing Barcelona for the first time. She agreed to explore flights and times and also to do some reading up on mushroom poisoning. She did not seem to think it a strange request. Or if she did, she did not say so. The arrangements to meet with Margarida's father and with Batlló-Sabé and the journalist were also made very straightforwardly, for Wednesday of the following week. In the meantime Staverley was determined to press on with his interviews with people involved in defending Agüiamolls and Palamós.

*

The journey to Barcelona was relatively easy. Staverley left his ciclo outside the station in Sant Celoni and caught the train directly to *Passeig de Gracia* in the centre of the city, one of the main shopping streets. It took about an hour. He knew he had not long for sightseeing and would be spending some time in the city when Monica came, so limited himself to a stroll down Las Ramblas and a quick detour into *El Barrio Chino*, Barcelona's infamous red-light district, before his appointment with Margarida's father. The apartment was close to the historic buildings of the University of Barcelona, as distinct from the Autonomous University. It turned out to be an *áttico*, a top floor flat with terraces all around that offered amazing views across the Chinese quarter and toward the sea. Margarida's father was very welcoming and set about making coffee while Staverley wandered and enjoyed the views. He was about sixty and had an amazing mane of unruly silver white hair that spilled over his shirt collar, reminding Staverley a little of pictures he had seen of Albert Einstein. His face was full and round, a smiley face. He was wearing loose twill trousers, a checked shirt and a voluminous grey cardigan. He was a pipe smoker and held a pipe tightly between his teeth while talking and preparing the coffee. As Margarida had explained, he spoke English well and had lived for a time in England, and in several other European countries. They drank their coffee in a study that was almost entirely filled by a huge desk, and the desk was almost entirely covered with neat piles of papers. Against one wall was a set of ancient wooden pigeonholes, each of which was filled with further piles of papers. The older man saw Staverley looking at this.

"My life and my work are rather complicated, and to manage those complications I have found it necessary to be well organised." He gestured with his pipe toward the piles and the pigeon holes. "Orderliness is not my natural inclination, so over many years I have had to train myself to think and behave like an orderly person, and to be honest this has now become a fetish. Any degeneration into disorder, however minor, makes me uneasy. So my piles and holes are now my friends, they keep me sane and keep me in a sensible relation with the world. I have a similar arrangement with my use of time. My various activities are allocated to different days of the week, or parts of the day in some cases. Wednesday is my day for seeing visitors, and so here we are, and I am pleased to meet you Senyor Staverley. My daughter has told me about you and your research and your, how shall I say it, your quest regarding your father. She felt that perhaps I could be of some help to you with that. I would be pleased if that proved to be so."

Staverley already liked Margarida's father. He seemed like a serious man who did not take himself too seriously. He spoke with a gentle sense of irony and self-deprecation.

"Well, I am trying to piece together the story of my father's time here in Catalunya during the Civil War, and to make sense of this." Once again he handed over his father's note. Each time the note was handled it became a little more tattered. Margarida's father looked at it quizzically and tapped the stem of his pipe on his teeth.

"I can see why this might intrigue you, and I understand from Margarida that you have already spoken with the three men named here. One of whom I know by the way, Subirachs, and another, Batlló-Sabé, I have certainly heard of."

"They were all very helpful and I have learned a lot about what happened to my father from talking with them. But some things are still not clear to me. Margarida explained that you are a trustee of a Fundación that is collecting accounts of the victims and perpetrators of atrocities during the Civil War, and I wondered whether there was anything in that material that might relate to my father or the people he encountered while he was here."

"That is a possibility. Fundación Puig, with the support of Senyora Puig's money, has been recording the testimonies of witnesses and victims for over five years now. Of course through the Fundación she also funded various of the social movements and environmental groups that are opposing the large scale hotel developments on the Costa Brava, which is also something of interest to you I believe. Of the victims' testimonies we have almost fifteen hundred recordings to date, and there could be many, many more if we had the resources. The process of interviewing and recording and transcribing the accounts is expensive and time-consuming. But of course the number of those who experienced the war directly is decreasing year by year. We are trying to recover a history that might otherwise be obliterated by forgetting and by mortality. You know of the Pact, I think, and the Amnesty. So our efforts are mainly focused on collecting and cataloguing. For the moment, we have almost no funding for the proper examination and collation of the materials, and even less than none to follow up on specifics, where we think that is needed. We have taken up just three incidents so far which are particularly egregious and tried to put the testimonies related to those into the public arena. These were incidents so horrendous that we felt the need to do something more than file the materials away for the future. But the current laws and the Amnesty severely limit what can be done. We are also urging the Catalan government to make our archive an official collection, and perhaps create a museum of memories, but there is little political support for these ideas at present. So the problem is, that with a few exceptions, or without relying on the recall of those who conduct the interviews, there is no systematic way of tracing the people referred to by those we have interviewed, good or bad. And of course the interviews are almost all in Catalan or Castilian."

Staverley was disappointed. He had hoped for some further lines of inquiry to follow from the Fundación materials.

"I supposed in a small way in trying to make some sense of what happened to my father I have been doing something similar to the work of the Fundación, eliciting testimonies from eyewitnesses. But the loose ends and inconsistencies are very frustrating. Perhaps I am expecting too much. Perhaps there will always be unknowns, blanks?"

Margarida's father examined his pipe and dug into the bowl with a small penknife.

"Well you can ask your questions, Senyor Staverley. It is possible that someone in the Fundación can be of help. We will not know if you do not ask."

Staverley began to wonder whether he was making himself into a nuisance. What is the importance of one man's experience, a man who survived the war, as against the tens of thousands who did not and who had no one to speak for them, and who were at risk of disappearing into the mists and convenience of forgetting? This was the moment when he could say he knew enough now about his father, and concentrate on the present and his proper research. But he could not help himself.

"Well there is one person I was hoping to know something more about, a man who kidnapped my father and may have brutalised him, a Russian, an NKVD representative in Spain during the war. His name, or the name he used, was Orlov."

Margarida's father made some notes on a pad on his desk.

"That is very interesting, and the name is faintly familiar to me. If you can wait a few minutes I will phone Adriá Planells, who is in charge of our project of remembering. Why don't you take your coffee and enjoy the views of Barcelona for a few minutes."

Staverley did that. From the terrace he tried to identify some of the few landmarks he knew in Barcelona. It was a clear day and it was possible to see both the mountains in one direction and the sea in the other. He reminded himself that if there was time he wanted to go to the Post Office and Telephone exchange where the CNT Trade Union militia had fought with the Republican Assault Guards. Margarida had said that the marks made by bullets during the battle were still visible on the walls. He was impressed by the project of remembering, as Margarida's father had called it, and agreed wholeheartedly about the importance of recovering the stories of those who had suffered in the civil war before those stories were expunged by time. Without an acknowledgment of the scars of the past there was always the possibility that the past would repeat itself, he thought. The failure to acknowledge and confront the imperial past in all of its ugliness was something that created continuing problems in his own country. Fantasies and lies, the lingua franca of modern politics, were no good basis for the future. He was aware from the work of one of his colleagues at Watermouth of the struggles going on in and around Margaret Thatcher's government about what school history should look like, and the lobbying of those who wanted that history to portray Britain's past as one of benign enlightenment – the Empire as a civilising process. If they succeeded, children in school would be taught a history of triumphalist myths, adding a further iteration of symbolic violence to the physical violence on which the Empire was built. The truth and power are always inextricably linked, he was thinking, when the voice of Margarida's father recalled him from his reverie. He sounded pleased with himself.

"I have something," he said, waving his notebook, "I was right, I had heard the name Orlov."

Staverley returned to the study and sat again. Margarida's father seemed quite excited.

"An extraordinary story, extraordinary. Orlov was a dangerous and evil man and a very devious one. It seems that he does appear several times in the accounts we have elicited according to Adriá. Shall I tell you?"

Staverley was also excited and nodded accordingly. Margarida's father referred to a page of notes.

"You are right that Orlov was NKVD. He was a Major of State Security and a veteran of the Russian Revolution. In Spain he was responsible for hunting down Trotskyites and Anarchists, as well as Roman Catholic supporters of the Nationalists and other supposed enemies of the Republic. In 1937 he arrested and tortured and executed many members of POUM including their leader Andreu Nin. This was by extension all part of Stalin's Great Purge. But in 1938 several of Orlov's colleagues came under suspicion themselves and were also purged, Orlov was ordered back to Russia and feared the worst. He fled with his wife and daughter to Canada, and thence to the United States. He remained undiscovered there until after Stalin's death in 1953, from which time he began writing about his life and exploits, and about Stalin, and much of what we know of Orlov after he left Spain comes from his own words. He wrote several articles and books. I must find copies. At present then, most of what we know of him comes from these sources, so in respect to that we must be circumspect. He was eventually interrogated at some length by the FBI but went on to live freely and had a modest career as a university researcher. He died in 1973. Quite incredible, but also very disappointing that such a man should never have had to face the consequences of his horrible crimes. I must find out more." He threw the notebook onto the desk top.

Staverley was silent as he thought about how it was that his father had met this man, if met was the right word. Joan had told him a little of what had been done to his father by Orlov, but he was sure that Joan had spared him the grisly details or did not know them.

"So in a way my father was one of the lucky ones. He was taken by Orlov but survived -while from what you are saying, most did not. I can understand now even better my father's reticence about talking about his time here and his sense of being betrayed. I'm sure he shared those feelings with the others who were subject to Orlov's witch-hunt or had things done to them by others like him. And all of this in the name of the Republic. I find that difficult to grasp, it seems grotesque." Staverley paused. "You have given me a lot to think about."

Margarida's father nodded and set about emptying the dottle from his pipe and refilling it. He did this with great concentration and precision. The he spoke again.

"Well, Adriá says he will speak to other colleagues and try to find any more specific references to Orlov and his cohorts in our interviews, but as I explained that will not be a systematic search."

"I do understand, Senyor, and much appreciate anything that might be done. But I would not want to distract from the work of the Fundación. That wouldn't be right."

"Don't worry about that. Adriá thinks that there is something here that we should pursue. He is now also bothered by faint memories of other references to Orlov, but for the moment neither of us can identify those memories properly. Perhaps this will gain some attention and support from elsewhere for the work of the project? Why don't you telephone me in a few days."

Staverley agreed to do that, and left Margarida's father deep in thought and in a fug of tobacco smoke. The pipe, he had explained, helped him to think, like Sherlock Holmes.

Chapter 9

Jack found it difficult to adjust to being back in London. He was pleased to be reunited with Edith, and realised how much he had missed her love and support and companionship. She was fully recovered from her illness now and was for the time being the sole breadwinner. Jack's hand was slow to heal and it was obvious that it would never function normally again. He was unable to make a proper fist, or to pick up and hold anything other than small, lightweight objects. He knew he would never be able to wield his trowel again. All of that was depressing, but so too was the state of British politics and the stubborn refusal of the Prime Minister and most of his Cabinet to recognise the threat of fascism or to acknowledge the horrors being perpetrated in Spain and elsewhere. The same complacency and ignorance was apparent among ordinary people. They had dangerous faith in the reassurances that they were given that there would be no war in Europe and that Hitler could be appeased with a few reasonable concessions. What added even further to Jack's despondency was the lack of interest of those of his friends who did share his political views in hearing about his experiences in Spain. They were happy to be told about the valiant struggles of the Republic and the atrocities of the Nationalists and the complicity of Germany and Italy but did not want to know about the role of the Russians and Spanish communists in acting against the militias. The Communist propaganda that portrayed the unionists and anarchists as deluded criminal elements was never questioned. *The Daily Worker* was unremitting in its condemnations of the non-communist left. Reading the vitriolic pieces Jack worried a great deal about the friends he had left behind and what was happening to them. He agreed to speak at two meetings that were called in support of the Republic but as soon as he tried to explain the internecine struggles on Republican side the Communists in the audience shouted him down. They followed the line taken by *The Daily Worker* that labelled POUM as Trotskyite spies working for Franco. In the second meeting he had been accused of being a deviationist and was only able to silence his accusers by showing his hand and asking who else in the audience had fought for the Republic and been wounded in battle. There were no replies but he was not proud of having done that. To his credit one of the men who had criticised him had come up after the meeting and apologised. He had even offered to find Jack a job, which Jack was still thinking about. He had to find something. His idleness was something else that weighed upon him. He found himself struggling with his moods. He tried his best with Edith to be even-tempered and positive but when he was alone or awake at night he could feel despondency washing through him like a wave. More than once he had cried. And when he did sleep he was beset with nightmares and woke sweating and agitated. Edith told him that more than once he had cried out and screamed in his sleep. She was worried about him and wanted him to see a doctor but he was reluctant. He had told Edith most of what had happened to him, with a little editing out of things that he felt he should not burden her with, and her outrage was vocal and loud. She had encouraged him to speak at the meetings and was also deeply disappointed by the lack of interest and the resistance to what he was trying to explain.

Jack went to speak with Manny Shinwell, the MP who had been partly instrumental in his joining the ILP contingent of the International Brigades. Shinwell was willing to listen, and sympathetic to an extent, but talked about the political realities of opposition to Fascism and the need to maintain a united front. Which Jack took to mean that he should keep quiet and toe the Party line. Shinwell also offered to help in finding him a job. John McNair, the ILP representative in Barcelona, was back in London and had also agreed to meet with Jack but after Shinwell's response he was unsure if that was worthwhile. Jack had also thought of contacting Orwell but had learned that he was very unwell and in a sanatorium, although working on a book about his experiences in Catalunya. Jack wondered if he should try to write something himself, but found it difficult to begin. Eventually he decided to contact the man who had accused him at the meeting, who turned out to be a Transport and General Workers' Union organiser operating in the Thames Dockland. Through his contacts and using his influence he was able to secure Jack a job as a radiotelephone operator for the Port of London Authority. Jack accepted, and he liked the job, although he sometimes regretted the long hours of sitting, and missed the physical activity involved in his previous work. Edith and he made up for this by joining the Ramblers Association and spending their Sundays on long walks in various parts of the countryside around London, and Jack became a member of his local branch committee.

...

Staverley's second meeting of the day was nearby, at Café Nuria just off the Plaça Catalunya, only five minutes' walk from Margarida's father's apartment. He was meeting with Ponç Feliu, a young journalist who was making a name for himself from his writing on corruption in Catalunya. The journalist was waiting when Staverley arrived, sipping a beer, a thin angular man with a full but neatly trimmed beard. His hirsute face was offset against a virtually bald head. Feliu stood and they shook hands. Staverley had already explained his research over the telephone and he had painstakingly worked through some of Feliu's newspaper and journal articles in the library in Sant Celoni. Feliu had written a great deal about Pujol and the *Banca Catalana* but also a series of articles on the hotel and resort developments along the Costa Brava. In particular he had investigated the role of foreign investment in places like Lloret de Mar and the kick-backs offered to local politicians to acquire permissions and compulsory purchase orders and to ensure the provision of local infrastructure to serve the new developments. The offers were not infrequently accepted. The argument made by the local politicians who supported the developers was one that Staverley had heard several times already - that the developments provided jobs, pumped money into the local economy, and ensured the modernisation of local services. Over a set of tapas – mushroom *croquettes, pa amb tomàquet, tortilla de patatas, escalibada* and cheese and olives – Feliu described the sorts of money and the sorts of people who were the investors in these developments. A lot of money came from Germany, from France and Italy and Sweden and even Russia. Most of it came from legitimate sources, but Feliu suspected, though he was still investigating, that some of it was being recycled, or laundered, from criminal activities in those countries. He was trying to follow the trail of some of the investments back to their source. In particular, he had found that some money from Germany was passing through a set of holding companies that were owned by Italian businessmen in Calabria, who in turn appeared to be funded by the local Mafia – the *N'drangheta*. The *N'drangheta* was a centuries old, military style criminal organisation that had become widely known when in 1973 they kidnapped John Paul Getty III, who had his severed ear mailed to a newspaper and was eventually released following the negotiated payment of $2.2 million by his grandfather. In recent years, Feliu explained the *N'drangheta* had diversified and extended their activities and was estimated to have annual global revenues of billions of dollars. There were now groups and branches in many countries around the world, and in Germany these branches were established primarily for clandestine financial transactions. Feliu had made a contact in the criminal investigation department in Stuttgart and someone there had told him that the *N'drangheta* was now the single largest criminal organisation in Germany. One of the banks suspected of being involved in laundering money from the *N'drangheta's* drug businesses was a major investor in Catalan tourism. Staverley recognised the name of the bank as one of those participating in Batlló-Sabé's investment group.

Feliu and Staverley had agreed that nothing that Feliu told him would go further - partly because Feliu was intending to publish a further set of articles once his investigations were complete but also because such investigations were not without their dangers. Speaking quietly from behind his beer glass Feliu said

"These are dangerous people, ruthless people, who have a history of violence. The most recent *'N'drangheta war'* in Calabria between rival factions in the organisation left over 200 people dead, and many local politicians and judges and police have been killed or have disappeared when they have attempted to investigate or prosecute the *N'drangheta.*"

All of this was difficult to take in. Staverley had become aware that there was in Catalunya and in Spain generally an ingrained culture of political and financial corruption – Pujol was a prime example – but he had no idea that this might in some instances relate to large-scale criminal activity and international money laundering schemes. He began to think that his own research needed to take more account of money and its flows and exchanges. His PhD, focused on the arrival of a large holiday camp in a small English seaside resort, had included a brief examination of the finances of the holiday company and their dealings with local councillors and officials, but perhaps he should have paid more attention to where the money for the camp had come from and where it went. Feliu skewered a piece of cheese and smiled.

"Do not be too alarmed, my friend. I am perhaps being over dramatic. I think sometimes that I spend too much time in these murky worlds – murky is an English word, yes?"

Staverley smiled back and nodded. Even so, he had noticed that Feliu remained careful to speak quietly, and frequently glanced over his shoulder and around the restaurant as though looking for someone or something out of place.

"It is possible that I have become a little paranoid, but some of the people I have tried to talk to are very clearly not just reluctant, they are frightened. On one of my visits to Lloret last year I was convinced that I was being followed. But then a reasonable level of paranoia is a good thing. So, you too Staverley must take some care, some precautions. Be circumspect." Feliu had some trouble with the word and tried it several times before it came out right. He smiled again briefly.

"Now I am serious."
"I understand, I do," Staverley replied.
After some hesitation Staverley asked Felui whether he had come across the name of Batlló-Sabé during his work on the coastal developments. He had, but knew little about the man, and he seemed to be mainly involved in the management of building work rather than in the money side of things. Which was what Batlló-Sabé had told him. Staverley found himself relieved that his father's friend was not involved in the things Felui had described, at least not directly.

They diverged into some lighter subjects while finishing their tapas – the struggles of the Barcelona football team to retain their *La Liga* championship, the refurbishment of the huge *El Corte Ingles* department store across the *Plaça* from the Café, and the implications for Catalunya of Spain's accession to the EU the next year. Before parting, they agreed that if Staverley came across anything that might be of help to Feliu they would be in contact again. Feliu reiterated his plea for care in asking questions on the coast, and with another look around the Café and at its clientele they left separately.

It was now 2.30 and Staverley had an hour and a half before his appointment with Batlló-Sabé. It seemed like a good moment to visit the Post Office building. He crossed *Las Ramblas* and walked along it until he stood outside the imposing frontage of the *Hotel Rivoli Rambla*, which had been until 1937 the Executive Building of POUM. He then turned into a side street and entered the *Barrio Gótico*. He zigzagged through the narrow, dark and sometimes rather smelly streets, looking at the small shops. The history and artisanship and specialisation of some of the small shops was amazing. He saw one that sold scissors, another fans, and another wicker and cane baskets. As he got closer to the harbour there were more workshops and a variety of seedy lodging houses, serving the needs of the port. He realised that somewhere here was the workshop in which Joan spent 17 years of his life hiding. He wished he had asked the address. He walked through the dilapidated *La Plaça Tripi* where he knew Orwell had lived briefly, and twice he was approached by young women, well one young and one not so young, both offering personal services of an intimate kind. He scurried away, embarrassed. It was a first for him. He also saw some exchanges that involved money and small plastic bags. After a couple of wrong turns and a bold approach to a passer-by in ungrammatical Castilian, he found the Post and Telegraph office. It was a large, very grand building in a mix of *modernista* and classic styles, built in 1927 he had read. He walked around it. The scars of bullets and other weapons could clearly be seen. He tried to imagine what it must have been like to be at war with your own side and the horrible political rivalry and hatred that were played out in places like this and which led to so many deaths. Before leaving for his meeting he looked inside. The main hall was huge, with a vaulted ceiling, much more like a cathedral than a post office. The whole edifice spoke of a combination of classical tradition and modern confidence. It was a hallmark of Primo de Rivera's dictatorship, the man who founded the *Falange*. He decided he would bring Monica to see it and also to read again the passages in Orwell's *Homage to Catalonia* describing the events that took place here

Staverley made his way back through along the *Via Layetana,* a broad street full of traffic that led from the harbour to *Plaça Urquinaona.* Batlló-Sabé's office was a few streets north of the Plaça. It shared a corner building with several other businesses, and occupied most of one floor. Staverley was surprised by its modesty. The furnishing and decoration was new but entirely functional: metal and plastic desks and chairs, photographs of completed hotels on the plain white walls, and banks of steel filing cabinets. Batlló-Sabé's secretary signalled him into a chair and offered a coffee, which he declined, always being suspicious of institutional coffee. Exactly two minutes after the scheduled time of his meeting, the door of the inner office opened and Batlló-Sabé ushered him in. He seemed a little harassed. The office repeated the basic functionality: no fripperies or ostentation.

"I hope this is not a bad time," Staverley said. "I could come back when you are less busy."

Batlló-Sabé gave the suggestion serious consideration for a moment.

"No, no, let's go on. A conversation would be some respite from the problems of delivery of materials and the disappearance of key workers. Hangovers, I suspect. These Andalusians are heavy drinkers, unreliable."

Batlló-Sabé's irritation was evident and his stereotyping not unusual. Staverley did not respond but tried to find a more neutral topic.

"I am sorry we did not speak at the ERC event. I was surprised to see you there. Was that a social occasion for you or a business one?"

Staverley was intrigued by Batlló-Sabé's presence at the event, but realised as soon as he asked the question that it was probably rude. He apologised quickly but Batlló-Sabé waved his apology away.

"To be honest with you I am unsure why I was invited. The invitation came in the post and I assumed from Subirachs and that I might see him there, but he was indisposed, so I understood from his daughter. It is always useful for someone like me to be able to meet with and talk to the politicos, and especially those on the left who tend to be suspicious of the intentions of persons such as I. But to be truthful I was not in the mood for lobbying. I enjoyed my mushrooms and my wine and some pleasant conversation. A nice change." He shrugged.

"Did you speak with Senyora Piug by any chance?" Staverley asked. "I wanted to, but now of course it's too late."

Batlló-Sabé shrugged again.

"Yes, we spoke briefly, and oddly she asked me some questions about the war, as you had done. So many years without speaking about such things and now two people who want to know about those times. It is strange. In truth I do not know much about the Senyora, but I realise that she is, or was I should say, held in great esteem by those on the left. She wanted to know if we had ever met in the war, she and I, in Barcelona, and whether I had been to her house. That was a very odd thing to ask. I had to explain that I was a lowly infantryman, one of many young volunteers in the Militias, and before that I was a clerk working for an import-export company down by the docks. Her social circles were very different from mine."

Staverley was somewhat perplexed by that and wondered about the Senyora's motives in asking such questions.

"Did she explain why she asked?"

"Not really. I did consider that perhaps at her age and with her infirmity that she was, how would one put it, losing her firm grip on the present and retreating into a world of memories. But that was not the impression she gave. Her mind seemed clear and sharp and the questions and the memories seemed to give her energy. I think she had her reasons for asking but she never made them clear. She wanted to talk more about the June Days, the things I told you about, but people who wanted to pay court interrupted us. It is most sad that she did not survive the illness. I shall attend the memorial event that is to be held if I can. But Senyor Staverley this stirring up of things from the war, although I understand why you are asking your questions, is disturbing. And to be honest they make me feel old. It was a long time ago. I am ambivalent about the Act of Forgetting but sometimes I do think that it is a good thing to leave the past buried and to live for now and for the future. I see my buildings as part of that future, and that pleases me." Batlló-Sabé's comment was the prefect opportunity for Staverley to move on to the other things he wanted to explore.

"Senyor, I wanted to ask you a little more about the buildings and how your investment syndicate works. I read your prosectus and that was helpful, but I have been trying to understand what is happening in *Palamós,* for instance, where there are conflicts between local people and the developers, like yourself. For an outsider like me, who does not speak the language very well, it is very difficult to grasp the seriousness of these differences."

Staverley was using a ploy he sometimes resorted to in his research, which was to feign ignorance and position the interviewee as someone who can instruct and inform. Few people can resist an opportunity to explain what they know to others. Batlló-Sabé could not.

"Ah well. It is a difficult situation. We are very aware of the sensibilities involved in places like *Palamós.* But when you say that local people are opposed that is only true to some extent, it is some local people yes, others, many others, see the plans for the resort on the beach as providing an important boost to the local economy. The local council and the Mayor are generally in support of the scheme. But we can do no more than present our plans and abide by decisions taken by local politicians. It is all very transparent." Batlló-Sabé spoke with growing confidence. It sounded like something he had said many times before, a pat answer intended to deflect concern, and not a little disingenuous. Staverley tried a gentle probe.

"So if I understand what goes on, you identify a location that might be developed, contact the owners of the land, draw up plans, submit these for approval, and await the outcome. If approval is forthcoming you make offers to buy the land, and if accepted then work begins. Is that right?"

"That is correct, more or less. It can be very complicated. Ownership is not always clear-cut."

"So at any point the process might be halted by landowners who refuse to sell or the refusal of planning permissions?"

"That is also correct. But you must be aware that during all of that my involvement is minimal, that is not my main responsibility, my work focuses on getting the buildings started and completed within a set budget. There are others who survey the land, draw up plans, and liaise with the local authorities and then put together the necessary financial package. All of that is complicated enough but I have different problems to overcome once building work is started. Although based on my experience on the coast, I am able sometimes to suggest new sites that might be explored for development, but nothing more."

"And the local council?"

"Of course, I have to deal with council officials in relation to many aspects of the building work – upgrading of local services, approval of building standards, those sorts of things. But they are practical issues rather than political ones."

"And the protests and opposition? How are they dealt with?"

"Dealt with sounds s little loaded. The protestors have every right to speak their piece and make their objections known, as long as they stay within the law. We are always eager to listen and to compromise whenever possible. But some of these people are troublemakers, with little real interest in the causes they espouse. They have a different agenda, they are agitators. We have had to contact the police when there has been damage to our equipment or trespassing on our sites. We now know one or two of them by sight and our watchmen keep an eye open for suspicious activities. They are a nuisance and can cost money to deal with as you put it, but as I say, if they stay within the law..."

Batlló-Sabé spoke with assurance and reassurance, and was now leaning back comfortably in his chair. Staverley decided on a change of tack.

"I have been reading some articles in the newspaper that suggest in some instances that the processes you describe are – I am not sure of the appropriate word here – are facilitated perhaps, by payments made to local officials and politicians. Is that something you are aware of?"

Batlló-Sabé quickly sat upright again and his demeanour shifted.

"If that is an accusation young man, I resent it. Are you suggesting that my business or I are involved in such things? I think our conversation is at an end."

Staverley did not want the conversation to end and tried to placate the now irate builder.

"I am not intending to be provocative, Senyor," although that was exactly what he was intending. "I wanted to know what you thought about what I had read. I realise that there are different interests and points of views involved in these issues, and the newspapers are interested in stirring up controversy, but I believe that at least one mayor has been prosecuted for accepting payments from development companies, but not your company."

Batlló-Sabé seemed to be considering this; his very pale, watery eyes were now narrowed. He looked suspicious rather than confident.

"That may be the case. There are some problems in our country with corruption, that is true, but I can assure you that these are exceptions and this is not the way my company and our business works. Our investors are reputable: several banks, for example, as you know. They would not tolerate such behaviour."

This gave Staverley another opening he had been hoping for.

"Of course, and I saw some very prestigious names among your investors, but I did notice that until recently the *Banca Catalana* was a major local participant. They would hardly live up to the standard of reputable."

Once more Batlló-Sabé shrugged and pursed his lips, but he had a response ready - again, Staverley surmised, one that he had deployed on other occasions.

"What has happened to the *Banca* is regrettable, and clearly there may be some irregularities in their financial management procedures that the States Prosecutor will want to pursue further. We must wait for his report. Our company is one of many in which the *Banca* invested, and others were misled, as were we. But the *Banca* no longer exists and we had already severed our relationship with it. All of that has been unfortunate, and we have had to bear some costs, but it is in the past."

Staverley wanted to move on again but also avoid a premature end to the interview.

"Several other investors are German, I read in your brochure. Does that come about from your own contacts in that country?"

Batlló-Sabé leant forward and put his elbows on his desk. He hesitated slightly before answering this time.

"To some extent. In one or two cases I have worked with these institutions previously in my German businesses. We have had a good working relationship, and they see the possibilities for investment in the new Spain. It is only natural that they would be interested in working with me again."

Staverley said nothing.

"In at least one case, a small investment bank, the relationship goes back many years."

Staverley waited again. Batlló-Sabé seemed much less comfortable with these questions. He was now neither confident nor irate.

"The German economy is buoyant and there is a growing interest in overseas investment opportunities."

Staverley saw another opportunity.

"So, do the banks - for example, the one with which you have worked previously - get involved at a local level here, dealing with the financial aspects of planning and permissions process you described? You had said that that was not within your remit?"

Batlló-Sabé hesitated again and Staverley thought he could see a sheen of perspiration emerging through his thinning hair.

"Of course, to some extent, they have the right expertise to deal with such matters and also want to ensure that their monies are being used appropriately. But I don't see how these things are of relevance to your research. I think I must excuse myself. I have other appointments."

Staverley had one more move to make.

"I wonder whether it might be possible to speak with someone who represents the German investors locally? I am keen to make sense of what is happening on the coast from all perspectives, both local and foreign. It would give me a better grasp of where the money comes from and the interests and motivations of the foreign investors."

Batlló-Sabé had moved quickly from discomfort to nervousness.

"I do not think that would be at all appropriate, not at all. I would not want my partners and investors bothered with that sort of questioning. These are private matters and delicate matters and cannot be opened up to public scrutiny. If I had known that you were interested in such things I would never have agreed to these meetings. I think, Senyor Staverley, you have misled me. To pursue this any further on your part might be..."

Batlló-Sabé was at a loss for a word.
"Dangerous?" Staverley suggested.
"What? Not at all. I was going to say..." But the word would not come.
"I was going to say... disruptive." Batlló-Sabé had found a word that worked. "I really need to impress upon you, Senyor Staverley, that my colleagues would not appreciate such a disturbance. These are serious people, very serious. You need to be very circumspect." Feliu had offered the exact same warning.

Batlló-Sabé shifted again from nervous irritation to something that might be pleading but could also be heard as a threat. Staverley knew that now he needed to be the reassuring one. Batlló-Sabé's reaction to the previous question was telling in itself, and Staverley knew that he would learn nothing more from probing further. He wondered whether what he was seeing now was a man who was actually frightened or just upset by the abuse of his willingness to help.

"Of course, Senyor, I understand entirely. You have been more than frank with me," which was perhaps not true at all, "and I now know everything I need to know, I will not bother you or your business partners any further with my questions. Absolutely not."

Batlló-Sabé's relief was very obvious, and he sat back again in his chair. He extracted a handkerchief from his trouser pocket and wiped it across his head. Staverley stood up and prepared himself to leave; he put away the notebook and pen he had been using. He did have one more thing to say, an attempt to placate.

'Senyor, I wanted to say again how grateful I am for your help in telling me about your friendship with my father. I have now spoken to Joan Canoes-Mas, and he has been able to tell me more about what happened to my father after you last saw him and he disappeared, and how he got back to England. They were not good things to hear but I think I now understand my father a little better. I also know now why you were unable to find him in Barcelona."

Again Batlló-Sabé looked disconcerted.

"Joan has never told me of these things, although as I explained when we meet we do not discuss the war. But even so I am surprised that he never mentioned your father. He was always the person missing when we met. I am sure we were each aware of that. As I said to you, I wish I had been able to do more at the time."

This was another opening that Staverley wanted to use.

"In relation to that time there was a name that has come up, someone involved in my father's disappearance. I wonder if you ever heard of a man called Orlov, a Russian, NKVD?"

Batlló-Sabé's expression was difficult to read. He rehearsed a classic set of memory-dredging looks, with quizzical eyes and head shaking.

"I don't believe so. Certainly afterwards, when I was in the Engineering Battalion, there were many Russians. They came and went, and were generally dislikeable, but I do not recall an Orlov, sorry. Now with apologies I must move on. I still have my missing Andalusians to deal with."

He escorted Staverley from the room. They indulged in a cursory handshake and the door was closed. Staverley hurried off to catch his train.

Staverley got to the station with minutes to spare before the next train to Sant Celoni. It was crowded but he found a seat and began to flip through the notes he had made in each of his meetings and added some further thoughts while everything was fresh in his mind. It had been a very productive day. He drew some diagrams in the notebook -

lines and squares and circles, joining up different issues and concerns and questions. It was a technique he always found useful to organise his thinking. There were three distinct topics he had been addressing - his father and his disappearance, Senyora Puig and her death, and the developments on the coast and the possibility of illegal or criminal activity. As he drew his primitive mind maps he recognised several ways in which the three were, or rather might be, inter-related.

On the one side, Staverley wondered whether his father had met Senyora Puig somehow in 1937. On the other, Senyora Puig was involved in funding the archive of memories and also some of the organisations protesting against the new hotels on the coast. If the sorts of people and organisations that Feliu had suggested were actually pumping money into those building projects, then it was possible that Senyora Puig was viewed by them as an obstacle to their activities. Then again Senyora Puig was also interested in things that took place in Barcelona in 1937 and it might be that she had stirred up things that some people did not want brought to public attention. Margarida had explained to him that there were many vested interests involved in maintaining the Pact of Forgetting. The Amnesty offered legal protection to those involved in atrocities but there were other things at stake – position, reputation, influence. His father had been one victim amongst many in what had taken place in 1937. Orlov was dead but he certainly would not have acted alone. According to what Joan saw, apart from the civil guardsmen there were at least two others who had had a role in the kidnapping of his father. For the first time, Staverley wondered if either of those other men was still alive. They might even be on the train. There were several men of the right age in his carriage. Or one of them could be the guard or the ticket collector. He speculated as to whether other survivors or victims' families ever looked around railway carriages as he was doing and wondered whether the person sitting opposite had been a torturer or a collaborator or a spy.

On the other hand, there was nothing concrete to any of the possibilities he had considered. He only had suspicions and hypotheses. He might be joining up things that had no relation to one another at all. He also had no further avenues to explore for the present, unless Margarida's father and his Fundación colleagues were able to find out more about Orlov from their archives. As regards to what was happening in Palamós, he could continue talking to people on the coast. The protestors might know something about where the hotel money was coming from. The other people he talked to, the waiters and local shopkeepers and farmers were hardly likely to be aware of international financial machinations. But as both Feliu and Batlló-Sabé had made clear, he needed to be careful about asking those questions. He was not brave enough or foolhardy enough to ignore their warnings. As the train pulled into Sant Celoni, and the people stood up – this was the end of the line – he did think of one way forward. He had an idea of something he could do, but he would need some help. He also had an idea about who could provide that help, if they could only be convinced.

With some difficulty, Staverley extricated his ciclo from the piles of bicycles outside the station, and pedalled off toward Sant Pere. Senyora Budó had promised to leave him another tortilla for supper, a courgette one this time. He was looking forward to it. He stopped at the bakery and bought a fresh baton of bread to go with it. He would eat, drink some of David's wine that had come direct from one of the barrels in the *bodega* and make a plan. The tortilla was delicious.

He still had Nuria's telephone number, and he rang her next morning from the *Granja*. She answered immediately. She had a formal manner but Staverley put that down to her job as political aide and party functionary. He asked if they could meet that evening, and he offered to buy her a coffee. She sounded surprised by his invitation but after a moment when he could hear her rustling through some papers, she agreed. She asked if he would collect her from the ERC office in Sant Celoni at 6.00pm, he agreed. Between times, he declared the day as a day off and went for a walk. He had seen signs in the town square that pointed toward the *Castillo Montclus,* and he was intrigued. The walk led him through some parkland, over a river and up a steep escarpment on the outskirts of the town. He was soon breathing heavily. After fifteen minutes' hard climb he emerged from the trees below a steep walled castle keep. It was in surprisingly good condition given its age, and there were impressive views of the valley from the battlements. He spent an hour pottering around, exploring the dungeon, some tunnels and the towers.

The ERC office was easy to find. It was a shop front. The window was covered in political posters - in part, he assumed, to provide some privacy for those working inside. He knocked and entered, and could see Nuria seated at a desk at the back of the long narrow room. She waved him in and began to tidy her desk. Nuria was a couple of years older than him. She wore a business suit that looked fashionable but serious. She was the only woman he had met so far in the locality who wore shoulder pads. Her hair was cut quite short, in the style he thought was called a bob. Her face was round and her nose small, and her eyes were charcoal black: perfect for delivering withering looks. If he believed in national stereotypes, which he did not, he would have said she was French, and he remembered that she had been brought up there. That would hardly account for how she looked, but it might account for the haircut and the clothes. Once in the street, Nuria quickly dismissed the idea of a coffee and stated firmly that she required a very large gin and tonic, and maybe more than one.

"Politicians are probably the most frustrating, annoying and ridiculous people on the face of the earth," she explained. "Some days I could happily strangle them all, my father included, especially my father in fact. I don't know how I put up with them. I should get a proper job."

Staverley had never heard her speak so much, and certainly not so frankly. In her father's company she tended to stand slightly behind him, to one side, speaking only when absolutely necessary but always alert. The perfect aide. He was pleased that she was more relaxed now. She led him to a bar that had obviously been recently refurbished and modernised and was decorated in steel and leather rather than the usual wood and tile. Jazz was playing quietly in the background.

Staverley boldly ordered gin and tonic for them both and a plate of olives, in his best Castilian. He was pleased with himself. They chatted for a while about Nuria's job, giving her the opportunity to rant a little more and dissipate the accumulated frustrations of her day. By the time they had finished their first drinks and ordered seconds she was calmer and ready to hear the reason for Staverley's invitation. He provided a relatively undramatic version of what he had learned about the unsavoury relations between mayors and developers on the coast, omitting any mention of the Mafia, and asked her whether she knew how he could find out more about the buying and selling of land in the coastal towns, specifically Palamós. Similar unsavoury things had happened in England, he added. He was thinking about the prosecution and jailing of local politician T Dan Smith in Newcastle ten years previously and told her about that. He thought she appreciated the gesture.

"Such sales and purchases are registered locally and can be consulted in the council offices. In practice however there are often delays in filing changes of ownership, and sometimes a reluctance on the part of officials to be as cooperative as they should be when enquiries are made. You might find some difficulties."

"Ah," Staverley said, "yes, I thought as much, so, what I was wondering was whether you might go with me." That made Nuria laugh.

"What a strange suggestion," she said, but did not dismiss the idea. She laughed again. "Why not? Perhaps a day on the coast will improve my mood, and I have earned a break. Yes, I will come."

"That's brilliant, thank you. What about tomorrow?"

That made her laugh even more..

"Not tomorrow. I will need to rearrange some commitments. The day after I think. And I have seen you on your cycle machine. I will drive us."

Staverley tapped her glass with his and downed the rest of his drink. Nuria consulted her watch.

"I must go soon. I am going to the cinema with some girlfriends."

The Nuria who left was much more light-hearted than the one he had collected.

Staverley rode his ciclo back to Sant Pere very carefully. The gin for the gin and tonics had been generously poured, without the aid of a measure.

The following morning in *El Pais*, the Barcelona newspaper he most often read, or tried to read, Staverley found an article referring to the death of Senyora Puig. Despite his best efforts he could not make out what it was saying. Dani, one of the waiters in the *Granja*, who was doing a part-time course in English at a language school in Sant Celoni, was happy to help out. He explained that the police investigation into Senyora Puig's death had been concluded, and based on their recommendation the *Medico Forense,* the rough equivalent to a coroner as far as Staverley could tell, had ruled the death to be of natural causes. That perplexed him. He did not exactly know why, but what little he had heard about Senyora Puig's collapse had not seemed at all natural. The news made it difficult for him to concentrate properly on his work that day.

Nuria collected him as arranged, and they stopped for a quick coffee in Sant Pere while Staverley explained a little more about what he hoped to achieve. Nuria seemed to take it as an odd but interesting challenge. She was dressed more casually but no less fashionably, and had brought with her a large brown leather briefcase. Briefcases always daunted clerks and officials, she said. En route they chatted, and Nuria recounted something of her life and upbringing in France. She had actually been born in the Dominican Republic, she said, but had almost no memory of the island. She had attended school first in Laon, a medieval town in northern France, and then in Vitry-sur-Seine on the outskirts of Paris. She had also attended university in Paris, at Sciences Po, one of the Grandes Ecoles of France. Her father had been offered a job in the wine trade, by a Republican comrade, which was how they had ended up in Laon, but after a few years another comrade had recruited him to edit and write for a political magazine produced by Catalan exiles. Her father had been drawn more and more into the politics of exiles, and from a very young age she remembered men arriving at their various apartments late at night, always seemingly in dark raincoats – carrying messages, or seeking a bed for the night, or conducting long disputatious meetings with her father that they were careful she should not overhear. Her father would sometimes go away on mysterious trips, and return either excited or depressed by whatever had taken place. When she was older her father had explained that these activities were all in some way connected with maintaining the ERC as a viable political party in exile, but she always suspected that there were other clandestine activities in which her father was engaged that might have involved travelling back to Spain illegally. While at university she had begun working as a volunteer for the ERC and when she and her father and others had returned to Catalunya in 1976 that work had turned into a permanent job. She balanced the seriousness and silliness of her political work with a lively nightlife, she said. Staverley reciprocated to her account of herself with a quick resume of his life and times. His personal history sounded very dull in comparison, he thought.

Once in Palamós they found the land registry office quite easily. It was in an annex to the town council building. As Nuria had predicted, the initial response of the young male clerk at the counter was studiedly unhelpful. Their requests were impossible and inappropriate; too time consuming; presented on the wrong day; and probably unlawful. Nuria listened to the well-honed dismissal and then opened her briefcase and withdrew a large text that was, Staverley gathered, the statutes and laws of Catalunya as related to all matters to do with land and its ownership. She then quoted various extracts, referred to her father several times, to the relevant government minister, who she called by his first name, suggested penalties ensuing from the illegal refusal of legitimate enquires, and concluded by complimenting the young man on his shirt – its style and colour. He was overawed, out-manoeuvred and smitten all at once. The files and documents Nuria had asked to see were quickly produced, and she and Staverley were offered a desk to work at and a coffee, which they refused.

From the large file of recent sales and purchases of land involving transfers of ownership, they first identified those related to the area on and adjacent to the beach that was the focus of dispute between the locals and environmentalists and the developers. From these they paid particular attention to six plots that had changed hands more than once in the past three years. Four of the six had been bought initially by a company called CBSB Holdings. All four had then been quickly sold on to different individuals, all of whom happened to share the same postal address, and they were then sold again, at a significant profit, to Batlló-Sabé's investment group. Nuria left Staverley working through the files to make a telephone call, and returned within fifteen minutes to confirm what they had both begun to suspect. CBSB Holdings was a company entirely owned by Batlló-Sabé. Batlló-Sabé had first bought the parcels of land himself via the holding company and then sold them on to his partners through fictitious intermediaries. In effect he was acting both as seller and buyer of the land, making financial gains at both ends. While Nuria was away, Staverley found another property purchased by CBSB and sold on, but it had not yet been bought by the investors. This was a pattern of double-dealing similar to that identified among the directors of *Banca Catalana*. Staverley now had the basis for another interesting conversation with Batlló-Sabé, one the man could hardly refuse to participate in. Nuria was keen to speak to the office of the prosecutor about what they had found, she knew people there, but Staverley persuaded her to wait until he was able to speak with Batlló-Sabé.

They were pleased with themselves, and decided that a good lunch was in order. The day had begun with a thin mist drifting along the coast but it was now sunny and very warm. They found a restaurant on the beach which specialised in fish, and for once Staverley decided to relax his dietary regime. They began with some whitebait and then a locally-caught grilled fish with steamed potatoes and lots of parsley, very simple but very fresh, and full of flavour – some local white wine went with it perfectly. Nuria, intrigued by what they had found, asked more questions about what Staverley had already discovered and he explained the possibility, it was only a possibility he emphasised, that some of the investment money flowing into the coastal developments might originate from Mafia drug and weapon sales. Nuria was shocked. Staverley also shared the words of caution offered by Felui and Batlló-Sabé. He thought that she took this seriously. Over coffee, and based on their evolving complicity in dubious matters, Staverley very hesitantly, decided to ask Nuria another favour.

"I was reading about the outcome of the investigation into Senyora Puig's death."

"I saw that," Nuria said, "and it made me think that I must have been one of the last people who spoke to her before she was taken ill."

"Well, I have been wondering, and I know it's probably crazy, but the *medico forense's* conclusions seem odd to me, not right. Do you know what I mean?"

Nuria looked both dubious and shocked.

"I am sure the investigation was very thorough, particularly given the high esteem in which the Senyora was held by many people."

Staverley hesitated again.

"Do you think you could get hold of a copy of the post-mortem report?"

Nuria put down her coffee cup very slowly; she looked Staverley directly in the eye.

"You're serious, aren't you?" She said.

"I am, and I know that it's not a small thing to ask. I am prepared to hear you say no, and if you do I will not mention it again, promise."

There was a very long pause, during which Nuria finished her coffee and stared at the sea for a few moments.

"I'll think about it," she said finally. She gestured toward the beach. "You know, we should have brought our swim suits. It's a lovely day."

Staverley recognised that the subject had been decisively changed and that he would have to wait for the outcome of Nuria's thinking.

"You know, I have been here for several weeks now and I haven't been to the beach once. I'm not a very keen beach person but the sea does look very inviting."

The afternoon proceeded as though Staverley had not asked his favour, and when Nuria dropped him back in Sant Pere she said how much she had enjoyed the outing, and that she definitely wanted to hear about what more Staverley might learn from Batlló-Sabé. He promised to report back to her. That spurred Staverley into action and he returned to the *Granja* to make the call. As soon as Batlló-Sabé's secretary heard his voice she said that her boss was unavailable and was likely to remain unavailable. But before she hung up Staverley deployed his newly gleaned information.

"Can you say to Senyor Batlló-Sabé for me that I want to discuss CBSB Holdings with him? Can you tell him that please?'

She said nothing but he heard the phone being put down on the desk top with a clunk. Two minutes later it was picked up again.

"Senyor Batlló-Sabé will meet you tomorrow morning at 9.00am at the Café Rebost in *Arenys de Mar*."

She put down the receiver before he could reply.

Staverley was getting used to the many bends and curves on the road to Arenys. As usual the ciclo stuttered slowly up the inland side of Mont Negre with the reward of a long and exhilarating coast down the seaward side accompanied by remarkable views of the sea. At the back of his mind, as on previous occasions when he had made this journey, was the hope that the rather primitive brakes on the ciclo would do their job when needed on the steep descent. He decided to put his trust in Salvador's mechanical expertise and enjoy the ride.

The journey also gave him time to begin to have doubts about the wisdom of going ahead with the meeting. It could be a big mistake, he could be putting himself in danger, although he assumed that Batlló-Sabé would not want any of his business colleagues to know about the activities of CBSB Holdings. He tucked his doubts away. Once in the town the second person he asked understood his query and directed him to the Café Rebost. He parked the ciclo outside and could see that Batlló-Sabé was already there, sitting inside in the corner furthest from the door. He had a coffee and a small brandy on the table in front of him. Staverley ordered a *cortado* as he passed the bar and sat down across from Batlló-Sabé. There was no friendly greeting this time and no offer of a handshake. Batlló-Sabé frowned and stirred his coffee vigorously.

"And so, young Senyor Staverley. I am here." He sipped the brandy.

Staverley considered various polite openings but realised they were redundant.

"I visited the Land registry office in Palamós yesterday with a friend and we spent an interesting morning examining recent sales and purchases of land on the beachfront, the beachfront on which your investment company is intending to build. It would appear that you have been buying some of those plots, and through some dummy owners have subsequently re-sold them to your company investors. Very unusual, I would think, although there is perhaps a perfectly straightforward explanation for these dealings. But then if there were such an explanation you would probably not be here."

Staverley had not planned to mention a friend but as he said it he understood that he was actually protecting himself - from what, he was uncertain. Batlló-Sabé now knew that someone else had access to the information that had precipitated the meeting. Batlló-Sabé stabbed his spoon several times into the packet of sugar that sat on the saucer of his coffee cup, spilling the contents across the table.

"And what will you do with this knowledge you have gathered so ingeniously? Or should I say, what do you want in exchange for not sharing this with others?"

Staverley took that to mean that Batlló-Sabé was expecting to be blackmailed in some way, and it was true, in a sense, that was what Staverley had in mind.

"My price, Senyor, if that is what we are talking about, is answers to more of my questions, nothing more, certainly nothing financial. I have no interest in sharing what I know or deriving any gain from it, I just want those answers." He found himself playing out a role that he had seen many times at the cinema in detective movies. He was the hard-boiled private eye extracting information from a reluctant villain with veiled threats. He tried to look mean and determined and imagined the hard outline of a leather holster in his armpit. He struggled not to slip into an American accent or to curl his top lip onto his teeth à la Humphrey Bogart. But as these notions whirled in his head he knew he should not be enjoying himself. This was serious, possibly deadly serious. It was obvious that Batlló-Sabé was resigned to doing what Staverley wanted, but Staverley also searched the man's face for some sort of relief. He saw none.

"Ask then."

Staverley turned slightly sideways in his chair, imagining himself as Lee Marvin in Point Blank.

"It's simple really. I want to know if I am correct in concluding that at least some of the money invested in your syndicate, the German money specifically, comes originally from another country and from organisations whose businesses are, what can I say, of dubious legality."

Staverley did not quite know why he was speaking in such indirect terms, but it seemed like the right thing to do, it seemed in character. Batlló-Sabé leaned back and looked up at the ceiling. He seemed to be waiting for some kind of divine intervention that would tell him what to do or whisk him away.

"You do realise that this conversation could be very dangerous to us both. You do know that?" Batlló-Sabé pointed his finger at Staverley. "You do know that?"

Staverley said nothing. Batlló-Sabé looked very
frustrated and very nervous.
"You are correct, my foolish friend."
Staverley expelled a long breath.
"Which bank?"
Batlló-Sabé was the epitome of conflict. He looked around the bar hoping for a way out of his predicament and the café.

"The *Sparkasse Ehingen*. All right. Enough? Are we done here?"

They were both in role now, speaking lines straight from a Dashiell Hammett story, but this was real, no one was going to shout, 'Cut, it's a wrap.'

"Yes. We're done."

Batlló-Sabé stood up and pushed the table roughly away. He picked up the brandy, drained the glass, and left the bar. Staverley realised that he was trembling slightly, and was tempted to order a brandy for himself, but decided on a walk instead, he paid for the drinks and then wandered around the harbour watching the fishing boats landing the last of their catch. A flock of seagulls was taking a close interest in leftover bits and pieces of fish. It took a while for his stomach to settle and his agitation to pass. He determined that he would report back to Nuria and to Feliu as soon as he could, despite his promise not to share. In part he felt that the more people who knew of what he had learned the safer he would be. But that still begged the question of what else he would do with what he knew.

He retrieved the ciclo and set off on the steep ascent back toward Sant Pere. While the tiny engine chugged and stuttered he tried to shuffle off his movie persona and think like a university lecturer, in a foreign country, who had gone out of his way to obtain information about the illegal financial operations of a highly secretive and violent Mafia organisation, putting himself and others at possible risk. And this was not the first time he had done such a thing. He finally got to the top of the mountain and switched off the over-heating engine for the descent, he used the brakes frugally to keep his speed within the limits of safety on the downhill stretch. About half way down he heard a car approaching fast from behind. It clipped the back wheel of the ciclo, knocking it and him off the road toward the edge of a deep tree-lined ravine. He tried to hold on to the handlebars but could not. The front wheel hit a bank of sand and stone, and he was propelled headlong over it. It felt as if he was airborne for a long time and he tried to brace himself for a painful fall on to the rocks in the ravine below, but his forward momentum was stopped dead when he hit a tree. He hit it hard and was knocked unconscious.

When he woke two men in workman's overalls were kneeling beside him. One was holding his head and the other was checking his arms and legs, for broken bones he presumed. They seemed to know what they were doing. One of them spoke, first in Catalan and then Castilian. Staverley understood that he was being asked if he could sit up. With some difficulty he tried but his shoulder hurt, it hurt a lot. The two men then helped him carefully and slowly to his feet. He was very dizzy and slightly nauseous. He heard himself saying thank you. He repeated it several times. The two men were concentrating on the task of keeping him upright. Beyond the pain in his shoulder he could now feel several other points of pain in other parts of his body, some sharp, some dull, but the shoulder was the worst. The two men lifted him into the cab of their small lorry, which was parked half way across the road. A van stopped and the driver of that got out to lend a hand. Between the three of them they got Staverley settled in the front seat of the lorry but he was having difficulty staying conscious. There was a short discussion and the van driver heaved the ciclo into the back of the lorry. The front wheel was bent out of shape. One of the men sat next to Staverley with an arm around him to keep him from falling, the other drove away fast. He realised he must have passed out again when the next thing he knew he was being lifted from the lorry onto a stretcher. As he was wheeled away he saw the sign for the Sant Celoni hospital above his head. He tried to speak but lost consciousness again and missed entirely being examined and treated.

"Staverley, Staverley, are you awake?"
Was he? He was not sure. Possibly. He tried to open his eyes. One opened, the other did not. The one good eye took a while to focus but eventually he recognised Margarida. She was smiling at him.

"Hello, how are you feeling? You've been in an accident."

Had he? Yes, he remembered that, or part of it, but then the effort of remembering was overwhelmed by hurting - the hurt now came from virtually all parts of his body. The parts seemed to be competing for most painful.

"I hurt," he tried to say but his lips were not working the way they should, they seemed to be someone else's lips, they would not do what they were supposed to. He tried again.

"I hurt." It still did not come out right.

"I am so sorry," Margarida said, "but the good thing is that nothing is broken. You look terrible but it's all cuts and bruises and no concussion. Your shoulder is the worst thing but there is no permanent damage. The doctor says it will heal. He says you were very lucky. He will give you some more painkillers and a sedative and if you have a restful night you might be able to go home tomorrow."

Staverley was relieved and tried to smile back at Margarida, but smiling hurt.

"Do you remember what happened? Were you going too fast?"

What had happened? He tried to remember through the fog that seemed to have set itself up in his head. He was riding down the mountain. Was he going too fast? No, it was not him, it was not his fault.

"I was pushed off the road," he said through the other person's lips. "I think it was deliberate." Deliberate was a very difficult word to say with those other lips.

"It was a car, it didn't stop. Men helped me. I must thank them."

Margarida patted his arm and he winced.

"Sorry. I checked. They left an address, because they have your ciclo."

That made Staverley feel better. He had a great need to thank them.

"I will ask about the car," she said. "You rest now. I'll be back tomorrow."

Staverley began to recite more thank-yous but after three or four he drifted off again and ended up somewhere deep and dark and peaceful.

Chapter 10

Staverley spent the first part of the next morning conducting an audit of his body, trying to distinguish the bits that hurt from those that did not. The number of the former heavily outweighed the latter. Nonetheless, when the doctor came he tried to downplay the pain and discomfort and make a case for being discharged. He had just spent his first ever night in a hospital and did not want another. After staring at his chart for a long time and a careful examination of his eyes and his shoulder and various extremities, the doctor signed the discharge and prescribed more painkillers. He was instructed to return in two weeks for a follow-up. Staverley was painfully elated. A nurse explained that Margarida had volunteered to collect him and would be arriving soon. He then spent a very frustrating half an hour trying to dress himself. Being unable to properly bend his legs or move his shoulder or lift anything or do up buttons made it very difficult. He nearly gave up on his shoes. His clothes were dirty and torn.

Staverley was sitting on the bed when Margarida arrived, and she hesitated in the doorway with a sharp intake of breath when she saw the state of his face. The bruises and swelling had developed further overnight. Even so she kissed him on both cheeks, very gingerly. Staverley had not looked at himself yet.

"You look…" she said, and paused, weighing up the possibility of various adjectives, "really, really terrible."

"Thanks," he mumbled between that other person's lips. There was then a long slow shuffle down the corridor and the stairs, holding on to Margarida's arm. He had suddenly aged forty or fifty years over night. Getting him in the car also took time and resulted in several loud exclamations of pain. He began to wonder whether being discharged was a good idea after all. As they finally set off Margarida explained what had happened while he was in the hospital.

"Salvador has collected the ciclo, and he says that it's repairable. The front wheel will need to be replaced but the rest of the damage is superficial and he has some parts from other ciclos that he can use. He also has your bag with your money and notebooks. The men who found you looked after everything and wanted to know how you were. The *Policía Local* have been to interview them and evidently they confirmed that a large black car overtook them immediately before you were knocked off the road. They didn't see the impact because it was round the next bend, but it appears that there is fresh black paint scratched onto the rear mudguard of the ciclo. So from what I understand a report has been passed on to the *Policía Nacional*. We will wait and see. They will probably want a statement from you."

Staverley contributed various grunts and groans to all of this, noises that did not involve having to move his lips but expressed his understanding and throbbing. In Sant Pere there was another protracted process of getting out of the car. Senyora Budó appeared and her hand flew to her mouth to stifle a scream when she saw him.

"*Pobrecito*," she said. She and Margarida helped Staverley into the house and up the stairs so he could wash and change. Forewarned Senyora Budó had prepared some pumpkin soup for lunch. The fields around the town were now full of them, many different shapes and sizes and colours. Staverley had eaten breakfast through a straw, and a spoon would be a new challenge, but he was up for it. He was hungry. Margarida and Senyora Budó watched him carefully and whispered to one another while he tried to eat with minimal dribbling.

Over the next few days Staverley's swelling and bruising began to abate and his limbs started to become moveable again. His lips and eyes were healing but remained startlingly black and blue and swollen. The shoulder remained very painful and stiffly locked in place, which made sleeping properly difficult. He could not find a comfortable position and tossed and turned. Sometimes he got dizzy and the painkillers made him constipated. It was all very frustrating and he could not work properly. He tried to walk a little further each day and by day three could manage the stairs pretty well. He could also eat almost properly. A postcard from Monica was delivered with the date and time of her arrival in eight days. Just enough time Staverley thought to reassemble himself into someone she might recognise and be pleased to see. He made a plan. He would meet her at the airport and they would spend one night at a hotel in Barcelona, to get reacquainted and 'do' the city, before coming to Sant Pere. Monica had five days before she had to be back to her laboratory and her experiments. A couple of days before Monica's arrival Salvador appeared at the front door with the reconstructed ciclo. He was pleased with the result. While not really understanding a word he said, Staverley understood everything. Salvador was very shocked and sorry for what had happened and was reluctant to take any payment for the repairs. Staverley insisted. Despite what had happened Staverley was pleased to have the ciclo back, if not quite ready to try it out.

As he began to venture out into town for coffees, his newspaper, a beer, lunch, Staverley became aware that his low-key presence had changed to something else. He was stopped several times on the street with solicitous greetings, and treated to smiles and nods by others he passed. It was clear that everyone now knew of his misfortune. These acknowledgements of his injuries and the well- wishing made visible the sinews of communality that made Sant Pere the place it was. It cared for its own. There was a tension of course between visibility and privacy but in the present circumstance Staverley was buoyed and gladdened by the care and concern of the townspeople. They were a tight-knit bunch, but somehow the incident had opened up a space for him in their complex social relations. The solicitousness might not last, but the incident and Staverley himself had entered the collective memory of the town and would be recalled in the future in the bars and shops. "Do you remember the strange Englishman who had that terrible accident on the ciclo?"

A *Policía Nacional* officer came to take a statement from him. He spoke English. But there was little to say. Staverley knew he had been hit by the car, he thought it had been done deliberately rather than being an accident, but he saw nothing and remembered nothing either just before or after the impact. That did not take long. The officer said that there would be further enquires and that if found the driver would be charged with leaving the scene of an accident at the very least. He said that the workmen in the lorry had thought the car had been a new model Mercedes but did not see the number plate, and with little to go on the police did not have high hopes of further developments. On one of his shuffling excursions Staverley had phoned Nuria and Feliu to tell them both what Batlló-Sabé had revealed to him and what had happened afterwards. Both expressed their concern, and Nuria was adamant that they should now go to the police and suggest that Batlló-Sabé should be questioned about the incident. Again Staverley persuaded her to wait, at least until he was a little better. She said she would come to see him to talk about things. Feliu did not exactly say I told you so but Staverley could tell that was what he was thinking. He also promised to visit.

On the day of Monica's arrival Staverley got a taxi to Sant Celoni, caught the train to the city and then another to the airport. He was eager and early. Monica's plane was on time and she appeared through the arrivals doors quickly. She looked lovely. Her hair had grown and her face was a little flushed. Staverley felt his heart swell as she rushed to embrace him. He had been worried that the damage to his mouth would affect his ability to kiss and be kissed properly but he need not have. The hello kiss was long and hot and very welcome, and the lips he was using were definitely his. They took a taxi to the hotel in the city and spent the afternoon getting reacquainted with each other's bodies. His was less flexible than before but eager to please. Monica undertook a thorough examination of his cuts and bruises. He had not explained to her the full extent of the damage. There were still a few tears. His shoulder was still very sore and stiff but he thought he managed the reacquainting remarkably well. As they recovered from their exertions Staverley was required to give a full account of the ciclo incident, as he called it, and everything that led up to it and was subjected to detailed forensic questioning. Monica was fascinated and appalled in equal measure by what he told her and spent fifteen minutes being very angry with him for putting himself in a dangerous situation. He was subjected to full on exasperation and then tears. If he had any doubts Monica's feelings for him were made very clear. They had both seen the two *Godfather* films but from what Staverley had gathered from Feliu and his reading, the N'drangheta were even more ruthless and vicious than the Sicilian Mafia portrayed on the screen by Marlon Brando and Al Pacino. They combined global financial expertise with a willingness to eliminate anyone who got in their way or threaten their interests. Once it was established that Staverley would never approach Batlló-Sabé again and would desist entirely from investigating his business partners Monica also wanted a clear explanation of who these two young women were that Staverley had been spending time with – Margarida and Nuria. Staverley wondered whether she was a little jealous, and hoped that she might be. Her response to his account of the women was grudgingly non-committal.

Later, as they walked around the city, Staverley began to tell Monica what he had discovered about his father. Then he wanted to know about her work and the research team that she was part of, but she deflected his questions.

"Totally uninteresting," she said, "although we might well have a viable battery up and running." Her Cambridge team were competing with other teams in Japan and the United States to make a battery that would be small enough and cheap enough to be sold commercially.

They undertook a whirlwind tour of the main sights of Barcelona and ended with dinner at *Els Quatre Gats*, a modernista style restaurant, where famous modernistas, including, it was said, Pablo Picasso, had gathered to socialise in the early decades of the century. It was clearly on the tourist trail but had not succumbed totally to cosmopolitan tastes. The menu was strictly and unapologetically Catalan but there was plenty on it for Staverley to eat and he was pleased to show off his language skills by translating some of the dishes and doing the ordering – he had been practising.

The next morning they ticked off a lot more places from their Barcelona must-see list. The city was a delight, full of architectural oddities, historic sites that represented the style and sensibilities of various invaders, and charming back streets and squares. Through his researcher's eyes Staverley could see that it might well become an even more popular tourist destination in the future, as flying got cheaper and feared that that might lead to changes that would involve damage to or the loss of some of its charm and oddity. Tourists invariably destroy what it is that they come to see and enjoy. He showed Monica the Post Office with its bullet-marked exterior, and they ventured into the notorious Chinese quarter, with its houses of ill repute and then up to the Castle of Montjuic. Franco had made the castle into a prison for his opponents and it was where Luis Companys, who had been president of Catalunya during the civil war, had been shot by a firing squad after being handed back to the Nationalists by the Gestapo from his exile in France. It was a grim and sad place.

They travelled to Sant Pere in the late afternoon, by train and then a taxi from Sant Celoni. Monica loved the house, with its simplicity and solidity, and took immediately to Senyora Budó despite the absence of a common language. Senyora Budó had made them a pile of mushroom croquettes, a jar of olive pate, and a plate of *escalibada* for their supper. She also had a large envelope for Staverley that had arrived that morning. When he opened the envelope he found an official looking document with a note pinned on the front. It said. "I hope you are recovering. We do need to talk." Below was another sentence, underlined. "It depends what you mean by natural!"

Apart from the fact that it was in Castilian, Staverley could make little sense of the technical language of the document. It was clear that it was the report of the post-mortem examination of Senyora Puig, but was written in a dense technical medical language. Monica, with her background in Chemistry was able to do a little better, despite having no Castilian.

"From what I can see here, the Senyora probably died of liver failure. That is the basis of the natural causes conclusion. She was otherwise in good physical shape for someone of her age. She had suffered a serious injury when much younger, which necessitated the use of a cane, but that was unrelated to her death. Although the thing is that some traces of *alpha*-Amanitin, a mushroom toxin, were found in her liver and elsewhere in her body – which were probably the cause of a massive hepatocyte necrosis that killed her - although identifying toxins from mushrooms is not easy. I did some homework as you asked me to. Diagnosis of mushroom poisoning is a bit hit and miss and is sometimes presumptive – the symptoms are nausea, vomiting, abdominal pain – and those could have many other causes. Alpha-Amanitin is a cyclic peptide. That means it's made up of a chain of amino acids and they occur naturally and are frequently toxic, but they also do have useful medical applications as antibiotics and such like. This one in the report is an amatoxin, and from what I read it is found in amanita mushrooms, like the aptly named Death Cap. Death Caps are easily mistaken for edible mushrooms but it only takes one or even part of one to kill a human. Most of the deaths from mushroom poisoning are attributable to them. Cooking does not destroy the toxins, as some people think, and they attack the kidneys and liver, as in Senyora Puig's case. Death usually follows one to three days after ingestion. The Death Cap is pretty widespread around the Mediterranean and particularly places like this with all the pines and oaks. Deaths are not frequent but they're not uncommon either. So given all of that, as your friend said in her note, it depends what you mean by natural."

"My God," Staverley said. "You are amazing. I knew there was a good reason for inviting you!"

Monica batted him with the report.

"But that's horrible. I had no idea that mushroom gathering was so dangerous. Picking and cooking with mushrooms is a really big thing around here. People drive up from Barcelona at the weekends to collect them. You see them wandering about in the forest with wicker baskets, and in the town the shops are full of trays of the things and all the restaurants have them at this time of year. It makes you wonder exactly how many people are polished off every year by these Death Caps."

He took the report back from Monica and waved it back and forth.

"So what this is saying really is that Senyora Puig was poisoned by a mushroom and that that mushroom was somehow missed or mistaken by whoever collected it and whoever cooked it, and that it got into one of the dishes at the ERC dinner and that any of us might have eaten it, but it just happened to be Senyora Puig."

Monica nodded. "I guess that's it. One deadly mushroom and she was the unlucky one."

Staverley thought for a moment. "But can the poison be administered indirectly?" "Well the toxins can be extracted by using liquid fungal cultures, but you would need some serious lab equipment and perhaps a sterile environment. It wouldn't be easy."

Staverley had finished waving the report and now threw it down on the table.

"Mmm! I still don't buy it. Why her? Why the woman who was arguably the most controversial and best-known person in the room? Why now when she has only relatively recently returned to Catalunya, and when she is asking questions about the civil war, and funding the project of memories, and supporting environmental organisations that are frustrating the ambitions of the people building hotels along the coast? It's all too coincidental or convenient or whatever. It's too much to accept, at least it is for me."

Staverley realised that he had not yet told Monica about all of the things he had learned about Senyora Puig.

"I haven't got round to telling you about her Fundación. I will. I just have the strong sense that something is not right here. I know now that I should have made more of an effort to speak with her and ask about my father, and the fact I didn't is very frustrating. Maybe that's part of what's upsetting me, I don't know."

Monica put her arms around him and edged very close to him. He rested his head on her shoulder. It made him feel part of her. He knew that she understood him and his inability to leave things that bothered him alone, and his need to ask questions and to not accept the obvious, even though those things had got him into difficulties in the past. The courage of truth could be risky but it was a manner of being that afflicted him. Monica stepped back and placed one hand on each of his arms. She looked him directly in the eyes.

"The question is, if you think that there is something not right and you have those questions, what happens next?"

He looked back directly at her.

"I really don't know. Let's eat our mushroom croquettes."

They both laughed even though they both thought it was not funny.

The next morning Staverley took Monica on a guided tour of Sant Pere. Even at a slow pace that did not take long. He introduced her to David and to Salvador and to Dani in La Granja, where they stopped for coffee. He took the opportunity to telephone Nuria. He told her that he thought she was right about speaking to the police about Batlló-Sabé but suggested they do it after Monica had returned to London. He also promised to tell her everything that Monica had said about Senyora Puig's post-mortem. Nuria suggested that Inspector Rodriquez would be a good person to see about Batlló-Sabé, and he thought that very clever.

"I can see why you work in politics Nuria." They agreed to talk again on Tuesday.

On the way back to the house Staverley and Monica did some shopping, and bought some wine, in a proper bottle this time. Monica had an idea for lunch. They pottered about in the kitchen together, peeling, chopping and frying and enjoyed the result, pasta with courgettes. It was time for a siesta. Staverley had explained the well-established health and well-being benefits, and Monica was willing to give it a try.

After their rest they walked again, out of the town this time and up onto a sandy ridge covered in Mediterranean pines that ran along the southeastern edge of Sant Pere. It was both serene and impressive. The sandy soil was almost totally covered in a thick carpet of pine needles. There were plenty of mushrooms of all sorts of shapes, sizes and colours but neither of them was inclined to picking. As they walked Staverley told Monica more about Senyora Puig's history and the work of her husband's Fundación. He also tried out on her in more detail some theories that he thought might explain Senyora Puig's death as being from unnatural causes.

"I have no evidence for any of this, it's all speculation, but it stems from what I was saying before – it seems to me that her death is of benefit or convenience to too many people, and the likelihood of her eating the one poisonous mushroom in a gathering like that seems too remote. And the people I have been talking to about my father, they were all there or nearby on the day - Batlló-Sabé was there, Subirachs' daughter was there, although I don't for a moment have suspicions about Nuria, her father was unwell and sent apologies, and even Joan was down from the mountain on that day. He was delivering his cheeses to the bodega and left some for me and for Senyora Budó. It's even possible that the Mafia might have had a hand in it. I'm sure they would have the resources to arrange for toxin to be extracted, and they could have bribed one of the kitchen staff or a waiter to put it in a drink or something. If they were responsible for the ciclo incident then they might also have wanted Senyora Puig got rid of."

Staverley paused and Monica put a hand on his arm.

"I'm still having a lot of trouble coming to terms with the idea that you might have been killed that day, and even more with the possibility that it could have been some kind of Mafia hit-man who did it. Our lives are not like that. We're, well, we're ordinary."

Staverley pulled her close.

"I know. In my dreams I keep seeing myself hurtling toward that tree and I think about what might have happened if I had hit it head on or missed it entirely and fallen into the ravine. Either way I would probably not have survived. But in the dreams it's like looking from the outside, watching it happening to somebody else. Perhaps that's some kind of sub-conscious defence mechanism to avoid having to deal with the reality – both what did happen and what might have happened, and even that it could happen again. I've been telling myself that it was just an accident and the driver panicked but that would be another big coincidence. Even so, I can't really believe that I am some kind of threat, despite what Feliu and Batlló-Sabé said. What harm can I do? But equally if it's all true, if I was a target and they did kill Senyora Puig as well, what can I do about that? I can tell the police what I found out but I don't think it's going to be easy to convince them that the Mafia or someone else is on a killing spree. The only other possibility is that I pack up and return to England with you, but even then who knows? If they're after me, the N'drangheta have branches in countries around the world, like some kind of multi-national corporation. And I can't do that, I can't run away. I'm not finished here. There are too many loose ends. There are things I still need to know. And other people are involved."

Monica hugged him tighter.

"There's also a very strange symmetry to this. My father came here and put himself in danger, and he was wounded and beaten. In a different way I may have also put myself at risk, and become a target for outside interests, just like him, although much more by chance in my case, but I've been wounded or damaged. It's a bit far-fetched I know but I was thinking that he and I both became entangled in foreign invasions, my father with the Nationalists, and the Germans and Italians and the Russians, and me with all of these foreign investors, also Germans and Italians, wanting to pillage the Costa Brava. Then it was about politics, now it's about profits, but poor Catalunya is at the receiving end both then and now. It could even be that what happened to him and what's happening to me now are actually related, although I don't know how. There're still questions In my mind about his note and the names. Lots of people have theories about the betrayal he wrote about and most of them make a lot of sense but I still feel that there's more to know, just as there is with Senyora Puig. And I know he was very ill after I was born and I know, as my mother said, that he didn't want to burden me with his experiences here and with his politics and disappointments, but I do believe that he wanted me to find out about those things for myself, or at least he hoped I would. I've already got plenty of material for my research but if I left now I would feel I would be letting people down, my father most of all but myself too."

They began to walk again.

"You know you are a very strange person Staverley," Monica said.

"You have no idea," he replied, and she dug him in the ribs with her elbow.

"But you are my very strange person and I wouldn't change you. It's probably at least partly your strangeness that makes me love you. You know I've had several boyfriends and a couple of lovers before I met you, I told you that, but they always ended up being boring. I have a very low boredom threshold. Some of them were great, I liked them, we had fun, I enjoyed their company, but every time we got to around three months I would begin to be bored by them and find myself wanting to be on my own and then either they ended it or I did. I'd more or less resigned myself to being on my own for the rest of my life or making do with a series of unsatisfactory, temporary relationships like those. And then I met you, and you may have lots of faults Staverley, and we can work on those". She poked him in the side with her finger.

"But one thing that you are not is boring. Strange yes, frustrating yes, but not boring, and quite lovable really."

They walked in silence for quite a while before Monica
spoke again.
"That's it, you see."
"What's it?"
"We're walking and nobody is saying anything, but we're together. We're not talking but I'm with you, and I know you're with me. We're together and it's not boring. It's never boring. And that makes me very happy."

They walked more and were silent again.

"One thing though," she said. "Please, please be careful. Be very careful. I don't' want to lose you now."

The rest of Monica's visit was studiedly devoted to not talking about research, deaths or betrayals. They enjoyed each other. Staverley introduced her to some of the culinary discoveries he had made, they drank far too much of David's wine, and explored more of the surroundings of Sant Pere. It was good for them both. Staverley could concentrate on healing, and Monica could forget about batteries. She had got very tired after many late nights in the laboratory in Cambridge, minding her experiments. She wanted to stay longer and promised to come back as soon as she could. They both felt that their relationship had moved on, that there had been a step-change. They knew and understood and trusted one another better than before, and loved each other a little more as a result. They did have some disputes over kitchen rights - who would do what and the proper way to chop onions - but those were also part of the growing intimacy and multi-dimensionality of their relationship. They both knew that any real relationship would have its up and downs. When it was time for her to leave Monica insisted that she would find her way to the airport on her own. She argued that if she was going to come back she needed to be able to do things independently and it would be good to get to know for herself how things worked. Salvador organised a taxi for them and they travelled together to the station in Sant Celoni. As he waved goodbye to the departing train Staverley felt a wave of deep sadness that she was gone, followed by one of joy – she was coming back. He spent a couple of hours exploring Sant Celoni and replacing his torn clothes before catching a bus back to Sant Pere. On his way to the house he again made use of the telephone in La Granja. He called Nuria and they arranged to go together to speak to Inspector Rodriquez the next day.

Nuria had made an appointment and picked Staverley up at nine. Once at the police station they were again directed to the Inspector's office. He was alone this time and seemed more relaxed without his Guardia colleague standing behind him. Nuria translated this time.

"Senyoreta, Senyor, what can I help you with? Do you have more information regarding Senyora Puig?"

Staverley let Nuria tell their story. He could follow part of what she told the Inspector because he knew what she was going to say. Soon after she began, the Inspector's expression shifted to surprise and then concern and he started to make notes on a pad in front of him. When Nuria had finished he then spoke for a long time and asked a series of questions, at which point Staverley frustratingly lost track of what was being said. Whatever the Inspector said, it clearly shocked Nuria and she covered her mouth with her hand. The Inspector picked up his phone and made a short call. Nuria took the opportunity to explain to Staverley what was going on. She was upset.

"I don't believe this."
"What? What's going on?" Staverley asked.
"It's Batlló-Sabé. He's dead. He was found in the marina in Santa Susannah on Sunday morning. He was wrapped in an anchor chain taken from one of the boats. His death is being treated as murder."

After the Inspector's telephone call everything got more formal and complicated. Both Nuria and Staverley had to make statements explaining everything they had found out about Batlló-Sabé's property dealings, and Staverley was asked to describe in detail his three meetings with Batlló-Sabé. Several times he had to go through his theory of the possibility that the *N'drangheta* might be involved as investors in Batlló-Sabé's building syndicate through a German bank, and how that related to what Batlló-Sabé had told him when they met for the last time. He did not mention, though, his meeting with Feliu, having decided that the journalist would not welcome his name being introduced. Staverley resolved to speak to him first. That led on to him having to rehearse again the ciclo incident and his suspicions about the perpetrators, but he was careful in making it clear that they were just suspicions. He did not want to sound like a crazy conspiracy theorist. But he did take the opportunity to air his speculations about Senyora Puig's death. He got the clear impression that they were not taken entirely seriously. He was also asked to account for his whereabouts on Saturday night and Sunday morning, a matter of procedure he assumed and hoped. Monica could vouch for him if needed. Staverley's statement required an official police translator, and it was over three hours before he and Nuria were able to leave the station. They decided to stay in Granollers for lunch and exchange ideas and experiences from the morning.

Nuria was still shocked but she said nothing about how things might have turned out differently if they had gone to the police about Batlló-Sabé earlier. They both knew the other was thinking about that. Staverley it was who had insisted on the delay, they both knew that. Staverley was also aware that he may even have triggered Batlló-Sabé's murder by asking him questions about the investors in the syndicate. They might have been observed or followed. Inspector Rodriguez had told Nuria that given their statements it was very likely that the case would be reassigned to the *Guardia Civil*, both because it involved possible financial crimes and the international aspects, if the *N'drangheta* were involved. There were specialist divisions of the *Guardia* that dealt with such things. She also said that the Inspector had intimated that Batlló-Sabé died after he entered the water but had probably been unconscious. Very gruesome. That made Staverley feel even worse,

"Don't forget, though," Nuria said, "he was embezzling the *N'drangheta*. It might have only been a matter of time before they found out, maybe they already had. Think about it, how would they know you were meeting with him? Or maybe they were already following him or there was someone in his office working for them. There was no way they would know what you were talking to him about. As far as anybody else knew it was to do with your research and your father."

Staverley thought about that and was a little reassured but he could feel a nugget of guilt growing in his mind and asserting itself over and against his insatiable curiosity. If only he had not asked so many questions and stuck to the main focus of his research. He also felt the need to apologise to Nuria for getting her involved in the first place. He should never have asked her to go with him. She dismissed that with a wave of her hand.

"I'm a grown-up, Staverley. I could easily have said no. I wanted to get involved, and to be honest I enjoyed what we did. Obviously I regret the consequences, but as I said we don't know that the murder was a consequence. The man was taking an enormous risk in cheating these people. It's up to the police or the Guardia to investigate now, and it's good that they will look again at what happened to you, but even with that we don't know for sure that it was connected to your meetings with Batlló-Sabé. His death may have nothing at all to do with you."

Staverley knew she was right. They did not know anything for sure, either about Batlló-Sabé's death or Senyora Puig's or the ciclo incident, or in fact about his father and his father's note. Everything was conjecture or subject to competing hypotheses.

Staverley had recently begun to read some work by French post-structuralist theorists and he tried to convince himself that this was a good moment to embrace the indeterminacy, complexity and openness that some of them saw as making up the social world. He could accept, as the theorists asserted, that the world was always changing, inherently unstable and intractably unpredictable, and he knew the belief in the possibility of certainty was comforting but also very misleading. He also knew that Nuria was right, that their involvement in what had happened to Batlló-Sabé was probably contingent rather than causal. He was eager to embrace these ideas at an intellectual level, though it was a little more difficult to get his conscience to cooperate at an emotional level.

As they ate they circled round various possibilities for what might happen next. Just as Monica had, Nuria asked him to be careful, and he asked her to do the same. She said she would do her best to find out how the investigation was progressing but with the caveat that that it might be difficult if the *Guardia* and Madrid took over. Her networks and contacts did not extend that far. When they had finished their coffees and got up to leave they both took a moment to look around. Staverley knew they were both now on the lookout for suspicious foreign-looking characters and big, black Mercedes cars, and that it would become something they did routinely, at least for the foreseeable future. They were both quiet on the way back, lost in their own worries. The morning had left them with a lot to digest. Nuria said she would contact him in a few days or sooner if there was anything important to report. They exchanged kisses.

Back in the house Staverley decided to spend the afternoon working through his research materials and attempt some initial writing up. He did not usually write in the afternoons, nine till twelve in the morning and a couple of hours in the evening were his preferred and most productive times to write, but now working would serve as a distraction from darker thoughts. When immersed in his research he was able to bracket away worries - a temporary but welcome respite.

Chapter 11

A few uneventful days passed. Apart from his research work Staverley had intended to try and speak again with Joan and with Subirachs, but given what had happened he did not quite have the heart. He was also concerned that they would be mourning their friend and would probably be appalled if they found out about the role that Staverley may have played in precipitating his death. He did telephone Feliu to elicit his take on the murder, and the journalist had been reassuring. He had said that if it had been that easy for Staverley to find out about Batlló-Sabé's double-dealing it would have been equally easy for any other interested parties. Feliu was also very grateful for Staverley's discretion in not mentioning his name to the police, but said that he intended to report to them what he had uncovered about the Mafia involvement in Batlló-Sabé's business activities. He also admitted, rather guiltily, that the murder of Batlló-Sabé would provide a dramatic conclusion to his series of articles on corruption on the coast, the first of which was due to appear in the next Sunday's newspaper.

It was a welcome break from work and self-recrimination when Margarida re-appeared at the door of the house late on the Friday afternoon. She always brought a flurry of energy with her when she entered a room and Staverley was pleased to see her. She did not disappoint.

"Let's go out for a drink," she said, "I have made some good progress with my thesis this week and had a good meeting with Professor Montoliu, and I have some news for you, and anyway you look down and dumpy. Is that what you English say?" That made him laugh.

"It's down in the dumps, but I like down and dumpy better."

"English is such a funny language. I often wondered how any of you understand each other. Anyway let's not be down and dumpy, or in the dumps, or whatever, let's drink some cava. Come on."

She grabbed his hand and pulled him through the front door. It was a mild evening, a classic of early autumn, and they sat outside a bar in the old main street, where Margarida did indeed order a bottle of cava and some olives and crisps.

"So, what's the news?"

Margarida held up her hand to stop him. The waiter came, opened the bottle and poured two glasses. Margarida clinked hers against his and took a long swallow from her glass.

"Ah. That's good. I was looking forward to that. And I deserve it. News yes. But first you must tell me something about Batlló-Sabé, one of your father's friends. It was terrible news."

Staverley's heart sank a little at having to go through his story again and he proffered a rather heavily edited version of events which failed to mention any Mafia involvement and the real reason for his last meeting with Batlló-Sabé. He felt a little ashamed of putting pressure on the man and only alluded vaguely to possible criminal involvement in Batlló-Sabé's business activities. That seemed to satisfy Margarida, and the subsequent speculation as to who might have committed the murder was brief. He was relieved and tried to change the subject again.

"Come on, on to more positive things, I'm keen to know about this news."

Margarida took another long sip from her glass and re-filled both his and hers.

"Well my father asked me to come and tell you what's been happening with the archives and the questions you had asked. Evidently it's caused quite a stir at the project. It's the sort of work they've wanted to do for a long time with the memories, but there's never been the time or the money. So Adriá says... let me get the notes I took."

Margarida dug deep in her voluminous bag and came up with a battered leather notebook. The notebook was stuffed with papers and envelopes and what looked like newspaper cuttings. She riffled through the pages.

"Right, Adriá spoke with some of the interviewers, they're all volunteers, I think there's around ten of them at the moment, and he said that he was surprised by their detailed recall of the interviews they had done. Anyway, from that he's identified four interviews so far in which there's a mention of Orlov or someone who could be Orlov. My father explained to me who he was. What an evil, disgusting man."

A look of disgust crossed her face. "He was clearly hunting down people involved in organising the anarchist militias and the CNT units - the trade unionists - doing Stalin's dirty work. So Adriá then read back through the four interviews and I've got some details. Do you want to hear? They are grim I warn you."

Staverley certainly wanted to hear.

"Okay. There is one woman and three men who talked specifically about Orlov. The woman was a CNT activist and a branch organiser in Terrassa, that's a small town outside Barcelona. So 1937, the Civil Guards raided the union offices. Everyone was taken away, six people. The woman never saw again any of the others who were taken that day. She was interrogated and severely beaten by Orlov and by another man, and there was a third man watched everything but did not participate. The two other men were definitely Spanish, she said and she described them in the interview. She was beaten several times, and the interviewer said that she was almost sure that the other man who did the beatings had sexually assaulted the woman, but she didn't want to talk about that. The interviews are difficult and bring back all sorts of issues and some memories that people want to avoid. They want others to know what happened to them, they want to be heard, but some things are just unsayable. It can also be hard for the interviewers as well sometimes and they need support. Some of the stories are horrific."

Margarida took another sip of cava and consulted her notebook again. Staverley refilled her glass.

"So, the questions Orlov asked were about various CNT officials and their whereabouts, which she could not answer in any case. She was nothing more than a clerical worker. After a couple of days she was taken in a car from the place she had been questioned by one of the Spanish men and dropped in the countryside. She was sure that she was going to be shot and doesn't know why that didn't happen and it seems almost certain that none of the others who were snatched with her survived. There is no record of any of them at all from that time. They are probably among those tens of thousands still buried out there somewhere in unmarked mass graves."

She sipped again. The story, even in the re-telling, was having an effect on her mood. Her energy was seeping away.

"The woman was taken in by a farmer who sheltered her and looked after her. She was in very bad shape and physically it took months to recover properly, mentally even longer, who knows what something like that does to a person. The physical scars may heal but the ones inside probably never do. The one nice thing about her story is that she ended up marrying the farmer and they were still together when she gave the interview. They have three children."

Staverley interrupted.

"Are you okay with this? You don't have to go through everything now. I can go to the Fundación next week."

"No, I want to do this, I want to do it for myself. Other people like me, people of my age, we need to know these things, we need to be exposed to the things that happened and were done. All this stuff about forgetting, it's rubbish, it's not healthy. And it's not fair that the people who suffered should be silenced, they are being tortured all over again. They need to be listened to. In a way it's a privilege to share these experiences. I'm grateful in a way, so I'm good to go on if you are."

Staverley understood exactly what Margarida was saying and he shared her sense that they were being allowed access to something special, and something important. It was a privilege and an obligation.

"I am yes, go on."

"The second one is a man, Guillem, one of three as I said. Again someone working for the CNT, I'm not quite sure what he was doing, something to do with collectivised agriculture, near Girona. There will be more details in the transcript. He was also part of a round-up, seven in all this time, six men and one woman, but from different locations. They were all thrown into a van or lorry of some kind. Again, there were some Republican soldiers involved, and Orlov, from the description Guillem gave, and two other men, one who smoked cheroots, and could be the same man from the first account who did the beatings, and another one who never spoke. The only other thing Guillem remembers about him is that he wore a hat the whole time. The cheroot smoker was referred to by the soldiers as *Chafa*, or something like that, some sort of nickname anyway. The whole group were taken to a workshop or storehouse and locked in a basement. They were harshly handled but then left to await their fate, with guards outside they assumed. And they waited. But no one came. Eventually they tried the door and managed to force it open and the whole place was empty. Something had happened in the meantime obviously, and they had become unimportant, so they left and scattered. They were just pleased not to have had to face Orlov and whatever he had in store for them. Guillem thinks that at least three of the others may have survived the war but he's not sure. He certainly did meet one of them many years later. He never did find out why Orlov and his men never came back and for him, he said, it was a lucky day. Those were chaotic times. More?"

Staverley was totally engrossed and was trying to imagine what it must have been like to find yourself in such a situation, as his father had, but he knew his imagination was incapable of recreating the fear and other primitive emotions that these people had experienced. Knowing about the past was one thing, experiencing it was something entirely different. He wondered how he would have coped, how he would have dealt with the pain – again, his imagination was inadequate. You can be brave and stalwart in the abstract but the reality might be very different. He was just grateful that he had never had to face such a reality.

"Yes, more, please."

"Right then, next is Arnau. These are all traditional Catalan names, which tells you something in itself I suppose. Arnau was a junior officer in one of the Confederal Militias. His background was in the Syndicalist Party, that's one of the anarchist parties that were heavily involved when Catalunya declared itself independent from Spain. Sorry this is complicated. These are bits of history that most people don't know much about."

"No it's fine, go on. I have been picking up some of this from the reading I have been doing. I'm almost through Hugh Thomas' big book on the civil war."

"Arnau ended up in the Harriers Column, one of the militias, they were anarcho-syndicalists." Margarida stumbled over the words. "That's really difficult to say in English! The Column was based in Barcelona and then they were on the Huesca front, and I think you said your father was there also."

Staverley nodded.

"Arnau was arrested on the street when he was back in Barcelona to bring a new contingent to the front from their barracks. A similar story to the others, but Arnau was almost sure that he was being followed before being picked up and he was targeted in some way, he thought. When he was questioned they knew all about him and his history. But they weren't just interested in him, they wanted to know about Juan Garcia Oliver. Have you heard of him?"

Staverley shook his head.

"He was interesting, larger than life. I've been reading about him. He started out in life as a waiter and got involved in the waiters' union and the CNT, and he is supposed to have designed the red and black CNT flag. I don't' know if that's true. In the 1920s he was part of a plot to assassinate Mussolini, and in the early '30s he was involved in an anarchist insurrection in Catalunya and was imprisoned. He was released in '36 and took part in setting up the Committee of Antifascist Militias of Catalonia, but he ended up as Minister of Justice in the Spanish government and he made some significant reforms, especially in the handling and treatment of prisoners. There's a great picture of him I found sitting at his desk in the Ministry wearing a holster and gun. He would clearly have been someone on Stalin's list of dangerous characters and he did leave the government in '37 but he continued working in Barcelona until the end of the war. He then went to France I think, then Sweden, and ended up in Mexico. It sounds from Arnau's account that Orlov took a different tack with him, at least initially. Orlov and another man, who could be our *Chafa* again, took turns in questioning him, keeping him awake, no food or drink but no violence, not at first. Arnau knew of Oliver and had some contact with him through the Harriers Column but the questions were about whether Oliver had some kind of relationship with or links to Trostsky, which Arnau knew nothing about. After a couple of days and nights he was handcuffed and hooded and taken outside and he was told he was to be executed by executive order. He was stood against a wall and he could hear the order to load and aim and he heard the weapons being cocked, but when the order to fire came the guns clicked without firing. It was all mock, another attempt to break him down. Other people interviewed have reported the same thing, mock executions. But after that he was fed and allowed to sleep and then transferred to an ordinary police prison. He was there for a few more days and then he was released. But even then he said he was sure that over the next few days he was being followed. He returned to his duties with the Column but things had changed, many of the senior officers were gone and the Column had been militarised and was incorporated into the 125th army brigade, who fought later in the Battle of Ebro. After the defeat what was left of the 125th retreated across the French border. After the war Arnau initially became involved in smuggling people back and forward across the border and then he was part of the French armed resistance against the Vichy government and the Nazis. He sounds like quite a character. After the war he became a schoolteacher in France and also wrote books for children. Some of them were published here in Castilian after 1975."

Staverley had started taking his own notes and had some questions.

"Did he say anything else about this *Chafa* person? Who he was?"

Margarida searched through the pages of her notebook again.

"I may have to ask Adriá for more details or get him to ask the interviewer again, or speak to Arnau himself perhaps. Adriá said that Arnau had no problems talking about the war and that he had written a kind of memoir but that's not been published. Again people don't want to know. The only thing I've got here is that Arnau believed the cheroot man, *Chafa*, was Spanish secret police. Adria told me that they were set up in '37, trained by the Russians and they were vicious – SIM was their name, Military Information Service would be a rough translation. They operated outside the law basically and carried out executions and torture. Mostly they were rooting out fifth columnists and Nationalist spies but also they were used by the Communist Party to persecute their political enemies, people like Arnau and Oliver."

"How do you know all of this?" Staverley asked.

"You have to blame my father. I grew up hearing about these things and reading what he was writing. I was even thinking that I should write a book about the repressive republic, or something like that, but no one would publish that either, and I must finish my thesis first. But your questions and the stuff from these interviews has got me all stirred up again."

"One other question."

"Sure, but let's order some food first, I'm starving. And we've finished the cava."

Staverley waved over the waiter, thinking about Juan Garcia Oliver as he did so. Did the waiter belong to a waiters' union, he wondered. With some help from Margarida and indulgence from the waiter he ordered some tapas and a glass of red for each of them.

"Your question," Margarida said.

"It's *Chafa*. What does it mean? Is it a proper name?"

"I was wondering about that too. My best guess would be that it's short for *Chafardero*, which is slang for a busybody, someone who pokes their noses into other people's business or watches people. If that's right it seems an appropriate name for a secret policeman."

"And there's no indication of his proper name?"

"Not in anything Adriá told me, but I could ask him to check if there's anything else about him that people remember from the interviews."

Staverley was thinking that *Chafa* and the man in the hat could well be the two men Joan had described to him as coming out of Senyora Piug's father's house when his own father was dragged away.

"And the other one, the man in the hat?"

"There's no sign of him in Arnau's account, but he does reappear in the final one. I hadn't thought about it but now you ask, he's there again I think. Do you want to hear the last one?"

"Let's do it, but a short eating break would be welcome."

And they set about their tapas and the wine.

When they were adequately fortified Margarida checked again in her notebook.

"I find this one the most difficult and the most evil in some ways. I cannot begin to understand how the men who do these things, and I mean men, live with themselves. They must get some deeply perverted pleasure from inflicting pain and humiliation." She sighed very deeply. "This took place in April of '37. Iker worked for POUM in the headquarters building. He seems to have been some sort of secretary, nothing very important, but he worked in the office of Andreu Nin, the founder and leader of POUM. He saw Nin every day. He had worked with him previously when Nin had been Minister of Justice in the Catalan government, and moved with him back to POUM when the Communists forced Nin out of office. So Iker and his friend Albert were snatched off the street during their lunch hour. I think they may have been more than just friends. Anyway, Albert was a sign writer and not really political at all. They were bundled into a van and blindfolded and taken to some kind of disused workshop - somewhere near the port, as far as Iker could tell. They were tied to chairs and confronted by three men. From what he describes they must have been Orlov, *Chafa* and the man in the hat. Again the man in the hat never participated directly in what happened but watched everything and Iker thought he was suggesting questions that the other two should ask. They wanted to know all about Nin, his telephone calls, his contacts, his movements and appointments. They already seemed to know what to ask and how Nin's office worked. Iker was determined not to say anything. He admired his boss and had always been treated well by him. He said that Nin had never lost a sense of his class background, his father had been a shoemaker evidently, and he treated his staff as equals, as comrades. Iker remained silent so Orlov and *Chafa* began to beat Albert. Orlov used some sort of truncheon and *Chafa* used a knife. Albert shouted that Iker should say nothing, but that made them angry and they worked harder on him. Iker thought that the beating and the cutting went on for hours, but he had lost a sense of time. Albert lost consciousness several times and the men would throw water over him and start again. Every so often Orlov and Chafa would stop and consult with the man in the hat and change places. Albert's face was reduced to a pulp. Iker's resolve collapsed and he agreed to tell them everything he knew about Nin if they would leave Albert alone. He told them everything he could think of, and then they asked some very specific questions. As he talked, the man in the hat took notes. Iker told himself that what he knew about Nin was mostly unimportant. He was torn between his loyalty to Nin and his feelings for Albert, and he felt he had betrayed them both, that he had allowed Albert to be tortured and still ended telling about his boss. And the terrible thing is that he still feels that way: he has spent almost fifty years feeling ashamed and guilt-ridden. The interviewer said that that was more harrowing than the physical abuse."

Staverley had felt a knot developing in his stomach as Margarida talked. He wanted to ask what had happened next. At the same time did not want to know. But he asked.

"And then?"

"And then Orlov garrotted Albert. Iker was untied and taken back to the van, driven away and thrown out in the street. He suffered a fractured skull and a broken collarbone but he recovered. He was sure that they had left him alive to remember everything he had seen and to relive it every day for the rest of his life, which is what happened. When he was fit enough he joined the army and waited to be killed, he said. He wanted to die, to be with Albert again, but he didn't, he survived. When the war ended he was rounded up with thousands of others and spent four years in a work camp in Mallorca, building roads. He couldn't get a proper job after that, Republican soldiers were blacklisted, so he moved from one odd job to another doing anything he could. But he also began to paint. It was a way of expressing the things he could not say out loud was how he described his work. He's had three or four exhibitions in the past ten years and he lives in an artists' colony in Castelldefels, that's just south of Barcelona on the sea. He's quite well known."

Margarida bowed her head when she had finished and they were both silent. They drained their wine glasses and were both tempted to order more but did not.

"My god, that's so awful. What must happen to a person when they are made to watch someone they love die like that? It's like you said, it's evil, nothing, nothing at all can justify that, or any of the things you've told me about. And what's worse is that they're still going on. Things just like that are happening now, everyday, in countries all around the world. And people just like Orlov and *Chafa* get away with it."

"Well that's what the project of remembering is about, at least in part. It's trying to make it a little more difficult for people to get away with it."

Staverley was tired now and so was Margarida, he could tell. Her earlier exuberance after a good week had been deflated by the terrible stories. But he had one more question that was bothering him.

"We know Orlov is dead, that he died in the United States, but what about *Chafa* and the man in the hat? They could still be alive. Do the people working on the project have any ideas at all about who they might be and what happened to them?"

"Not really. As I said before, they will do some more digging through the interviews and look for others but it really takes a different kind of expertise to identify and trace people, and you need to have access to archives, which is not always easy. A lot of the documents from the war were destroyed and more again disappeared after Franco's death, and are still hidden. There's still a lot of fear and secrecy and guilt. My one thought is that you might go and speak with Arnau yourself. From what Adriá said I don't think any of the others would want to talk to anyone else. The interviews were very difficult for them. The talking may have been helpful in some ways, but I get the strong sense that they have said enough. But Arnau is still full of a passionate anger, and he might let you read his memoir. That would be a good way forward if you want to pursue this. He lives, let's see…" Margarida flipped through some pages in her notebook. "He lives near Tarragona."

Staverley did not have to think.
"Great idea, I will go."

They paid the bill and began to wander back to the house.

"You know I don't think I can drive back to Barcelona tonight. I'm too tired and I have definitely drunk too much. I'll stay over."

Staverley was taken aback by Margarida's announcement. Was it a suggestion? A proposition? What was he supposed to say? He liked Margarida, he liked her a lot, and she was a very attractive woman, but he thought of her as a friend. Margarida caught the change of expression on his face and seemed to read his dilemma. She laughed out loud.

"Sorry, sorry, Staverley, your thoughts are so transparent. Senyora Budó will put me up for the night. She's done it before. I do like you, I like you very much, you are a gentle and interesting man, but you are still a man and on the whole, in terms of romance I prefer women more, if you understand me."

She was still giggling now. Staverley did understand and he was greatly relieved. He joined in with Margarida's laughter and they shared a big hug. It felt good to hug a woman with no strings of sexual tension involved. And it made them both feel a little better after the harrowing stories. At the door of the house they exchanged kisses and headed for their respective beds.

Staverley found it difficult to sleep properly. Images from the accounts Margarida had relayed displayed themselves in his head like garish flash photographs, each one ugly and shocking. Every time he drifted toward sleep another image would suddenly appear and jolt him back to consciousness. He tried to think about other less disturbing things, but as soon as his mind relaxed the images would reappear, demanding his attention. In the early hours he gave up the attempt to sleep properly and began to rehearse what he would say to Arnau, if the man was willing to meet with him. Perversely that did the trick and he slept peacefully for the last three hours of the night. In the morning, somewhat the worse for wear, he washed and dressed and tentatively knocked on Senyora Budó's front door. She opened the door and touched his cheek with her hand. Staverley assumed that was an expression of sympathy for his dishevelled and worn state. He could see Margarida moving about in the kitchen, and suggested breakfast in

La Granja, to which she agreed. He needed coffee and wanted one of their *tortilla de patatas* bocadillos, but also hoped that he could persuade Margarida to make some telephone calls for him. He asked and she agreed. She first called Adriá, and then they waited and chewed away at the sandwiches. The tortilla was still warm and the bread fresh and crunchy, straight from the bakery, delicious. Adriá called back and Margarida immediately made another call. She wrote something down in her notebook and returned to the table.

"Done. Here is the number and the address. Arnau says you are welcome whenever you want to see him."

Margarida handed him a sheet of paper and told him about trains to Tarragona, Staverley decided to go the next day. She phoned again.

"You're expected at 12.00, and your secretary needs another café con leche."

"I'm sorry, I know I'm exploiting your good will. You need to think of something I can do for you for a change."

Margarida smiled. "I will. In fact, I have a couple of ideas. But after the coffee I must get back to Barcelona, I need a change of clothes and I'm meeting friends for lunch, and I have a father to keep amused and out of trouble."

Trains to Tarragona left once or twice an hour from Sants station in Barcelona. The journey took around an hour and a half. Staverley had got up early, somewhat warily ridden his ciclo to Sant Celoni, and caught the train to Barcelona from there. He was still nervous on the ciclo and could not stop himself from looking behind every time he heard a car approaching. But he got to the station without incident. The line from Barcelona to Tarragona was mainly along the coast, often right next to the sea. The train stopped at Castelldefels - where Iker lived, he remembered, -and at the seaside resort of Sitges. Tarragona was a port city and had been a Roman colony. It had, Staverley read in his guidebook, many Roman ruins, including an amphitheatre and necropolis and some traces of the forum. He told himself that he would return to see those. From the station he took a taxi, as Arnau had suggested. The journey took around ten minutes, most of it through the old centre of the city. The taxi driver was very adept at picking his way past wayward pedestrians and bustling street stalls and awkwardly parked lorries. The final part of the ride was steeply uphill, and when Staverley exited the taxi he could see right across the city below and down to the port and the sea beyond. Arnau lived in a small modern block of flats on the top floor, which meant even more dramatic views.

Arnau was, as Staverley already knew, well into his eighties. He was a large man with a jolly demeanour, bald except for a neatly barbered ring of white hair above his ears. His cheeks were full and ruddy and his eyes were a very pale blue. He wore an elegantly crumpled linen suit. It had a yellow silk handkerchief protruding from the top pocket. He spoke to Staverley in French, which he hoped would do as a medium for their conversation, and offered a *vermut*, which Staverley accepted. Arnau explained that while he was generally healthy his eyesight was deteriorating and his ability to manage on his own was being tested. Staverley was heavily drawing on the vestiges of his O-level French to follow this but Arnau spoke clearly and slowly and encouraged Staverley to interrupt him if he could not understand. Staverley cobbled together a messy mixture of French and Castilian to explain his interest in Arnau's experiences and the men who had kidnapped and abused him. Arnau understood that he wanted to know more about *Chafa* and the man in the hat, and was willing to oblige as far as he was able.

"I will tell you what I can and if I can be of help I will be pleased. I have returned in my mind to those experiences many, many times and as you may know I have written down my memories. I tried to interest several publishing houses in my account but they were all reluctant. They would publish my children's books but not my memories. You know - I think? - what was done to me by the men you seek. You also know that after the war I found myself in France and I worked with the French Resistance. There were others like me who had fought Fascism in Spain and were then fighting it again in France. The uniforms were different but the vile wickedness was the same, the same disrespect for freedom and difference and for human life. The Resistance wasn't a single entity, you understand. There were many different groups, some of which refused to cooperate with others, some of which operated entirely independently. Some aligned themselves with De Gaulle, others with Moscow. I worked for a time with a group that were Boy Scouts. Can you imagine that? But they were very successful in rescuing Jewish children from the French police I admired them very much. I wrote one of my children's book about them, as a sort of adventure story. I will give you a copy. I tried to keep away from the Communists, given my previous history, but wherever I was and whoever I was with, I always asked about *Chafa* – 'Have you seen Chafa?' Does anyone know if Chafa got out?' – that sort of thing. For all I knew he had been killed in the fighting in Catalunya, or had fled elsewhere or had stayed on. There were rumours that some of the SIM agents had been taken on by Franco's secret police, *La Brigada,* who were key actors in the White Terror, that was the Nationalists' campaign to punish or eliminate all loyalists. You probably know that people refer to the things that the Republic did to Nationalist supporters and its own supporters as the Red Terror. The Left was also intolerant and also responsible for the deaths of thousands of innocent people. I accept that and regret it deeply. Perhaps you can tell my friend that I have had a long time to think about these things, maybe too long. But I am digressing, I have few people to talk to these days and I ramble a little. Do you want to know of all this?"

Arnau was an engaging speaker, and Staverley was more than happy to allow him to tell his story as he wished.

"I do, yes, please Senyor go on. This is of great interest to me."

Arnau sipped his *vermut* and nibbled a small almond biscuit from the plate he had brought. He re-settled himself in his chair, dabbed his lips with the silk handkerchief, and resumed his narrative

"I came across several men from SIM in the resistance, and indeed one woman. She was infamous for her cruelty but she was a very effective resistance fighter. I heard she was captured by the Gestapo and she perhaps experienced some of the torments that she had inflicted on others. I continued to ask my questions and one of the men from SIM, who was part of a raid that my group participated in, did recognise the name *Chafa.* They had, he said, worked together for a short time in Barcelona and by pretending a friendship of my own with *Chafa* I managed to get the man to tell me his real name."

Staverley tensed. He had not really expected this. He had anticipated that Arnau would be able to provide more details or clues to *Chafa*'s identity but not that he would actually know his name. This was another of the men who had kidnapped his father. His heart was beating fast and he leaned forward toward Arnau.

"His name was Enrique Cruz, he was from Valencia." Arnau lifted his arms in a gesture of resignation.

"But what could I do? In a way I was satisfied I knew the name of my nemesis and I continued to ask after him but I heard no more. After the war while I was working as a schoolteacher I began to write my memoir and in that I named him but apart from a few friends no one has read what I wrote. I had done what I could and I moved on with living my life as best I could. But after Franco's death, by which time I was retired from teaching, I decided to return to my home, to Tarragona, to enjoy my remaining years in familiar surroundings. Some of my stories were published here, as well as in France, and they provide me with a decent income, as you see."

He gestured to the flat and the view.

"But once I had settled back here the memories of Enrique Cruz began to gnaw away at the back on my mind. 'What if he is still alive?' I thought I realised I needed to do more. So I hired a private detective, a very resourceful man. I paid him well but his father had fought for the Republic and my account of Cruz and what he had done gave further impetus to his investigations. Indeed he was relentless. For almost two years he asked questions, visited archives, read documents, pestered officials, and eventually he found him, he found Enrique Cruz. He was alive but had changed his name. He had changed it more than once, in fact. He was then Alejandro Chacel, and I knew exactly where he was, after forty years, I knew."

This was even more incredible. Staverley had to ask.

"What did you do?"

"I did nothing, well nothing much. I contemplated visiting Cruz or Chacel, acting out a cliché of confrontation and resolution, I thought about standing before him and accusing him, but I did not. I have restricted myself to sending him a series of postcards, pictures of

Barcelona with cryptic messages – 'I know who you are', things like that, quite childish really, but it was enough. There was no need for more."

Staverley did not understand this.

"After so long and so much effort, did you not want at least for him to know that you knew who he was and what he had done? Or perhaps find a way of exposing his past."

"I thought of many possibilities but I realised that I was content as things stood. And in a way, as much as I hate the man he has also been a positive influence on me, and my life. That may sound very strange to you and it was something that took me a long time to realise. That night in the courtyard when the triggers were pulled and the hammers fell I was ready to die. You will die bravely I told myself. Let them see how a true Republican can die. When there was no other sound and no pain, when I did not die, it was as though I had been given a new life. Not the one I had had before, but a new start, a new set of possibilities for who I might become, and what I might become. And I never feared death again. I had stood eye to eye with death and overcame it, defeated it, and from then on I would cherish life and I had the chance to be a decent human being. I think that's what I carried with me during the rest of my time in the army and then the Resistance. I came to relish danger but always emerged totally unscathed. I volunteered for dangerous missions but was always unharmed. I began to think that I had been spared for a purpose. And later as a teacher and then a writer I savoured each day as an extra day, a day of the life I might not have had. And each day I tried, and I still try, to take time to think of something – something I did or ate or saw - that was special, that is worth valuing. It is a kind of a ritual, a habit, one that means that every day I remember the opportunity I was given when I stood in front of that firing squad. What happened to me was meant to demean and destroy me, break me, but it didn't; it made me more resilient. It was many years later I read the philosopher Nietzsche and came across his well-known aphorism – 'that which does not kill you makes you stronger'. I was shocked when I read it because it explained that moment, that half a second, that changed my life rather than ended it and made me into a different person, or allowed me to become a different person. I am not saying that it made me into a better person, but a different one, with different weaknesses and flaws yes, but with a zest for life and for living a good life, a proper life. Does that make sense to you Monsieur Staverley?"

Staverley did not know what to say. What Arnau had described did not make sense to him, but then he had never had such an experience. How could you understand second-hand such a life-changing event? But then he stopped himself, because of course he had had such an experience, albeit not in such dire and dramatic circumstances. The sense of the tree in the Mont Negre rushing toward him, or him toward it, that still recurred in his dreams, had confronted him with the possibility of death, at least thinking back now it had. It was not the same as what Arnau had described but it was not entirely different. He wondered whether he had not considered properly the significance of that moment of confrontation with death and its implications and opportunities, as Arnau had put it. Arnau was not made guilty by his survival; he celebrated it. That was not the case for many others who had gone through such experiences, but Arnau's response was uplifting. Staverley knew an answer was pending.

"I was going to respond by saying that it does not make sense to me, but that would be wrong. You have presented me with something that I will need to think about and I am grateful for that. And what you have said does explain in part your ambivalence toward *Chafa*, but I don't think I could be so restrained. I think I would need to do something more. I would like to do something now, on my father's behalf. Not something dramatic or violent, I don't know what it would be, but something, a gesture at least."

Arnau smiled.

"Ah, the impetuosity of youth. In that case, I would suggest to you that you visit this *Chafa* and make a decision then as to what you might do, what that something might be. He still lives. I can provide you with his address."

Arnau left his offer hanging between them. He looked at his watch.

"But while you think about that I believe that we should lunch together. There is a very decent restaurant just down below, where I often take my meals. They have a very good *menú del dia* and if you were to take my arm I will manage the stairs very nicely. Over lunch I will tell you about Tarragona and its history while you decide what should happened next. Yes?"

"Yes indeed."

Arnau, Staverley decided was a delightful man and a very special one, someone to learn from. They enjoyed a long, leisurely lunch and before parting company Arnau gave Staverley the childrens' book about the boy scouts.

On the train journey back to Barcelona, Staverley stared out of the window enjoying the changing colours of the sea in the early evening sun. The sky was beginning to redden and reflect back from the light clouds to create what looked like a good approximation to a Turner painting. Even as he gazed, somewhat sleepy from the two large glasses of Terra Alta white wine he had drunk, recommended by Arnau, from a local vineyard, he was very aware of the folded piece of paper in his inside jacket pocket. On the paper was the address where he would find *Chafa*. He had not looked at it yet. He was still not sure that he would look at it. Arnau was content with what he had discovered, so why should he not be also? If he did confront the man, what would he say? What would he do? Perhaps he needed to say no more than what Arnau had written on his postcards – 'I know who you are, I know what you did.' By the time he had arrived back in Barcelona he had made a decision. He would do nothing more. By the time he arrived back in Sant Celoni, he had changed his mind. By the time he arrived back in Sant Pere he again did not know what to do, or not do. He needed help. Yet again he used the telephone in *La Granja*. Yet again he was phoning Margarida. She answered. He explained what Arnau had told him and she was astonished.

"After all those years to be able to find the man, that's incredible. But to do nothing more, that's also incredible."

"So you think I should confront him?" Staverley asked.

There was a long silence before Margarida replied.

"I thought I was going to say yes, of course, but before I could say it all sorts of doubts and caveats and cautions flooded into my head. Like you, I am not sure. I think you have to think about what you want to achieve and exactly what you are going to say to him or do. Why don't I speak to my father, or better still Adriá? He might have some experience of such things. Shall I?

"Please, I need help with this. I keep changing my mind. It's not something I have any experience of, so yes, Adriá might be just the person."

"I'll do it now. Will you be there for a while?"
"I can be."
Staverley took a table and ordered a brandy. He did not really want more alcohol but he thought the brandy would steady his nerves. The series of changes of mind was unsettling. He tried not to think any more, and engaged Dani, the waiter, in an impromptu language lesson. They took turns to ask and answer questions in the other's language. Staverley realised that Dani was making much faster progress with his English than Staverley was with his Castilian, and he was now using even more of the Catalan words he had picked up. The mix of the two languages sometimes made Dani laugh, for which he apologised. But Staverley understood how he must sound. Otherwise Dani was patient and serious with their lesson. They both enjoyed the process and decided that they would have more sessions together. Then the telephone rang.

"Adriá understood your dilemma," Margarida said. "It has come up before in the work of the project and in interviews. His advice is to take things step by step – find out more, go to the address and watch and ask and then decide what might be the right next move at each point. You don't have to decide in advance, he said. You will know when the time comes you will know what is right. So what do you want to do?"

"I suppose the first thing is to look at the address. He might live at the other end of the country, and that might be an issue."

"Go on then, have a look."

Staverley took the folded sheet of paper from his pocket and spread it out on the bar.

"Okay, it says - *Residencia Las Acacias, Plaça Mercat, Olot*. I'm not sure what that means and I don't know where Olot is."

"A *Residencia* is a home for old people," Margarida explained, "and that would make sense. *Chafa* must be in his late 70s or 80s like Arnau, maybe even older. And Olot is a small city in Girona province, about twenty-five thousand people at a guess. It's famous for its volcanoes and its *ratafia* and it's very Catalan. Listen, if you decide you want to go and see where Chafa lives then I'll take you. I would say it's about two hours drive from Sant Pere, maybe a little more."

"That's too much Margarida, I can't ask you again. I'll find a way, really."

"Listen, Staverley, you got me involved in this quest of yours and now I'm in, I'm in. After those accounts I went through with you, I need to know about *Chafa* as much as you do. In fact if you don't want me to take you I will probably go on my own anyway."

Staverley laughed. "All right. If you put it like that then I would be very grateful if you could take me, thank you."

"Good. Apart from anything else it's a very difficult place to get to. The railway line was closed back in the '60s, so you would have to get on and off lots of buses, which would take forever. And there's no way your ciclo would make it all that way over the mountains."

Staverley could hear pages being turned.

"I'm at the university tomorrow all day. What about the day after? We could make an early start."

"That works for me. In fact I've got a couple of interviews with protesters in Palamós tomorrow."

Staverley was relieved that he did not have to make a firm decision, at least not immediately. Just as Adrià had suggested: step by step. He decided to spend the evening reviewing his notes and ideas about Palamós in order to prepare for the interviews, and trying to find some music worth listening to on the small radio he had bought in Sant Celoni. He was missing his collection of LPs, which were back in his flat in Watermouth. He hoped that the visiting American academic he had rented the flat to was taking good care of them. He had left a vinyl cleaning cloth at the front of the cabinet as a reminder.

The journey to Palamós, and the interviews there, went well. Staverley was still a little nervous on the ciclo but he managed. The protesters, one local man and a woman from one of the environment groups, were both very helpful. Their groups were working together to oppose the beach development, but from slightly different points of view. The man did not want his town despoiled and overrun by the proposed resort and hotels, and the woman was concerned with the impact on wildlife and the access to the beach for local visitors rather than tourists. They each explained their concerns and their tactics, and were both scathing about the foreign investment monies that were behind the building plans. They were both aware of the death of Batlló-Sabé and the police investigation. Indeed, the woman and some of her colleagues had been interviewed by the police, but neither was able to summon up a lot of sympathy for the man. The local gossip had it that there could well be some kind of relation between the murder and the resort plans but equally others were suggesting that it might have been something more personal. Staverley knew nothing about Batlló-Sabé's private life, even, he realised, whether there was a Senyora Batlló-Sabé. He was certainly not going to share his suspicions that the Calabrian Mafia were involved. These interviews and the others he had done, in Palamós and elsewhere, along with the other material he had collected, were a solid basis for a case study of tourism, and economics versus the environment and local culture, that would be one part of the book he was planning to write. He had already drafted out a rough structure and contents, and was quite pleased with it. Whether he would be able to make use of what he had discovered about the Palamós investors remained to be seen. It seemed as though he was making good use of his sabbatical.

Chapter 12

Margarida arrived early, as she had said she would. They stopped at *La Granja* for a very quick coffee and promised themselves an *almuerzo*, an early lunch, or more accurately elevensies, en route. Margarida decided to drive through the Montseny and then Vic rather than going back to the eastern valley. She said it would make a change for her, and that Staverley could see the rest of the Montseny. He had not yet been further across than the turn-off to Joan's house. Margarida's small car laboured up and up to *Coll Formic*, the highest point of the road, and then more easily down the other side. The views on both sides were dramatic. This part of the mountains was almost totally covered by forest, but with a few cleared meadows here and there around small farms. The farmhouses, called *macias*, were large, multi-generational, all-purpose buildings – for families, storage, and in the winter animals. They almost all followed the same design: low and wide with gently sloping roofs and rounded stone-lined windows. Above the tree-line was a mix of gorse, broom and heather, each of which flowered at a different time of year. It was an unusual, special and very precious place with several unique species of plants and insects. Staverley was determined to do more exploring before he had to return to England.

Once in the valley on the other side they drove north toward Vic. Vic, Margarida explained, was best known for its pig products – cold meats of numerous different kinds and shapes and sizes. There were dozens of them, she said: *fuet, chorizo, salchichón, sobresada, butifarra, llonganissa,* and many others.

"It's a pity you don't eat meat, Staverley. These are jewels of Catalan cuisine. We love our cold meats. Mind you, I'm not sure I would want to live in Vic. On some days, when the wind blows in a certain direction, you can smell the pigs everywhere."

They stopped at a roadside restaurant just north of Vic for their *almuerzo - cortados* and pastries - and then entered Olot at eleven thirty. It turned out to be market day, which made it very difficult to find anywhere to park. *La Plaça Mercat*, where the *Residencia* was, and all the roads around it, were closed to traffic and packed with market stalls. People had obviously come from all around to shop and socialise, and the whole centre of the town was crowded. They eventually found a place to park on some waste ground about ten minutes' walk from the square, and made their way back through the narrow streets jostling with shoppers. Many of the women had shopping trolleys or carried huge wicker baskets. The food on the stalls looked wonderful – the vegetables, cheeses, dried fish, eggs, herbs and spices and dried fruits, olives and of course lots of cold meats. There were also stalls selling clothes, shoes, tools and kitchen equipment. In one of the side streets, live animals where being bought and sold, and Staverley did not enjoy seeing the rabbits and chickens and chicks packed together in wire cages with little room to move.

Once in the Plaça Mercat they made a circuit and found the *Residencia* on the north side. It was a modest but recently modernised three storey building that announced itself as a Home for *Ancianos*, old ones. Staverley and Margarida retreated to a café for another coffee to decide what to do next. This was the point of a next step. Should they sit and watch, buy some food in the market, have lunch and go home? Or should they go in and ask after Senyor Cruz - or Chacel, as he was now called? After fifteen minutes of debate about what was the right thing to do, which resulted in no clear conclusion, they decided to go in and ask. Then they could decide. They crossed the square and entered through the highly polished glass and wood front doors, which led to a small foyer. There was a small hand-bell and printed sign on a console table standing beside an inner door. "Ring for attention," said the sign, Margarida explained. They rang. Quite quickly a large middle-aged woman wearing a pale blue pinafore uniform and paper cap covering her hair emerged. She was drying her hands on a towel.

"Preparing lunch," she explained. "Can I help?" She was brusque but not unfriendly. Staverley realised that they had probably chosen a bad time to call. Margarida explained exactly that to the woman, who dismissed the problem with a wave of her hand.

"Never a good time here. It's all go."

They had agreed that Margarida would say they were looking for a long-lost relative, a great uncle, who they thought might be a resident in the home. They were not absolutely sure but it was possible that a

Senyor Chacel was their great uncle. They had decided to feign uncertainty, in case they needed to make a quick exit.

"Ah," the woman said, "you mean Enrique. He's one of our oldest, and not in the best of health. I'll get Aina, she's the senior carer, she will be able to help you. Can you wait a moment?"

All of this was in Catalan and Staverley would need Margarida to explain later. The woman disappeared behind the inner door, and soon another appeared, Aina, she said. They introduced themselves. Staverley was explained as a distant family member from England. Aina invited them into a very tiny office. There was only one chair and most of the space was taken up with files and boxes of medical supplies and aides of various kinds. She apologised for the lack of room, they all stood..

"So you may be related to our Enrique? If that's the case, you would be the first we've seen. He's down in the files as having no living relatives, and in the time he has been here no one has ever come to visit. Not that it would make much difference. We know almost nothing of his previous life but all his costs are paid by a lawyer in Madrid, the money arrives every month without fail and his medical expenses are also covered. You're welcome to talk to him but don't expect too much."

They followed Aina up two sets of stairs and along a narrow corridor lined on either side with narrow doors. All of the doors were open and most of the rooms were empty. They were furnished identically – functional and in most cases anonymous.

"Most people are downstairs getting ready to have lunch," Aina explained. "A few of our less mobile residents, like Enrique, usually have their meals in their rooms. He's here." She gestured to the last door on the right. The three of them stood in the doorway. Inside an old man sat in a plastic-covered armchair. His head was bowed and he looked as though he was sleeping. Throughout the building there was a strong smell of bodies and cleaning fluids and disinfectant, but here that was undercut by something else - the odour of decay, Staverley thought. The old man roused himself and looked around the room but did not seem aware of their presence. He was shrivelled and dishevelled. His hair was matted and his skin, which hung loose from his face and neck, was grey and flaky. His eyes were vacant and watery and almost translucent. His limbs were trembling slightly, each one to a different rhythm. Around his neck he wore a cotton bib, a larger version of those worn by babies. It was soiled with a combination of food and saliva, a trail of which leaked from the right side of his mouth. This was a husk of a man, almost unrecognisable as a functioning human being. Seeing *Chafa* like this was a shock. It was not at all what Staverley or Margarida had expected. They looked at one another, and Staverley thought he could see tears forming in Margarida's eyes.

"Poor man," Aina said. "He's been this way for some time now. Every time I come up I expect to find that he has passed, but he hangs on, he won't let go. I don't know what keeps him going, it's no life. And he's difficult to deal with for the staff, difficult to keep clean and to get to eat and to move. We do our best. He has his moments but most of the time he just stares into space. On his good days he can manage a few words but he's better with old memories than anything in the present. He talks about someone called Conchita sometimes, or talks to her more like."

Neither Staveley nor Margarida could think of anything to say.

"If you want to talk to him and find out if he is your relative you should go ahead, but don't expect anything sensible. I don't think this is a good day. I've got to get back for the lunch, so I'll leave you to it." Aina hurried off down the corridor.

Staverley and Margarida looked around the room. It was stark and simple: easy to keep clean that way, they assumed. There did not seem to be any personal items except for a small photograph pinned on the wall next to the bed. Margarida went in and looked at it. It was of a small girl holding a large bunch of flowers and smiling. It was very old and faded, Conchita perhaps? There were no other chairs, so Margarida sat on the end of the bed and Staverley leant against the window frame. *Chafa* seemed to become aware of the movement around him and looked vaguely in Staverley's direction. The awareness did not last for long and his head began to sink back on to his chest. Staverley crouched down next to the armchair. He thought of touching the man's arm but could not bring himself to do that.

"Enrique? Senyor Chacel? My name is Staverley." Staverley said this in Castilian.

Chafa's head came up again.

"And my name is Margarida." Margarida crouched on the other side of the armchair and spoke in Catalan.

Chafa made a sound somewhere between a groan and a sigh, like a dog. They took that to mean that they had his attention. On the journey to Olot, Staverley and Margarida had talked about what they would say and what they would ask if they met with *Chafa,* but it was obvious that many of those questions would now be impossible. Margarida did her best.

"Do you remember the war Senyor Chacel?"

Chafa looked in her direction, turning his head very slowly, and he seemed to be trying to focus on her and what she was saying but he made no response.

"Do you remember SIM?"

His gaze moved and became fixed over her left shoulder in the direction of the photograph on the wall. Again there was no response.

"Do you remember your time in Barcelona?"
Still nothing.
"Do you remember Orlov?"
Chafa's gaze shifted again and he struggled to speak. What emerged was a kind of flat chuckle, hollow and mean sounding, and then he said, "Orlov." His trembling limbs were still.

"Yes, Orlov, do you remember him. You worked together in Barcelona."

Chafa looked to be making an effort to engage with Margarida. He gestured limply with his hand toward the glass of water on the bedside cabinet. Margarida picked it up and held it for him while he gulped down several swallows, a lot of the water spilling from his mouth and running down on to his bib.

"Remember," he said, dribbling more water down his chin, "remember Orlov". He spoke in Catalan and produced another sour chuckle.

"Orlov. The Russian. He ran away. Eau de Cologne. Truncheon. Bad times. Bad man."

Each word was an effort, and between them he sucked air into his lungs and his chest rattled noisily and alarmingly. The years of smoking cheroots had obviously taken their toll. At the end of the sequence of words he struggled hard for a breath. He struggled for so long that Margarida and Staverley both thought it was not coming, but he managed eventually.

"Who else, Senyor Chacel, or *Chafa*? Can I call you *Chafa*? Who else did you work with?"

Margarida was doing her best to maintain a connection with the man and his past and elicited another chuckle like response.

"*Chafa*. Long time. *Chafa's* dead and gone."
"Who else did *Chafa* work with, who else?"
There was another struggle, or rather two, in his body and his mind: a struggle to remember and a struggle to speak. This involved another series of ragged breaths and a lot of licking of his lips to get them moving. It was painful to watch.

"Unit. Team. Orlov and *Chafa*."
"And who else?"
"Orlov and Chafa and *El Traje*. Unit. Watch, take, act. Questions, always questions."

He attempted more words but there was no more breath, nothing more came. He seemed to be giving up the struggle to speak.

"Who was *El Traje*? Who was he?" Margarida persevered but she could see that she was losing Chafa's attention. His head moved again to her left and his focus drifted there. Whatever connection she had made with his past was broken; he had retreated into whatever netherworld or half-consciousness he now inhabited. His hands began to tremble again and his head dropped to one side, and another bubble of saliva began to build up in the corner of his mouth.

"That's it, I think. That's all we're going to get," Margarida said, and Staverley nodded back.

"Let's go," he said, "let's leave him."

They tip-toed out of the room, although that seemed hardly necessary. Downstairs lunch was now being served; they could smell the food and hear the clatter of plates and the murmur of conversation from the communal dining room. The staff were busy and no one noticed as Margarida and Staverley left the building. They felt bad for not thanking Aina for her help but they were both eager for some fresh air.

"I need a stiff drink." Margarida said, and Staverley agreed.

It was not easy to find somewhere to eat or drink on market day. People's minds were now moving from shopping to lunch. Staverley and Margarida walked through the narrow streets of the medieval centre of the city, jostling with the crowds, they turned down an even narrower side street and found the entrance to a restaurant at the bottom of a short flight of steps. Inside, the space was larger than seemed possible from the outside. It was a converted cellar with a low vaulted ceiling. The tables were packed close together, and the noise of talk and laughter was like a wall of sound, but there were two free tables in the furthest corner and they took one. The menu was chalked on a board on the wall and Margarida offered to order for them both. A waiter quickly appeared and after no more than a raised eyebrow, which Staverley assumed was a response to his dietary preference, rushed off again to collect bread, water and a carafe of red wine. They sat in silence for a while as they both quickly downed a glass of the wine. It was warm and fruity, and left behind a taste like sultanas. When the food came Margarida enjoyed her various parts and combinations of pig, and Staverley equally enjoyed his dishes of vegetables. Staverley was first to speak.

"I think I grasped most of that, it wasn't difficult, except *El Traje*, what or who was that?"

"Well, straightforwardly it means The Suit, you know, like a suit of clothes. I assumed it was another nickname, like *Chafa*. And if that's the case then my guess is that it most likely refers to the man in the hat, which makes sense if you think about it and the way the interviewees described him."

"I can see that. But does it help?"

"I don't know," Margarida replied, "but maybe that doesn't matter now. Here we are, we've seen *Chafa* and we've talked to him. How do you feel about it?"

Staverley gave a grim smile.

"I was hoping you weren't going to ask, because I'm really confused about how I feel, -or rather, I feel lots of contradictory things. I can't not feel sorry for him. What a way to live is that? But then at the same time I'm glad. I think he deserves it. Perhaps that's his punishment. He's being tortured now. He's a prisoner and he's suffering. But then I wonder, if he doesn't remember what he's done, there's no possibility of regret. If he doesn't know where he is and what he is, then maybe there's no suffering. And part of me wants him to suffer, while another part of me can't bear it. No human being should be reduced to that. He just exists. What's the point? Why is he still here? What makes him cling to life? What about you?"

Margarida finished chewing another piece of pig.

"I'm the same exactly. I was shocked to see him, it was sad. And then I remembered what his victims had described and, like you said, it seemed like some sort of retribution. His body and his mind have turned against him. Possibly at some level he was aware of the evil he had been part of and is punishing himself, at least I hope so, or maybe he's wiped out the memories of what he's done so he doesn't have to live with them. So, like you say, you can see it the other way as an escape, as not having to face or live with what he's done. Perhaps his mind could only cope by wiping out everything and existing in another place where there is no need to think about what he did, maybe with the little girl in the picture, whoever she is. That could be the one good memory he has. But it's all speculation. I don't think there's a simple resolution, at least I don't feel like there is."

Staverley was impressed.

"It may be speculation but what you say makes a lot of sense. I would go along with that. And you're right, there's no resolution here, and I can understand better now some of the things that Arnau said. I assume that he thinks that he doesn't need to do more because of what is being done to *Chafa* already, or what *Chafa* is doing to himself. Who knows? And you can pity the man, knowing at the same time that he had no pity for others. Mind you, what's happening to *Chafa* happens to other people. Bad things happen to good people as well."

They slipped back into their own thoughts until the waiter returned to offer coffees, which they both wanted. Then it was time to start back. On the way to the car Staverley bought some vegetables, they looked too good to miss, and some cracked green olives, that were just slightly bitter, and a piece of aged *manchego* cheese that crumbled as it was cut from a large round, and then some dried fruits. Margarita indulged her Catalan heritage with some strangely shaped sausages tied together with string. "Some for me and some for Papa," she said.

On the drive back they picked over again and again the things *Chafa* had said, even though there was not that much to work with, and they speculated further about *El Traje*. There were no great insights. They stopped in the car park at Coll Formic to give Margarida a break and to enjoy the views for a while.

"If you come up here on your own," Margarida explained, "you can either walk up to the left, to *Matagalls*, the second highest peak in the Montseny, which is a very steep climb, or to the right to *Pla de la Calma*, which is not so hard. They are very different, and the Pla has lots of interesting birds."

Staverley invited Margarida into the house when they got to Sant Pere but she was tired and wanted to get back to Barcelona. They agreed they would both think more about the visit and swop ideas later in the week. Staverley was also tired, emotionally rather than physically. He wrote a letter to Monica, telling her about the trip to Olot and what they had found, then made himself a sandwich with his Manchego cheese and opted for an early night. To his surprise, he slept very well.

The next morning Staverley decided to begin work on a preliminary paper based on his research on the coast, describing the background to the exploitation of the Costa Brava for tourism over the previous twenty years. That would be a way of trying out some of his ideas, and could also serve as the basis for an introduction to his book. When he returned to Watermouth, Lionel, his Head of Department, would expect to see some product from the sabbatical, and a draft paper and a book in progress would be a reasonable return to report. The days when sabbaticals were an opportunity to laze in the sun or catch up on reading were long gone. More and more it was expected that you would account for your time, and demonstrate you that were good value for money. Thank you very much, Margaret Thatcher, Staverley thought.

After nearly three hours of very focused and very satisfying writing Staverley was interrupted by a firm thump of iron on wood. He made his way down stairs and pulled open the heavy front door. A man stood outside. He was dressed in trousers, jacket and tie, and held a grey trilby hat in his hands. There was a large white car parked at the curb behind him - another man sitting behind the wheel. "Señor Staverley, good morning. May I speak with you?"

The man nodded formally and spoke in English with an accent that was not local. It took Staverley a second of two to recognise his caller. He opened the door wider to let the man.

"Capitán Lopez, please come in."

The Capitán turned and gestured toward the man in the car and then entered. He looked around.

"An interesting house, Señor, very traditional. I hope you are enjoying your time with us?"

"I am, thank you, very much indeed. Can I offer you a coffee?"

"Thank you, no. I require just a few moments of your time. Perhaps we could sit?"

"Of course." Staverley pulled out chairs from the kitchen table and they both sat. Staverley wondered if he should be worried. It's not everyday that an officer of the Guardia Civil pays you a visit. But the Capitán seemed friendly enough, certainly more so than when they had met in Inspector Rodriguez' office.

"Please, let me explain myself. This is not a visit that I would normally make and what I am going to say I would not normally share with a civilian, or at least not all I have to say. But Señor you have been of some service to my Department and in recognition of that I felt it proper to speak with you about various developments that may be of interest to you. My superiors have agreed."

Staverley had no idea what the Capitán meant by him being of service, or what it might be that was to be shared, but he was intrigued. The Capitán seemed to require a response before he continued. He carefully placed his hat on the table.

"Do go on, Capitán. I am listening carefully." That appeared to be the right thing to have said.

"Your activities here in Catalunya have required the attention of *la Policía* and *La Guardia* in a number of respects. You have been, shall we say busy, during your time with us. But on that we will not dwell. You have also acquired a number of friends who speak well of you, which is important. Such friends are always important in Spain. "

Another response seemed to be needed.

"I do appreciate their confidence," Staverley said. Again that seemed to be appropriate.

"Just so. Then I have four items to report to you, in fact. First, and perhaps most important to you, two days ago a Señor Montilla called at the *Policía Munipal* station in Sant Celoni in a state of considerable agitation. It turned out that he had been severely disturbed by his conscience for some time and wanted to make a confession. He confessed to having hit with his car a man riding a ciclo on the road from Arenys to Sant Celoni one morning three weeks ago, and then driving away without stopping. He was also most concerned to know whether the man he hit had been injured or even killed. He was, he said, prepared to face the consequences of his actions. Señor Montilla was extremely relieved to know that the man - you, of course - had survived the incident and was making a good recovery from his injuries. Señor Montilla was most anxious that the police convey to the man his most sincere apologies and to express the sense of shame he now felt for his actions both in causing the accident and in driving away from the scene. On behalf of the police and Señor Montilla I am now doing that. But I should also say that Señor Montilla has been charged with a serious traffic offence and faces the possibility of a term of imprisonment. Nonetheless, he feels more at peace with himself having made is confession."

Staverley was at a loss to know what to say. He had never expected to know who had almost killed him that day on the mountain. Neither had he expected that, if he did come to know, it would be a random motorist with no apparent connection to the Calabrian mafia.

"I am stunned, Capitán. I had assumed that I would know nothing more about what happened that day. Despite the best efforts of the police," he added. "I am pleased that the man came forward and I hope he feels better knowing that he had not killed me." That did not sound quite right, but the Capitán seemed to understand what he meant.

"Quite so, a satisfactory conclusion, at least as far as the police are concerned. Of course, you may want to pursue the matter further through your legal representatives." Staverley assumed that referred to some claim for compensation.

"I don't think so, Capitán, it is enough to know what happened, and despite everything I hope Senyor Montilla does not end up in prison."

The Capitán appeared to approve of that response.

"With your permission, I could convey your sentiments to the office of the prosecutor?"

"Yes, please do that."

"Very well then, the second matter. I know from Inspector Rodriquez that you have taken a certain interest in the death of Señora Puig and that your interest may have extended beyond the asking of questions."

Staverley assumed that this was a reference to Nuria getting him a copy of the post-mortem report. They exchanged a look and the Capitán continued.

"I wanted to say on behalf of my Department and the police that despite a somewhat inconclusive report from the forensic examiner the case remains open and under investigation, and some progress has been made. That progress I cannot share with you but be reassured that the case is active."

"I am pleased and reassured to hear that, Capitán. I can't accept that her death was accidental, I know that it is a possibility, but to me it seems very unlikely."

He could have said more but thought it best to leave the police and the *Guardia* to do their work. He would pursue his suspicions in his own way. He and the Capitán exchanged another look. Staverley understood now that there was a sub-text to this visit and the conversation, and that meant not saying things that he and the Capitán were nonetheless both cognisant of.

"Your concern is noted Señor." The Capitán nudged his hat forward a few centimetres with the tip of his fore finger.

"So then the third matter I will mention relates to another death. That is the brutal murder of Señor Batlló-Sabé, who we now know you met on a number of occasions."

"Yes, he was very helpful with my research and he had also been a friend of my father, a very long time ago. I wanted him to tell me about my father and their time together during the Civil War. They were comrades in POUM, the anarchist brigade."

'That I did not know, Señor Staverley.'

Staverley could see the Capitán making a mental note, and could imagine some comments being added to a file somewhere. The Capitán leaned forward and moved his hat very precisely a few centimetres to the right.

"I know that there was some discussion between yourself and Inspector Rodriguez that the murder of Batlló-Sabé might have some connection with his construction and financial activities and that some outside interests related to those activities might be complicit in his death. This was taken very seriously. Both things have been considered and investigated thoroughly, however for the moment we have dismissed both possibilities…"

Staverley was about to interrupt, but the Capitán raised his hand.

"We are at present pursuing a different line of inquiry which suggests that the murder might be a much more domestic matter, if I can put it that way, or closer to home I think is the English expression."

Staverley opened his mouth again to speak but the Capitán raised his hand again.

"If I may? I can say nothing more about our ongoing inquires as regard the murder, other than that we expect to make an announcement very soon, but there are other matters of interest that pertain to the information you were able to share with us: the fourth item that is."

The Capitán shifted his hat to the left and removed a speck of dust from the brim.

"The financial crimes division of *La Guardia* have identified a number of issues of concern regarding the buying and selling of land by Batlló-Sabé's consortium and some of the sources of their funding. The accounts of the consortium have been frozen, contact has been made with the appropriate police authorities in one other country, and the State's Prosecutor is preparing a number of indictments. His office and my colleagues are grateful to you for alerting them to these… What should I say, interferences from abroad. We are now expanding our inquiries to examine a number of other such interferences."

Staverley took the Capitán's guarded account to mean that the *N'Drangherta* were involved in some way in supplying money to Batlló-Sabé, and having that money laundered, and that the German foreign intelligence service was cooperating in tracing the sources of that money. But he was surprised that the involvement of the mafia in Batlló-Sabé's death was now discounted. He would have liked to ask more questions about that, but further questions were clearly not intended to be part of the very odd exchange that was going on. Staverley knew he was meant to be grateful for the latitude that allowed the Capitán to tell him things that would normally be kept in-house, and he was grateful, if a little frustrated. He was pleased, though, that for the time being at least the wonderful beach at Palamós would be safe from the greedy ambitions of the developers. The Capitán was already making a move to leave. He picked up his hat from the table and stood. He twirled the hat in his left hand.

"Thank you for coming, Capitán. I know that you did not have to, and I do appreciate it."

The Capitán managed a facial rearrangement that almost resembled a smile. It did not last..

"And thank you also for doing all of this in your excellent English. You put my language skills to shame."

The Capitán nodded.

"I had the opportunity to work on my English during a secondment to Interpol, and my ongoing contact with colleagues there has been of enormous help with our current enquiries into the international movement of money. But such an investigation is nonetheless fraught with difficulties, as I am sure you will appreciate."

Staverley took this to mean that he should not expect to hear of an easy resolution of the question of money laundering. From the reading he had done and from talking with Feliu he had begun to grasp how difficult it was to track and trace mafia money. They were increasingly adept at disguising their ill-gotten gains. Staverley opened the door and he and the Capitán shook hands.

"A pleasure, Señor."
"And for me, Capitán."
"Enjoy the remainder of your stay."
The man in the car got out and hurried around to open the back door. The Capitán tossed his hat inside and slid in himself. Staverley stood at the roadside as the car moved away, and as soon as it was out of sight he started to go through in his mind everything he had been told. If it were all true then he had to accept that many of the suspicions he had harboured over the past few weeks were misplaced. More than anything, though, he was pleased that he would not have to be constantly thinking about who might be behind him every time he used the ciclo, and he could not help but feel sorry for Senyor Montilla and his guilty conscience. He could imagine that what had probably been an ordinary and uneventful life was now in chaos and in doubt.

It was difficult to concentrate on work after the Capitán's visit. Staverley had planned to do some reading after lunch, but found himself instead drawn back to thinking about the implications of what had been said - and not said. After another *manchego* sandwich, with tomato, salt and olive oil rubbed into the bread, Staverley decided to take a walk. He headed toward the Montseny and the hermitage of Sant Elies. He had seen it signposted from the road, and had wondered what exactly it was. Whatever it was, after an hour and a half on an increasingly steep and fractured path it still appeared to be a long way off and a lot higher up, and he reluctantly turned back. An earlier start on another day, he told himself. The strenuous walking had cleared his mind somewhat and stretched the muscles in his legs. His inactivity since the ciclo crash had been a set back in his attempt to become a proper mountain walker. One thing he decided on his way back down to Sant Pere was that it was time to talk again with Joan. He knew he had to offer his condolences for Batlló-Sabé at some point, and that he should report on the meetings he had had with Arnau and *Chafa*. And Joan might have his own ideas about Batlló-Sabé's murder. Back in the village, Staverley called at the Bodega to ask David about Joan's next delivery. If that were too far off he would make another trip to find Joan on the mountain. As it turned out, Joan was expected the next day, or the one after, and David promised to ask him if he would call on Staverley.

Chapter 13

It was two days before Joan appeared in Sant Pere. He knocked on
Staverley's door mid-morning and explained that he had shopping to
do but would be happy to meet for lunch in the restaurant in the old
main street. Joan was already seated, working on some papers, when
Staverley arrived: his accounts, he explained. He looked thinner than
when they had met before but fit and healthy nonetheless, his cheeks a
ruddy brown contoured by deep wrinkles, his long hair pulled back
and fixed in a leather clasp.

"What did you deliver today?"

"It was a mixed load. Some cheeses of course but also several boxes of
mushrooms and some early chestnuts. There will be more in a few
weeks. The mountain gives up its bounty at this time of year."

Staverley had been wondering about Joan's visits to Sant Pere.

"I meant to ask you before how you managed to get your produce
down here. I remember you saying that you did not have a car or
truck."

"I'm lucky, I have a friend who has a small farm below me on the
mountain, the other side of the road. He lets me borrow his van when I
need it. The donkey, Platero, the one you met, carries the boxes down
to his farm and then waits for me there and carries my shopping back
up. It's simple really and Platero enjoys the outing."

They ordered some lunch. The waiter was used to Staverley's odd
eating habits by now and he started with a plate of potatoes and
acelgas. Joan declined the wine and Staverley abstained as well. He
was unsure how to begin with the things he wanted to say.

"Joan, I want to tell you how sorry I am about the death of your friend
Jordi, Senyor Batlló-Sabé. It must have been a shock."

Joan looked up from his plate of pig's cheek and gave a weary smile
and shook his head.

"At my age young Staverley death is never a shock. One waits for it; the
question is will it be you first or your friends? And you know I am not

sure that Batlló-Sabé was my friend. Our relationship had become strained by the passage of time and events. We never recovered the closeness of our time in the Militia. His life and mine had become very different; our values had become very different. And I did not like the things he was doing to Catalunya. But I will mourn him nonetheless and I am sorry for his wife and his sons. I only met them once but they seemed like nice people and he was a good husband and father, that was very obvious. The manner of his death is a different thing, that was a shock. Do you know whether anyone has been arrested?"

Staverley explained what he had discovered about Batlló-Sabé's business dealings and his business partners and his own suspicions about the *N'Hangdreta,* and he passed on what he had been told by the Capitán.

"That all seems quite incredible to me. I had no idea that Jordi might be involved in fraud and money laundering. He always seemed such a proper person, and careful about money and everything else. When we fought together we always said that if we were all killed that Jordi would be the last to go because he was much more aware of the risks than the rest of us. Not that he was cowardly, not at all, he was a brave man, but he never acted without precautions, which was good for all of us. He stopped us from doing foolhardy things. Like others we often acted with bravado rather than with strategy. But it seems I did not know him as well as I thought, or perhaps he had changed. I know while I was hidden away he was travelling and experiencing things I could only read about."

"So you don't have any ideas about who might have wanted him dead, other than the Mafia?" Staverley asked.

Joan shook his head and took another mouthful of his food.

"I can make no sense of what you were told by the Capitán. Jordi's family life was settled and I was never aware that he had relationships with women outside of his marriage or had enemies. His personal life seemed quite uneventful."

Staverley finished his vegetables and began to explain to Joan about the things he had found out from the project of remembering and the interviews and the accounts of Orlov and *Chafa* and the man with the hat, and his subsequent visits to talk with Arnau and see *Chafa* in Olot. Joan stopped eating and listened carefully. His expression was difficult to read. When Staverley had finished Joan pushed away the unfinished plate.

"I do not know what to say. When we spoke of these people, when you came to the mountain, I never imagined them being alive still. I thought of them as part of the past, certainly not part of the present. I had known that Orlov was dead and I assumed the others would be too. I don't know why but I suppose I thought of them as having too many enemies and too many secrets. So much has happened over the years, so many people have died. How were they able to survive?"

Staverley understood Joan's surprise. He had set out with the same expectation and yet all of the key characters in his father's story, apart from Orlov, were still living, or had been until Batlló-Sabé's murder. The only one not accounted for was the man in the hat.

"It does seem unlikely, who knows, perhaps even the third man still lives, we know nothing of him beyond the glimpses from the interviews. The one new thing, the only thing really that came out of the trip to Olot was a name, or a nickname rather. *Chafa* called the man in the hat *El Traje*, but I don't know what that means, or if it helps in any way in identifying him. Perhaps I should be content with what I now know."

Joan put both his hands on his head and scratched hard at his scalp. He seemed agitated but waved to the waiter to order a *crema catalana*. Staverley was not keen on deserts and asked for a coffee. Joan cracked the hard burnt sugar on the surface of his *crema* with the back of a spoon and ate quickly.

"I have thought about your father and the men who took him many times since you came to visit me. I have tried to remember more about what I saw and about what he told me afterwards. But perhaps it is not good to think so much. Perhaps there comes a time when the past should be left to its own devices. And now I must go, Platero is waiting, he will be anxious if I am late."

Joan's mood had changed and his departure seemed very sudden but Staverley realised that he may have upset his father's friend with so many sudden revelations and talk of Batlló-Sabé's death. They paid for their lunches and walked together to Joan's van. Joan said his farewells quickly and drove off. But after a few metres he stopped the van and waved Staverley forward.

"Next week, Friday, come to the farm. We will begin with your lessons in cheese making."

Joan did not wait for a reply but Staverley was pleased with the invitation and stood and waved as the van pulled away. He put Joan's abruptness down to the disturbing topics of their conversation and perhaps also the lack of company on the mountain and his many years in hiding. With no one to talk to but his donkey and the goats, social niceties were probably of little importance. Staverley could see that Joan had stopped the van again outside David's Bodega, to collect his provisions he assumed. Before he caught up Joan had driven off again. David was closing up for the afternoon as he passed and wished him well. Staverley returned home and lay down for a while. At four he planned to go to Sant Celoni on his ciclo to work in the library. The very helpful librarian had ordered up a set of old newspapers that reported the events around the successful campaign to protect *Aigüamolls* from the building of the marina. He also wanted to see if Nuria was in her office and whether she might want to meet for a drink. He wanted to tell her about the Capitán's visit.

The newspapers were useful and as before the librarian was very willing to help with translations of the words and phrases Staverley found impossible. There were a lot of those. When he had finished in the library he walked to Nuria's office but it was closed and there was no one inside. He wrote a message to Nuria on a page torn from his notebook, saying he wanted to see her, and pushed it into the letterbox. He sat in a café across the street for a while in case she returned, and sipped half-heartedly at a beer. Since lunch he had had the feeling in the back of his mind that he was missing something in all the recollections he had accumulated about his father's experiences in Catalunya: a connection, something or some things that he knew or had been told but could not join up. After half and hour he gave up waiting and retrieved the ciclo for his journey back to Sant Pere. The

afternoons were getting shorter and he was very careful driving back
in the fading light as the ciclo had no lights.

**

Joan did not change his routine but the calmness and contentment he
normally experienced during his excursions with the goats, and his
cheese making and his reading in the evenings, were proving elusive.
In the early morning he walked down the mountain into the trees with
his basket, to a spot he had harvested many times in the past, but there
were few mushrooms to be had, or perhaps his attention had
wandered and he was missing some prize specimens. That evening
also he could not settle into his book, a history of the French
Revolution, and changed it for a novel. He was working through the
books of Graham Greene, the English Catholic writer, and turned to
Brighton Rock and the sociopathic Pinkie Brown. The night was quiet,
the afternoon wind had dropped and the mountain had taken on a
mantle of heavy silence. He could hear an owl hooting nearby - or was
it more than one? The bells that some of the goats wore around their
necks tinkled as they moved in their pen. The rasping of one rock
against another at the side of the house might have been an animal
passing by, a wild boar or deer. Joan put down his book carefully and
turned out his reading lamp. He crossed the room and stood in an
alcove between two of his enormous bookshelves. There was normally
a small cupboard standing in the space, in which he kept his personal
documents, but he had moved it earlier in that day. He was all but
invisible in the low light from the oil lamp on the kitchen table. He
waited. Several minutes passed, and he continued to wait. There was a
soft but distinct clunk as someone put their weight against the front
door and moved the iron door handle. It was impossible to do that
silently. There was a further wait and the door began to open very
slowly. When there was space enough to pass through, a figure darkly
dressed, wearing what looked like a beret and carrying a shotgun,
slipped into the room and stood in the corner where coats hung on the
wall. It was impossible for Joan to tell whether it was a man or woman.
The figure raised the shotgun waist high and turned slowly to survey
the room. The barrel of the gun passed across Joan's alcove without

stopping and the figure crept forward, heading carefully on tip-toe toward the staircase that led up to the bedroom. As the intruder passed Joan's hiding place he stepped out and struck the figure on the neck with a cosh, a leather bag filled with lead shot. The intruder collapsed like the proverbial sack of potatoes and the gun clattered across the stone floor.

When Subirachs woke, he was tied securely to one of the heavy chairs in the kitchen. His neck ached and he felt dizzy and a little nauseous. Joan held a glass to his mouth so he could drink some water.

"Hello Jaume, as you can see I was expecting you. You obviously got my message. I'm glad you could come."

"Don't be foolish, Joan." Subirachs tried to move his arms but the leather straps, from which Joan made the collars for the goats, were impossible to loosen.

"You are right, I am foolish, I have been foolish for many years. Foolish to think you were my friend, foolish not to realise who you really were, foolish not to be able to make sense of what I saw that day outside the house in Barcelona. But now I've done being foolish and I want to know all about you and the things you have done, things now and things then. And when you have told me those things I will decide what is to be done with you."

Subirachs struggled again but the straps were tight and strong.

"Why should I tell you anything?"

"Why should you? I could say that I think you owe it to me, to us. But I think that we are beyond such an appeal. I can wait. We can sit. You can remain silent. There is nothing to do until morning. I can doze, but you might become uncomfortable after a while in the chair, I certainly would. Cramp would probably be the worst thing, especially as you are unable to move your legs. Cramp can be excruciating. And then there's the problem of the toilet. Men like you and I, men of our age, tend to need to go more often than we did when younger, and the feeling of a full bladder and the urgent need to empty it, that can also be very painful, and of course embarrassing in due course if we do not heed the call. It is your choice."

Joan waited, and Subirachs held out for a few more minutes.

"All right, what do you want to know?" His voice was husky and coarse. He still sounded reluctant and recalcitrant.

"Everything. I want to know who you are. Start with the Russians, start there."

"Then untie my legs."

"Not yet. You need to show me that you deserve something first. Isn't that how it works?"

Subirachs struggled again in the chair but his movements only seemed to make the ties bite deeper into his flesh. He stopped and asked for more water. Joan held the glass to his mouth again. Once he had drunk he fixed his gaze at a point above Joan's head and began to talk.

"I was recruited by a man I met in a café. The Russians wanted people who could find out things, who knew people, who could tell them when Trotsky was coming. They really believed that Trotsky was coming to Spain, or at least Stalin did. The NKVD recruited people through the Spanish Communist Party, people who were then encouraged to join the militias like I did, or work with the Unions. There was always a tension between the anarchists and the communists in Catalunya, you know that, and there were plenty of volunteers from the Party willing to go under cover and feed back information. That's what I did, and there were advantages. Many did those things, became informers, for their politics, they were zealots. I did them for myself and for money. When I wasn't at the front I could lead a different sort of life, I could buy proper clothes, go dancing, meet women, forget about the war and the killing and the constant drudgery. Even going to clubs and bars could be useful for gathering information. There were conversations that might be overheard, tongues loosened by drink, confidences shared. And I was good at it, getting people to trust me and to talk to me, just like you and Jordi and Jack trusted me. That's when Orlov took me on as part of one of his action units, that's what he called them. He was impressed by what I had reported. So for him I was supposed to identify targets for interrogation, people who worked with the Militia leaders or had contacts with foreigners of whom the Russians were suspicious. *Chafa* would follow them and watch them and then they were arrested and questioned. I didn't take part in the torture, I really didn't, I hated that part. If I was made to be there when it happened it was just to suggest questions, what would be best to ask about, what the person might know. And I tried to get them to stop when I thought there was nothing more to be known, and sometimes they did stop, but not always. And some people were just stubborn and wouldn't say anything. That was the worst. Orlov would get mad then, and things would get messy. I regret all of that, you have to believe me, I told myself I was doing it for the Republic, we were eliminating subversives. And I tried to make myself believe that, I did. It wasn't like I was working for the Fascists."

Subirachs began to cry, tears ran down his face and a line of snot dribbled from his nose. Joan said nothing. His one-time friend had become a pleading, drivelling wretch.

"Orlov encouraged me to get elected to the revolutionary committee in POUM, and that meant I got to know things about Nin and the other leaders and I could make trips to Barcelona for meetings. Orlov especially wanted information about the international brigaders who had joined POUM, particularly Orwell. He wanted Orwell badly. You know they tried him later, in his absence, after he had gone back to England. They found him guilty of rabid Trotskyism. Orlov also sent me to find out how the wounded POUM brigaders were getting out of the country and who was involved in that. I always tried to make sure that none of your names were included when I made my reports but there were other agents, not just me, and when Jack and you were sent to the hospital in Barcelona I knew that Orlov would come looking. He wanted Jack, he thought he could tell him where Orwell was, and he sent me to look for him. And I did look, but I was going to warn him, tell him to run, I was, but *Chafa* found him first, he was good at that, finding people. There was nothing I could do then, nothing. I did try."

"But why, Jaume, why? Just for money?" Joan's voice was shaking with emotion.

"Not just the money, I was different. I wasn't like you and the others, I wasn't political, I wasn't committed. I was there fighting because I wasn't brave enough to say no, I went along with things because I was weak. When the lorries came to collect volunteers I jumped aboard like my neighbours and friends did. I did what was expected, what others were doing. It all seemed heroic and exciting at the beginning and when I met with you three I wanted to be your friend and stand alongside you against the Fascists. I wanted to be like you. But I used to listen to the three of you talk and your convictions were clear in your voices, your certainty that you were doing the right thing, you were all there for a reason, you were defending freedom, securing a better future, all those grand ideals. I never said but I thought you were fools to believe that the world could change or could be changed, and that Franco could be beaten by our rag-tag, people's army, even with the Russians helping. I just wanted to be left alone, I wanted my old life back, the cafes and music and women. Orlov gave me that opportunity, and I was looked after, protected, and I was useful. Those times when I went back to Barcelona I could wear proper clothes, and I could afford good ones. Probably the best times of all were when I went to my tailor's, being measured up for a new suit, being shown the latest shirts from Paris, picking out a new pair of cufflinks. I could forget about the war and the dirt and the violence, I could be ordinary and live an ordinary life, my own life. That's all I wanted really, just to be ordinary and to be safe. And Orlov wasn't all that different from me, I began to realise that. It wasn't all about the Party and politics. He was a cruel man, but never cruelty for its own sake, except sometimes when he lost his temper. It was about efficiency, a means to an end, about getting things done for his political masters, for Stalin. Behind all of his Communist jargon about deviationists, counter-revolutionaries, his politics were a pretence, and he was fearful about his own future and the safety of his family. He knew Stalin was a tyrant, little different from Franco. You know that he ran away. He got wind that they were coming for him and he ran away."

Subirachs sniffed loudly and tried to gather himself. Joan wiped his face with a cloth and gave him more water.

"So what happened to you?"

"I tried to run away too, to disappear. POUM was gone and those who were left were integrated into the army and I didn't want that so I hid, but *Chafa* found me and he told me that SIM had things they needed me to do. I wasn't given much option, either to work for them or to be sent to the front. But then after Ebro, when the Nationalists marched into Catalunya, I was able to get away as everything fell apart and I crossed into France and eventually ended up in the Dominican Republic. There were people from the CNT there who helped me, and who later enabled me to get back to France. They saw me as a patriot, as one of them, a valued comrade. And things went well for me in France for a while. I met my wife there and I had a good job, until one day *Chafa* came calling, he found me again. He was BPS then, Franco's secret police, and there was another ultimatum, provide information about the exiles in France and their activities and plans or he would tell the people who had helped me and I had worked with what I had done and who I had been. I knew that would be a death sentence, so I worked for *Chafa* and the BPS reporting on the activities of the marquis, the Resistance, back in Spain and identifying *enlaces*, the helpers and supporters, and tracing the leaders and organisers, like *La Pastora*, *El Quico* and *Caraquemada* – they all had *noms de guerre*. But when *El Quico* and *Caraquemada* were killed in the early '60s the marquis were more or less finished and *Chafa* stopped calling. I wasn't useful any more. By that time I was becoming significant in the work of the ERC in exile. Ironic, don't you think, me a non-believer and a traitor becoming a respected politico, a man of integrity, fighter against Franco, and all the time I was giving Franco's secret police information that led to the torture and death of his real opponents! My life has been built on lies, I know that, and I've lived with it, and all the time I just wanted to be left alone."

His head sank on to his chest. He looked exhausted, and bitter and ashamed. Then he raised his head and looked at Joan.

"And now it's you, you won't leave me alone, you and the Englishman, you want to dig up the past, you want to know what happened. Him asking questions about who betrayed you and his father and making you think and Jordi think. And that stupid woman, who thought she recognised me, and then Jordi remembering things, and making me have to deal with them both. I didn't want to kill them, especially not Jordi, but I had to, I couldn't face it all being in the open. It was my life I was protecting and my family. It's too late for revelations and revenge or whatever. That's why there's an amnesty and the forgetting. I have a reputation, a daughter, and they were not going to take those things away from me. I had to stop them."

His head sank again.

"Well, now you know. It was me, I was the betrayer. I'm the one Jack wrote about. You've got me and you have to decide what to do with me."

Now there was defiance in Subirachs' voice, as if he was trying to challenge Joan. Joan remained calm. He felt a mix of pity and disgust.

"That is the question: What to do with you?"

**

Staverley was looking forward to returning to the mountain and to Joan's house and he was really intrigued by the idea of getting involved in making cheese. It was another of the things he could never have anticipated when he was planning his trip to Catalunya. He left Sant Pere early. He had bought himself a pair of walking boots and was better prepared this time for the climb up from the road. He hid the ciclo behind a rock as before and set off on the steep and rocky ascent. His various outings to walk on the Montseny were having a positive effect, building up both his leg muscles and his lung capacity. Mountain legs and mountain lungs, David had told him. Senyora Budó had insisted again that he take something to sustain him on his journey, and he stopped to eat on the way. He sat on a large rock and enjoyed the view across the valley while he chewed the artichoke tortilla sandwich. He could hear a raptor calling and was entertained by a pair of eagles soaring and tumbling in the sky above him. Eagles were fairly common in the Montseny, and using a bird book he had bought in Sant Celoni he had identified four different types. He had also seen his first hoopoe from the window of the house in Sant Pere – a bird designed by a committee.

His sandwich devoured, he continued up the track, stopping occasionally to listen for the bells of the goats, but he knew that Joan ranged far and wide with the herd, to find new grazing and so as not to over graze the area closest to the house. When he arrived at the house he had still seen no sign of Joan nor heard the goats, so he settled down to wait on the wooden bench beside the front door. It was surprisingly comfortable, having been worn smooth by centuries of use. He had brought a book for exactly this eventuality. He was reading an English Penguin translation of *Fortunata y Jacinta* by Benito Perez Galdos, that he had found in a second-hand shop. It was a key novel in the tradition of nineteenth century Spanish realism. He was enjoying it. He read on and off for nearly two hours, pausing occasionally to watch passing animals and birds, before he heard the bells in the distance. It was another twenty minutes before he saw the first of the goats and then Joan with his shepherd's stick, striding behind them.

Joan looked pleased to see him and they exchanged an embrace. Staverley helped to usher the goats into their pen and then Joan excused himself. He wanted to wash after the long morning on the mountain. He asked Staverley to make coffee and to toast some bread. As soon as he returned from his ablutions Joan put his hand on Staverley's shoulder and began an apology.

"I wanted to say sorry for my rude departure when we met in Sant Pere. I will explain more, but I was distracted by something in our conversation that I needed to think about, something important and difficult. I hope you will understand."

"Please, no, I was not offended. I thought you must have had a reason. I am intrigued now."

"That's good, I am relieved. Let's drink our coffee and eat a little and then we can make cheese and talk."

They ate their toast with oil and salt and rubbed with a clove of garlic. It went well with the strong coffee. Joan began to explain the process of the cheese- making. The milk had been left to curdle and they would now be collecting the curds and putting them into muslin sacks to drain. The sacks would be left for four to eight hours. The longer they are left, the more solid the cheese becomes, he explained. Different kinds of cheese could be made that way.

The milk was kept in large metal vats in an outhouse attached to the side of the main house. Inside, it was cool and dark. They used their hands, carefully washed beforehand, and large slatted ladles, to gather the curds and fill the bags. As they worked, Joan began to talk.

"In Sant Pere, it was when you said the name *El Traje*, at that moment, after all these years, what I saw on the day your father was taken made sense. You would not believe how many times I have revisited that day in my mind. There was always something that I knew I should have understood, but I could never quite grasp it. It was like chasing a butterfly without a net; every time I got close it eluded me. Why had I watched so attentively as the fifth man walked away? What made me do that? And then over lunch what you said made it obvious.. I had been a fool, trying to think about the man all this time. It was not the man, it was the suit. He was wearing the suit, and everything else with it, that Subirachs had described to us so many times when we were together at the front. I did not recognise the man, I could not see his face, he wore the hat, but it was the clothes, the suit. That was why I watched. I had heard Subirachs go into detail about the colour, the pattern and the cut of the suit, and the shoes, shirt, tie and hat that he would wear with it. So then it was clear, and then I knew everything else. It was Subirachs who had betrayed us, his friends, the militia, and who knows who else. He was working with the Russians, for Orlov."

Staverley dropped the handful of curd he had collected back into the milk. His heart was racing and he struggled for breath. He leant on the edge of the vat and put his forehead against the cool metal. He tried to think about his meetings with Subirachs and his feelings for the man. It was difficult to get his mind to digest and deal with the idea of Subirachs as a traitor.

"But he spoke to me about his friendship with my father, with you all, he seemed so sincere. And he is a respected man. I am finding this difficult to believe."

Joan put his hand on Staverley's shoulder.

"So did I. I kept telling myself that I must be wrong, that after so many years memories are unreliable, the mind plays tricks, I had made a mistake. But once the idea was in my head other things started to make sense - Subirachs' keenness to join the Revolutionary Committee, which was unlike him, and the visits to Barcelona that that allowed him. But even so I was still sure I was wrong. I needed to put my idea to the test. So I sent a message to Subirachs, through David. I asked him to pass it on through the daughter, Nuria. It said; 'Now I remember the suit and the man who wore it. The man who betrayed us.' And then I waited."

Staverley had recovered his composure but felt a little nauseous. He sat down on a small wooden stool used for milking the goats.

"And what happened?"

"It did not take long. Two days passed and then he came in the night. He came with a gun. But he did not know how difficult it is to be silent on the mountain. The night is full of sounds even when it is quiet, if you know what I mean. I have listened to the quiet for years and I know the sounds that belong and those that do not. So he was unable to use his gun. I knocked him out and tied him up and asked him questions. He told me everything."

Joan sat on another stool face-to-face with Staverley.

"He was going to kill you?"

"I was sure that was what he intended and he admitted as much. He had killed others who suspected him. He killed Senyora Puig and Jordi and maybe others over the years. He made it clear that he would do anything to avoid being exposed for what he was. He did not want to talk at first but when he understood that he had no alternative he answered my questions and told me the other story of his life, the one he has kept hidden all these years. I never realised what a weak, calculating and disgusting person he was. To hear him made me ashamed to have been his friend."

Staverley asked if they could go outside. He needed some air. They stood side-by-side and stared across the mountain into the distance.

"This is incredible. It seems unreal. When I started out to know more about my father and the meaning of his note I never imagined that it would lead to this. And if I hadn't started asking questions of you all then Jordi might not have been killed. I thought I had led the Mafia to him, but it was Subirachs."

Joan put his hand on Staverley's shoulder again.

"Don't think that. What about Senyora Puig? He killed her because she thought she recognised him. That was nothing to do with you. And Jordi's suspicions were as much to do with Senyora Puig's death as with what you were asking. He and I had both struggled with fragments of memory over the years and the missing pieces could have been triggered for him by anything. You have no blame here. If anything it was me not understanding all these years what it was I saw that day that has brought us to this point."

They stood in silence. The stark beauty of the mountain was calming. It had witnessed many dark deeds and could not be surprised by the doings of evil and calculating men.

"Shall we finish with the cheese?" Staverley said, and they did.

After hanging the remaining sacks to drip and drain Joan suggested they have lunch. The sacks would be left for at least two hours, and as Joan had explained, the longer they hung and the drier they became the harder the final cheese would be. Joan wanted both soft and hard cheeses so they would move the curds into moulds at different times in the draining process. Joan had prepared a rich and spicy vegetable stew for lunch and had left it to gurgle gently while he walked with the goats. He brought a carafe of red wine to the table, decanted from the barrel which stood in the corner of the kitchen, and poured two large glasses, handing one to Staverley.

"I think this might be necessary," Joan said.
Staverley nodded and drank.
"Can I ask more about Subirachs?"
"Of course, you have as much right to know as anyone.
This is what he told me."
Joan recounted what Subirachs had told him about being recruited by the NKVD and by Orlov, and working for Orlov and for SIM and then later for the BPS, and the further betrayals and deaths that had come about from that. He described as best he could Subirachs' motivations, his weakness and his duplicities. Staverley was horrified.

"He was responsible for so much, so many lives lost or destroyed, so much pain. It's difficult to reconcile that with the ERC politician that everyone respects."

Joan tapped his finger hard on the table top.

"It was all a lie, he lived a lie. He did not believe anything he said or did. He was able to fool people and fool himself. He told me that he just wanted to be left alone and be ordinary, but that was never possible for him. He always had to be something else, someone else, he wasn't allowed to be ordinary he said. I could almost feel sorry for him if he had not inflicted so much suffering on others and ruined so many other lives. He was a pawn, yes, but he allowed himself to be used. He was shallow and craven."

Staverley then got to the obvious question, but the one he had been avoiding.

"So where is he now? What will happen to him?"

Joan filled their large, red ceramic bowls with stew and cut chunks of bread from a huge round loaf.

"You might want to dip the bread and clean your bowl, dunk I think is the English word. It's a little old but better that way."

They both ate and dunked. The stew was thick and adhered wonderfully to the bread.

"While I waited for him to come, and while I had him tied to that chair, sorry it was the one you are sitting on, and asked him questions, I had not thought what would come next. I think I hoped that there would be some kind of explanation and all of my doubts and fears would go away and that we would laugh about the mistake and drink some *ratafia* and reminisce. But as soon as he began to talk I knew I would have some difficult decisions to make. I thought I could take him to the police and tell them what he had told me, or I could speak to the newspapers and let him cope with the humiliation of being exposed and everything that might follow. But neither possibility seemed right, it did not seem enough. So I made a different decision, and when I tell you then you will also have a decision to make."

Staverley stopped eating and looked intently at Joan, waiting for what he would say next.

"When Subirachs finished his confession he taunted me. I think even after everything I then knew he believed he could talk his way out and that I would let him go. But there was nothing he could say that could justify what he had done and any friendship we had once had was dead. I knew by then what I had to do. I untied him, and I took his gun and we walked out onto the mountain. It was dark but the moon was up. We walked for a long time and he talked more as we walked. He made more excuses, he talked about the good things he had done as a member of parliament, he told me about how much he loved his daughter. I know the mountain very well. With the goats I have covered just about every metre. Over towards Matagalls there are some old mines. They used to dig out minerals and crystals, but they have been abandoned for many years. It is a dangerous area, the ground is unstable; some of the shafts have collapsed, some are difficult to see, some are very deep. He pleaded at the end on his knees and cried. I shot him and I pushed him into one of the deepest shafts and heaved some rocks in after him, and left him to die there. I don't think he will be found for a long time, if ever. The creatures of the mountain will probably see to that. I realised as I walked back that I had done what had happened so often in the Civil War – an execution and an unmarked grave. It took me another couple of hours to find his car hidden down by the road. I drove it to the railway station in Seva and left it there. It was a very long walk back."

Joan started eating again. Staverley did too. Joan poured more wine. They ate in a companionable silence. The bowls were emptied and refilled. When the bowls and glasses were empty again they both sat back in their chairs, replete.

"You did the right thing," Staverley said. He did not have to think hard to come to that conclusion.

"Are you sure?"

"I have no doubt. It was right. But there will be an uproar when it is realised that he has disappeared: police, newspapers... and questions."

"That may be so, but if I am asked, I think I have nothing to contribute, I have no idea what may have happened to the man. I assume you have nothing useful to say either."

"You are right, I do not. I know nothing."
Joan stood and collected the bowls.

"We must see to the cheese."

Chapter 14

Staverley thought he would be troubled by what Joan had told him, but he was not. When he said that killing Subirachs was the right thing, he meant it, and thinking further afterwards he remained absolutely sure that it was. His only doubts were about the affect on Nuria and her loss and grief - but perhaps better that than to know her father was a traitor and a murderer. At least she could hold on to the good memories she had of him and would not be subjected to humiliation and ridicule. Staverley would try to contact her again.

He had enjoyed the cheese making and Joan's company, in spite of everything. Joan was, he decided, a very wise man. He had stayed the night and ridden back to Sant Pere the next morning, slipping back with surprising ease into his routine of work on his research materials. It was two more days before Subirachs' disappearance was reported in the newspapers. A massive police hunt ensued and various theories and speculations circulated. It was three days after that before the tenor of the news coverage shifted. Police sources, it was said, had suggested that Subirachs was wanted for questioning in relation to the death of his long-time friend Jordi Batlló-Sabé. It had emerged that the two had been seen together and heard arguing on the night of the murder. The coverage was now of the possibility that Subirachs had escaped abroad to avoid the police investigation. Ports and airports were being checked. His car was found abandoned at a railway station. Joan, Staverley heard, had a cursory visit from a police constable to ask if he had seen or heard from Subirachs. He had not and was shocked by the possibility that one friend may be involved in the death of another. Staverley was not contacted. He tried telephoning Nuria but unsurprisingly in the circumstances she was not at work. He left a message. He also phoned Margarida and they shared their respective amazement about the turn of events. Margarida wondered whether Batlló-Sabé's murder was related to some nefarious business between the politician and the developer that had to do with building permissions; others thought the same. She made no mention of the Civil War. Staverley was relieved, but in a way disappointed that he could not share what he now knew with her. Margarida had been so helpful and important in introducing him to the work of the project of remembering which had led to his meeting with Arnau and thence to *Chafa*, and ultimately to Subirachs. They did not speak about *Chafa*. Their uncertainties about what to do were left as just that, and *Chafa* would live on in whatever nether world he now inhabited, either oblivious of his past or constantly haunted by it. She did say that it looked as though Senyora Puig's estate would provide further funding for the project, and that would enable more testimonies to be collected and the archive to be catalogued properly.

Staverley finished his paper on changing patterns of tourism on the Costa Brava and sent copies to a couple of colleagues back in England for comment. He also gave a copy to Margarida and left one for Nuria at the ERC office in Sant Celoni. He was now doing a further set of interviews with café and bar owners along the coast and had started work in earnest on his book. That was a welcome distraction from thinking about acts of betrayal and torture and death, but he did spend an afternoon in the library in Sant Celoni looking at material on the Spanish marquis. There was not much; forgetting and amnesty were still very much in the ascendant and Spanish historians seemed to focus their attention elsewhere.

The weather was now on the cusp of autumn and winter, and changed dramatically from day to day; some days were misty and damp, others were clear and sunny. Now that it was cooler Staverley was doing more walking in the Montseny. Every four or five days Senyora Budó would make him a packed lunch and he would set off on the ciclo to various points along the road to Coll Formic from which he could then explore. He visited several hermitages, of which there seemed to be many in the mountains, and climbed part of the way up Turó de L'Homme. He could not make it all the way. He saw a lot of mushrooms but not the trumpets of death he had enjoyed so much. He felt fitter than he had for many years, and the walks offered a deep and serene peace that verged on something religious, although he had no time for religion. It was about being part of a natural world rather than over and against it. He began to wonder how he would cope with the inevitable return to England and to university life. Both would be constraining and frustrating compared to the freedoms he was now enjoying, both physical and intellectual. Even so there were plenty of things he missed - Monica, of course, football, his friends, his music and the cinema. The absence of cinema was like a dull ache, an unsatisfied addiction. He had twice been to local cinemas but everything that was not Spanish was dubbed. That made it almost impossible to follow the dialogue. The voices were wrong and did not follow the mouths.

Monica came for another long weekend. They spent two days in Sant Pere and another two in a small hotel further up the coast. Neither had yet managed to bore the other, and their relationship seemed to be set for a good while to come. He told Monica everything. She cried and asked a lot of questions but never once expressed doubts about what had been done. Her pity was for Nuria she said. Staverley's mother came for a few days at Christmas. They spent one day with Senyora Budó and her family, but they did not want to intrude too much. They also spent a long day walking around Barcelona. She pointed out places she remembered when she had visited Staverley's father. Staverley told her everything. She cried and asked a lot of questions but never once expressed doubts about what had been done. Staverley's father would be pleased that his son now knew something of his life and his politics she said. After his mother left he had drinks and dinner with David and his wife, and spent a boys' night out with Dani, which was an extension of their now regular language practice sessions, but with several beers. He also travelled to Barcelona to spend New Year's Day with Margarida and her father, and a few days later shared a celebratory meal on the mountain with Joan. They both drank too much brandy and suffered terrible hangovers, but they enjoyed themselves and walked off the hangovers with the goats the next morning. Staverley was able to taste the cheeses he had a hand in making, and felt quite proud on his newly acquired skill. They did not speak of Subirachs but they did raise a glass in honour of Batlló-Sabé and another for Staverley's father. Late in the evening Joan showed off his remarkable ability to recite poetry from memory: one of the few good things left over from his many years of hiding, he said.

**

Jack was very aware that his health was drastically failing. He had already come to terms with the idea that he was now an invalid, that he would never return to work and that he might be bed ridden for the rest of his life. It had not been much of a life, he decided, but he had his family, he had some good friends, and he had fought on the right side and for the right ideas. Some of the political changes he had hoped for and struggled for had come about with the establishing of the Welfare State after the end of the war, but he feared that some of many of the new social provisions could be too easily done away with by future governments. The NHS was certainly working well for him, and Edith got plenty of support as his care made ever greater demands on her. There had been some suggestion by one of his doctors that he be moved to a sanatorium but he was very glad when Edith said she was very much against the idea. If he did not have long left he wanted to spend as much of that time as he could at home.

It was increasingly difficult for him to read now, which was something he badly missed. More than anything he looked forward each day to the times when his young son would visit him and sit on his bed and sometimes hold his hand. His son would tell him about his day, the games he had played, the fantasies he had conjured up and the adventures he had had. Jack loved the boy's unfettered enthusiasm for play. In return the boy expected stories from Jack, and Jack did his best, for as long as his breath and energy lasted, trying to recall things from his reading that would be suitable for a small child. Many times he was tempted to talk about politics and war and his experiences fighting Fascism but he never did. He desperately wanted his son to know him and understand the decisions he had made in his life, but he also wanted his son to live for the future, for new possibilities rather than ones already missed. If the boy wanted to know more, then he would have to find out things for himself. Maybe that would never happen, but Jack did decide to leave him with something to start from, when the right time came.

> History is "neither 'past' nor 'other', but an
> extension of the present to which all people,
> whether they know it or not, are attached."

Sebastian Faulks (2019) *Paris Echo*, London: Vintage.

Acknowledgements

I have a lot of people to thank for their contributions, in different ways, to the writing of this book. Most importantly Trinidad Fructuoso-Gallego – discussant, critic, language and cultural adviser, believer and rock. Meg Maguire who is discerning and immensely supportive in equal measure. Monica Durall-Rivas for sharing childhood memories. Jordi Collet-Sabé for answering obscure questions and reading a draft. Steve Crump and Kate Hoskins also read drafts and asked constructive questions to which I tried to respond. Alex Moore read and corrected the whole manuscript with great care, stout fellow.

There are some terms and phrases from Catalan and Castilian in the book, mostly the former. The speakers use Castilian or Catalan forms as appropriate.

The sections of the book that relate to the events of May-June 1937 describe those events as accurately as possible. Two recently published books were enormously helpful in understanding the period, the International Brigades and POUM in particular. They are both in English.

Giles Tremlett (2020) The International Brigades: Fascism, Freedom and the Spanish Civil War, London: Bloomsbury.

Alexander Clifford (2020) The People's Army in the Spanish Civil War: A Military History of the Republic and International Brigades, Barnsley: Pen and Sword.

Re-reading *Homage to Catalonia*, was a pleasure and informed the descriptions of life at the front.

As Tremlett explains as of 2020 only two Brigade volunteers were still alive.

The International Brigades (*Brigadas Internacionales*) were military during the Spanish Civil War. The organization existed for two years, from 1936 until 1938. It is estimated that during the entire war, between 40,000 and 59,000 members served in the International Brigades, including 15,000 who died in combat. The first of the International Brigades were composed mostly of French, Belgian,

Italian, and German volunteers, backed by a sizeable contingent of Polish miners from Northern France and Belgium. The Abraham Lincoln Battalion was made up of fighters from the United States, Canada and Irish Free State, with some British, Cypriots, and Chileans from the Chilean Worker Club of New York. There were 2,100 British Brigaders, 500 of whom came from Scotland, and half of those from Glasgow, around 530 of the British volunteers were killed. Around 50 British volunteers fought for Franco.

Several of the characters who appear directly or are referred to in the book were real life participants in the Civil War.

Alexander Orlov (1895-1973) was NKVD resident in Spain, his 'work' in Spain and life after fleeing to the United States is as explained in the book.

Andreu Nin Perez (1892-1937) was a Marxist politician. In 1937, Nin and the rest of the POUM leadership was arrested by the Moscow-oriented government of the Republic on trumped up charges of collaborating with Franco's nationalists and tortured to death by Soviet NKVD agents. On 17 June 2013, 76 years after his death, the parliament of Catalunya officially paid homage to him and his political work with special emphasis to his reforms while Justice Minister.

Juan Garcia Oliver (1901-1980) was a Catalan anarcho-syndicalist revolutionary and Minister of Justice of the Republic. He was a leading figure of anarchism in Spain.

George Orwell (Eric Arthur Blair) (1903-1950) was an English novelist, essayist, journalist and critic. *Homage to Catalonia* (1938) is Orwell's personal account of his experiences and observations fighting in the Spanish Civil War for the POUM militia. He was wounded in the throat by a sniper's bullet while fighting at the front. The trial of the leaders of the POUM and of Orwell (in his absence) by the Republic took place in Barcelona in October and November 1938. There are some phrases borrowed and adapted from Orwell's book in the prologue, and other there from Antonio Muñoz Molina's novel *In the Night of Time* (SerpentsTail.com 2017).

Juan Negrín y López (1892 – 1956) was a leader of the Spanish Socialist Workers' Party (PSOE) and served as the last Loyalist premier of Spain (1937–1939), and presided over the defeat of the Republican forces. He has been vilified, not only by Francoist historians, but also by important sectors of the exiled Spanish Left, including the leadership of his own Socialist Party. He has been depicted as the principal responsible for losing the civil war, and charged with a dictatorial leadership style, selling Spain out to the Communists and robbing the Spanish treasury. The PSOE expelled Negrín in 1946, but he was posthumously rehabilitated in 2008.

Mannie Shinwell (1884-1986) member of parliament for the Independent Labour Party is also mentioned.

Jordi Pujol was President of Catalunya (1980-2003) and the growth and demise of *La Banca Catalana* occurred roughly as it appears in the book. In July 2014, Pujol released a note explaining that for 34 years, including 23 as the President of Catalonia, he had maintained secret foreign bank accounts inherited from his father. The note apologized for his actions and explained that the millions had been declared and taxes paid. In 2020 Judge José de la Mata of Spain's High Court (*Audiencia Nacional*) recommended that all nine members of Pujol's family should be tried for cashing in on their "position of privilege" in Catalunya's political, economic and social life and accumulating "disproportionate" wealth, allegedly through illegal commissions that companies paid to secure government contracts and other favours.

There is a recent film starring Jesse Eisenberg, based on the exploits of mime artist Marcel Marceau and French Boy Scouts during the Nazi occupation, as referred to in the book by the character Arnau - *Resistance* (2020)(available on Netflix).

The Endless Trench or *Trincheras Infinitas* (2019) is a film (now on Netflix starring Antonio de la Torre and Belén Cuesta) based on the stories of *'los topos'*, that is, those like Joan, who after the end of the Civil War hid for fear of reprisals from Franco's police. There was a violent campaign after the Civil War against known Republicans, in particular, those who had made public their politics, such as Manuel Cortes, the Socialist mayor of Mijas who hid behind a constructed wall in his village house for over 30 years. And there is also a Spanish documentary film, *30 Years of Darkness* (2014) that also explores the experiences of *Los Topos*. *Los Topos* were, as noted in the book, granted amnesty by Franco in 1969.

The bookshop Sempere and Sons is of course borrowed from the works of the late and lamented Carlos Ruiz Zafon.

The specialist divisions of La Guardia Civil mentioned in the book are as represented.

The struggles against building of a marina at Aigüamolls and a resort on the Palamós beach that Staverley researches in the book did take place and were successful.

All other characters and events are entirely fictitious and any resemblance to persons alive or dead is purely coincidental.

Printed in Great Britain
by Amazon